SHATTERED PARADISE

Book One

Salvaggio's Light

An Epic Contemporary Romance Serial

By C. L. Cattano

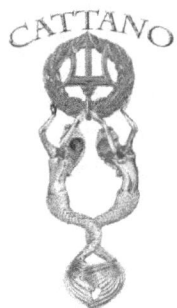

VAGARY PUBLISHING

Shattered Paradise
Book One
Salvaggio's Light
A Vagary Publishing Book
Copyright © 2017 by C. L. Cattano

Cover Art, Title Page Art and Typesetting Copyright © 2017 by Chynsia Hinesley

Published by:

VAGARY PUBLISHING

www.vagarypublishing.com
inquiry@vagarypublishing.com

Rogena Mitchell-Jones, Independent Literary Editor
RMJ Manuscript Services LLC *www.rogenamitchell.com*
Proofreading by Karen L. Jones

ISBN 13-978-0-9980906-4-1

First Edition

WARNING

It is suggested readers of this story be adults over the age of eighteen.

This dramatic romance series has many scenes describing sex as well as intense emotional scenes and acts of violence.

This is a serial story with themes that flow from one book into another with lots of twists and turns. Reading this series from the beginning is highly suggested, or the reader may not be able to follow all of the story lines.

Go to the Salvaggio's Light Facebook page to join other readers who are talking about the series.
www.facebook.com/SalvaggiosLight/

Join the C L Cattano mailing list and check out my website at www.clcattano.com

Acknowledgments

I WOULD LIKE to thank everyone involved in making this EPIC crazy drama happen from editing, artwork, and beta reading to just listening to me go on and on about the whole thing and make innumerable changes in plots and personalities. Without you and the help and encouragement you gave, the process would not have been such a great journey.

To all of you, I give my deep appreciation and thanks.

Dedication

For Marie – who listens and rolls her eyes.

Salvaggio's Light

An Epic Contemporary Romance Serial

Shattered Paradise
Blue Inferno*
Secrets & Rivalry*
Wildling's Claim*
Sowers of Discord*

*Coming Soon

I note clearly how the eternal light, already, shines back from your intellect, that, which, once seen, always sets love alight, and if anything else seduces your love, it is nothing but a trace of this light, wrongly comprehended, that shines through in it.
 — Dante Alighieri, The Divine Comedy

1

THE BRIGHT AUTUMN colors on the Canadian slopes surrounding the rental car were hidden in blacks and grays. Rafaella Salvaggio was driving down the dark mountain road with her daughter Bronte, who was babbling happily in the backseat. The moonlight was not enough to show the full majesty and danger of the pass leading down the mountain and away from the hotel with its tourist crowded lobby. Rafe relied heavily on the headlights lighting up the wet black road and made it sparkle under their light as the car hugged the curves along the road winding around the mountain.

Rafe looked back at Bronte through the rearview mirror and sighed. She had grown so much and was getting so smart. She wished her own mother could be here to see Bronte. Rafe was sure she would love her as much as she did. Her thoughts quickly fled from the pain the memory of her mother's death could bring flooding back if she dwelled too long.

Rafe looked through the windshield and saw they had made it safely into the little tourist town and stopped at one of the two stop signs in the village. She looked up at the sign and sighed heavily. The sign, with its bright word *STOP*, seemed to glow with an ominous warning under the bright beam of the headlights. She took this vision as a signal she was making another big mistake.

"What the hell am I doing? I'm running away." She sighed in answer to her own question. "Is running away what we want to do, Bronte?" She looked up into her rearview mirror at the vision of her daughter reflected there, but Bronte gave no answer. She only smiled as she played with her small stuffed bear. Rafe knew she had made a terrible mistake, one that may hurt Bronte and a lot of other people. "No, it definitely is not what we want to do. I remember what my papa said about things like this. He told me, 'per scappa non è mai la risposta[1]' and it 'è garantito per creare più problemi.[2]' So how am I going to fix this?"

Looking up to her left, she saw a brightly painted sign under a glowing yellow light, directing travelers to a petting zoo.

"I know, adventure time! Let's go see some animals and try to figure it out."

The gravel crunched under the wheels of the car as Rafe pulled into the parking lot of the petting zoo. It looked like it had been set up hastily just to extract a few bucks from tourist travelers. She parked and opened the back door to get Bronte from the car.

"Hey, *Bambina,* want to pet some animals? Let's go see them." She felt Bronte's arms hold tight to her neck as she gathered her up then made her way toward the small zoo entrance.

---

[1] to run away is never the answer

[2] is guaranteed to create more problems

"You made it just in time. We're just about ready to close," said the old, grizzly faced zookeeper as he took Rafe's money for entry. He led them to the small corral at a lazy pace. The brisk autumn weather seemed not to bother his old body at all. "You have a beautiful baby," he declared in his gravelly voice.

Rafe pushed back the hood of Bronte's toggled pea coat so she could see the fuzzy brown reindeer coming up to them looking for a treat. She smiled at Bronte and then at the old zookeeper. "Yes, she is beautiful. Thank you."

"What's her name?" asked the old man with a snaggletooth grin.

"This is Bronte," said Rafe with a smile filled with a mother's pride for her child.

"Hello, Bronte! I'm Nick, the zookeeper," he said shaking her small hand. He looked up at Rafe. "And what's your name?"

"Rafe." She smiled and shook his hand firmly.

"Bronte and Rafe!" He laughed. "They rhyme," he observed as the Italian 'e' in their names were pronounced like the American letter 'ā.' "That's very sweet. You're definitely a matching pair."

Bronte, like Rafe, had light olive brown skin and a head full of black wavy hair shining under the lights around the little zoo. While Bronte's eyes were like her mother's, a light brown with small golden flecks around their centers, Rafe's eyes were an intense steel gray with streaks of blue rays chased by black and were prone to shift from subdued to brilliant blue depending on her mood. In both cases, even with their unusual eyes, there was no denying their Italian heritage.

As other animals noticed them and started to come over hoping for treats, Rafe helped Bronte pet the reindeer on the nose with her small hand. The gray-bearded old man pulled an old Instamatic Polaroid camera from his pocket.

"Would you like a picture to mark the occasion of her first meeting with a real live reindeer?"

"Sure." Rafe smiled as she turned Bronte to pose with the reindeer. "Say cheese, Bronte," Rafe directed as the zookeeper took a picture and the flash washed over them. "Thank you," she said as she adjusted Bronte on her hip.

"No problem. It's what I'm here for," he said as he grinned toothily at them. He pulled the photo from the camera and began waving the picture as if it would help it develop faster. "I'll just put it inside one of our Lake Louise Petting Zoo photo holders for you, and you'll have a nice keepsake. That'll be ten dollars, please."

Rafe stared in shock at the old man for a second and then chuckled. She did say she wanted one without asking about price. Something she should know better than to do. She paid the old man and looked at the photo of her and Bronte with the reindeer standing aloof beside them, and then she put the picture in her coat pocket.

"Well, we had better get back to the hotel now," she said after Bronte had petted several more animals. "Say bye-bye to the animals, Bronte." Rafe held Bronte's hand and waved it at the reindeer and the other small animals and then at the zookeeper. The zookeeper waved back and then turned away to get back to the warmth of his shack and to close up for the night.

2

AFTER GIVING HER rental car keys to one of the hotel valets, Rafe Salvaggio carried Bronte inside the warm lobby tastefully decorated for the fall holidays. She un-toggled Bronte's coat and slipped it off her, revealing her pretty fall outfit and her sweet ruddy face. The small face looked at her and smiled as she babbled, pointing out the pumpkins and other fall decorations, made Rafe's heart ache. It ached for the lost life she had planned for their family. It ached because, even though she was not Bronte's biological mother, she felt she was still her mother in all other ways.

Bronte's biological mother, Eden, who Bronte got her eye color from, was, in Rafe's mind, the most beautiful woman she had ever met. The first time Rafe had seen her, she could not take her eyes away. She still reminded her of a woman from a renaissance painting with her golden blonde hair, the flush of pink in her cheeks with sweet pouting lips, and her golden brown eyes with flecks of gold. Not only was she beautiful, but until their break up, Rafe thought she was the kindest and most loving person she had ever met. She knew Eden was still loving and caring—just not for her.

She missed having Eden in her life.

Bringing Bronte into their lives was a long, heart wrenching, but in the end, magical adventure. They spent months deciding what traits they would want in a donor and months finding someone who fit all the qualities they wanted.

Then they spent even more time at doctors' offices and sperm banks looking through donor profiles.

During that time, Eden suddenly wanted them to go to therapy and to attend relationship workshops to make sure they were good. Rafe still didn't understand why Eden insisted they go through the therapy sessions. But Rafe would do anything for her, so she agreed to go to the sessions and hoped they would help get them through all the stress so they could have their family.

Rafe tried to be positive about the therapy sessions, but they just made her confused and unsure of herself. It also seemed as if Eden had grown even further away from her emotionally as well as intimately. It made her angry, so she stopped agreeing to go to therapy because she thought it was doing more harm than good.

After three unsuccessful inseminations, they were both under a lot of stress, magnified because they were going to have to go through the whole choosing a donor process again.

In October of the same year, Rafe was in New York on business for her architectural conservation and design firm, *Eroina Conservazione e Design,* and visiting her father who was sick and in the hospital again. The company had been her passion even when it was just an idea in her mind. With the help of her father, who agreed to co-manage the company with her while she was in college, and his real estate savvy, it became a reality. Because of their strained relationship, it was sometimes a fight for control. It had been difficult for Rafe to work full-time at the firm and handle the demands she put on herself for her education. It was especially hard when her father was buying property in other countries and demanded she travel there to work on-site. But the properties he managed to obtain always seemed to be amazing and they reeled her in, so somehow, she met all his demands and those of her education. As her education progressed, she took over more and more of the business.

Finally, after finalizing her doctorates, she took full control of the company from her father and moved to California. They still found projects to work on together, but by then, the partnership was less of a fight for control and more of a way to become closer.

Also by October, being closer to her father had suddenly become important because he was diagnosed with cancer again. When she visited him, he seemed fine and looked good. The doctor even said he expected him to be able to go home soon, so Rafe was relieved. They were working together on a project in Milano, and Rafe had spent time with him going over the project. He was, as always, excited and passionate about every aspect and had ideas and opinions about dealing with everyone and solving any problems that might arise. They were both in their element and loving their work.

While still in New York, Rafe got a call from her childhood friend who had traveled from Italy to America. He, too, was in New York on business and wanted to meet with her.

Gabrielli Braulio De Angelis was a very talented musician from Florence who had studied music at the *Conservatorio Statale di Musica Giuseppe Verdi*, Turin, Italy, where he studied piano, guitar, and voice. Gabri was a family friend of Rafe's since they were very young. They, along with their friend

Brettito, were always at each other's houses and they were the masterminds of many adventures. They grew up running the streets of Florence and went to the same school. Gabri's family was not as well off as Rafe's or Brettito's, but he was extremely talented and was able to work hard and get into his school of choice.

After she and her father moved from Florence to Milan and then to America a year later, Gabri studied harder thinking one day he would marry Rafe. But when Rafe went back to Italy to college, she had to let him know she was not interested in men. He took the news very well considering how he felt about her.

They had much history from their youthful adventures to the death of Rafe's mother. Then there was the death of their friend Brettito, which was hard on them both. After everything, they remained close friends and continued to be throughout their lives.

Gabri contacted Rafe and told her he was in New York for a music job and would like to meet for dinner to catch up on each other's lives. After taking him to visit her father for a while, they went to what Gabri called a 'real American restaurant,' and filled each other in on the latest details of their lives.

When Rafe told him about the process they were going through to have a child, he was surprised and happy for her. Then Rafe looked at him thoughtfully and asked him how he would feel about being the donor. He smiled and said he would be *onorato*[3], but he wanted to *incontra la bella donna che ami*.[4]

---

[3] honored

[4] meet the beautiful woman you love

Rafe was ecstatic, and Gabri was able to fly to California for the weekend to meet Eden at Rafe's birthday party.

Rafe remembered they had walked up to the house arm in arm and went inside where all of her and Eden's friends were gathered for the birthday party. She took him straight to Eden and introduced her to him.

"Eden, this is my friend Gabri. He's here from Italy," she told her with a smile as she hung on his arm then leaned close to Eden's ear. "He's agreed to be our donor," she whispered excitedly. She smiled back at Gabri. *"Gabri, si tratta di* Eden."[5]

"Ciao bella che è un piacere conoscerti,"[6] said Gabri and kissed Eden's hand then looked at Rafe.

"Eden sarà la madre di nascita,"[7] Rafe explained to him.

"Oh, non sei lo madre, Eroina?"[8] he asked disappointedly. *"I nostri bambini sarebbe bella e intelligente."*[9]

"Eden è molto intelligente, molto bellissimo e i suoi figli saranno parte di noi sia. Itlaliano e Americano,"[10] Rafe told him with a smile ignoring his use of her childhood nickname, *Eroina.*[11]

"Sono impressionato che siete in grado di trovare una bella donna e lei vuole avere il tou bambino."[12] He laughed.

---

[5] Gabri, this is Eden.

[6] Hello beautiful, it's nice to meet you.

[7] Eden will be the birth mother.

[8] Oh, you're not the mother, Eroina,

[9] Our children would be beautiful and smart.

[10] Eden is very smart, very beautiful, and her children will be part of us both. Italian and American.

[11] Heroine.

[12] I'm impressed that you're able to find a beautiful woman and she wants to have your baby,

"Lei è la donna più bella di America che ho visto."[13] He smiled at Eden

"He says you're the most beautiful woman he's seen in America." Rafe winked at Eden.

"Thank you." Eden smiled shyly. "It's so nice to meet you," she said as she looked uncomfortably from him to Rafe not following their conversation because she did not speak Italian.

"Lei detto che è bello conoscerti,"[14] Rafe told him then looked at Eden happily. "I'm going to show him around. He's good right?" She watched Eden nod slowly as she looked at him. Rafe was overjoyed her friend and Eden liked each other. "I'll tell him everything, and we can take him tomorrow!" Rafe turned back to Gabri. *"Venite. I mostrerà intorno a voi e vi introdurre i miei amici,"*[15] said Rafe as she led Gabri away holding his arm and leaning close to him.

Later in the night, Rafe told Eden all about Gabri and some of their adventures when they were young, but she left out her nickname was *Eroina*, which meant heroine in Italian. When her friends Gabri and Brettito found out her middle name was *Erodotie*[16], and her mother tried to explain, unsuccessfully, how they feminized the Italian name for *Herodotus*, a Greek philosopher, Rafe somehow got stuck with the nickname Eroina. Both her parents thought it was a very cute nickname, but Rafe didn't think it was at all and wished her father had liked a different philosopher than the one he named her after.

---

[13] She is the most beautiful woman in America that I have seen.

[14] She said it's nice to meet you,

[15] Come. I will show you around and introduce you my friends,

[16] Earrō-dō-tiā

In Rafe's mind, Gabri met all of their requirements for a donor plus the added advantage he was full-blooded Italian made him seem more than perfect. Their baby would be a reflection of them both, and Rafe could hardly wait to be able to make love to Eden and create their baby.

The next day, Eden and Rafe took Gabri to the sperm bank, and he deposited for them.

"Si dovrebbero avere molti bambini con tutto quello che ti ho dato!"[17] he told them proudly.

"He said, we should have many children with all he gave," Rafe whispered to Eden and laughed with her and Gabri, happy with the incredible gift he had given them.

Later in the day, Rafe and Eden took Gabri to the airport and thanked him again for helping them have a family. He looked longingly at Rafe like he did back when they were in college.

"Se questo è l'unico modo,"[18] he said with a small shrug. *"Questo la strada vi mostrerò il mio profondo amore per te."*[19] He hugged Eden then Rafe.

"Ho ameranno la sia la madre e il padre dei miei figli,"[20] said Rafe into his ear. They then kissed goodbye in their Italian way, then she and Eden waved as he left to catch his flight.

Everything happening in her relationship with Eden after the visit were like a roller coaster with peaks of exhilarating highs and valleys of terrifying lows that seemed like it would

---

[17] You should have many children with everything I gave you!

[18] If this is the only way,

[19] This is the way I will show you my deep love for you.

[20] I will love both the mother and the father of my children,

never end. When it did, they found they not only survived the rollercoaster, but their lives were changed forever.

They had Bronte.

Rafe smiled as she looked into Bronte's sweet face and saw a reflection of herself, and especially, her friend Gabri, but with Eden's bright brown eyes.

"Ready to go see Mommy?" she asked the wiggling child. "Okay, let's go," she whispered.

Nervously, Rafe made her way to the elevators to take the slow ride up to Eden's room. Their outing to the petting zoo was not exactly sanctioned. Taking Bronte out of the hotel was not approved, and if Eden knew before Rafe had come to her senses, she actually considered running away with Bronte and making sure she got full custody... Well, it would not go over well. She knew how it felt to lose a mother and knew she just could not do that to Bronte or to Eden. Rafe could only hope that Eden and Jake never found out the truth, and then she could try to keep on faking being happy about how her life was crashing in around her.

Rafe was devastated when Eden had decided she could no longer be in a relationship with her, or any woman, any longer—even after having Bronte. Rafe had hoped it was just a phase, and Eden would, at the very least, start dating women again, but after almost a year, she could see how serious Eden was about her new boyfriend. Rafe was sure Eden had her reasons for dating men again, but they would never be good ones in her mind. Eden being with anyone else besides Rafe was painful to think about. She also knew they were both equally to blame for their break up. *Almost equally*, Rafe thought sadly, believing more of the blame fell on herself.

It was in New York where she got fucked up—fucked up and fucked the wrong girl. She was there alone dealing with her father's death feeling cut off from Eden and not knowing what to do to fix things. Rafe could not understand why Eden was suddenly so distant and angry. Eden had left her there alone and gone back to California, unsure about starting a family with Gabri's gift to them.

After Eden found out and left the house, Rafe went back to New York. Everyone assumed while she was there, she kept fucking the girl. The biggest fuck up was she did not deny the accusations. At the time, she did not feel it mattered. There really was no excuse except for ego, maybe. Rafe could only believe she did it because the girl woke something up in her she wasn't feeling with Eden. It had to have been because it felt good to have someone want her again, talk dirty to her, tell her she was great, stroke her ego—and a little more—and who wanted to help her through the grief she was feeling over her father's death. She really could not think of any other reason for her actions. When she tried, it just made her feel sick and made her head ache, so she avoided thinking about it at all anymore—if it were possible.

It was like a break from the reality of her father having died and Eden not wanting her. The problem was reality came crashing in, and by the time it did, it was too late. Rafe knew she had betrayed Eden with the affair. She knew because of her betrayal, she and Eden just could not find each other again. Now Eden couldn't see her the same as she had before.

They tried to work things out after finding out Eden was pregnant. But, after Bronte was born, things got hard again. Eden said she was sure the reason was because they should never have been together in the first place. Then Eden confessed she thought she needed to be with a man, and Rafe's world was suddenly off center again.

The next thing Rafe knew, Eden had left and taken Bronte with her. The only thing left, after Eden and Bronte were gone, was a new reality—she had lost everything that really mattered.

Now, they were here in this hotel with their families and friends, everyone, trying to have a family vacation together for Bronte's first birthday. They were all working to show they could be a family for her, even though they were broken.

Eden was having dinner with her boyfriend, Jake, who was now apparently her fiancé. Rafe could not stand Jake from the moment she met him. She couldn't figure out what Eden saw in him. She felt he was pretentious and a fake and, in her opinion, Eden could do better. She did not think Jake would even qualify for the word handsome. He may be clean cut and somewhat fit, but those things were about all anyone could say about him. Rafe felt he was just nondescript. He had dark brown hair, cut close to his head, brown eyes and a farmer's tan from his short-sleeved shirts. When he smiled, his bright white capped teeth took over his face, and he looked like a freakishly animated ventriloquist doll to her. He claimed to be a graphic artist, but in Rafe's opinion, he was really just a pumped up pretender who replicated corporate logos and set type for handbills. Everything he did, in her opinion, was canned and unoriginal, so he was not an artist at all. In her opinion, his work lacked any kind of real talent and all his compositions were either stolen from others or poorly executed.

Rafe hated how Jake was always prompting his son Hunter to call Eden mommy and Bronte his sister. They were not even married yet.

In addition, he pissed her off because he was convincing Eden to stop the adoption process for her to officially become Bronte's parent and threatening to move her and Eden away.

They had done all of the home visits and covered all the requirements for the adoption, but Eden kept postponing getting all the necessary paperwork turned in. There was nothing Rafe could do but wait and hope Eden would not just dissolve the application.

Rafe calmed herself as she stepped out of the elevator, and heading left, she came to Eden's room. She knocked softly and rebalanced Bronte on her hip. There was no answer, so she knocked again a bit louder but still no answer. "Hmm, *piccolina*,[21] Mommy must still be at dinner. Let's go ride the elevator again, okay?"

---

[21] Little one

3

AT THE HOTELS' lavish front desk, the prim and proper night manager, Mr. Ellis, tapped on his computer keyboard as Eden Kingsley tapped impatiently on the counter with her room key. Fury burned through Eden and her golden brown eyes blazed as she thought about what she would do when she found Rafe. Her fiancé and her friends Abby and Julia were hovering around her awaiting the results of the managers' computer search.

The manager clicked his tongue and looked up at the agitated group and the angry woman with golden blonde hair and a red flushed face who stood in front of him.

"I am sorry, but leaving a message for Ms. Salvaggio won't be possible because our records show she checked out two hours ago at seven this evening."

"Did she have my baby with her?" Eden demanded angrily.

"I'm sorry, ma'am, but I don't know. I didn't check her out. The employee who did has gone home."

"Call him at home. Call him right now!" Livid was not even close to the word describing the emotions Eden was feeling at the moment.

To come back to the room and find her baby gone and the babysitter dismissed had detonated the most primal emotions of horror, anger, and motherly concern within her. Nothing short of throttling Rafe would satisfy and comfort her seething anger.

She had immediately started calling Rafe, but she didn't answer her phone. Rafe had set things up so all her calls were forwarded to her assistant so she wouldn't be tempted to work over vacation, and her assistant had not heard from Rafe. Even though Eden knew Rafe set things up so she could focus on being here, she was still angry she couldn't contact her.

Jake Thompson could see Eden was ready to jump over the counter and grab the hotel manager by the neck for not giving her the answers she needed fast enough. He didn't blame her. Rafe had crossed the line. She checked out of the hotel while the rest of them were having dinner and took Bronte.

"Eden, we know she has her. We don't need to call the employee at home. We need to call the police."

"Maybe Rafe is still in the hotel," said Abby who was standing behind Eden and Jake. "I mean, just because she checked out doesn't mean she's gone," offered the freckled faced woman sensibly. She nervously ran her hand through her strawberry blonde hair streaked with multi-colored blonde highlights.

Abby couldn't believe Rafe would be so stupid as to take Bronte like they thought she did. She had known Rafe for a long time, and though she was apt to do crazy things, she just could not see her doing something like this to Bronte, or to Eden.

She was there the first time Rafe brought Eden around to meet everyone. Abby didn't think Rafe would ever settle down, and she had a strong opinion about her and her ways with women. But the way Rafe looked at Eden, she knew she was in love with her. Abby admitted to herself she was jealous at the time, but after getting to know Eden, she decided she really liked her. Abby knew Rafe was unhappy with things that had happened over the past eight months, but she still just couldn't believe Rafe would do what they were accusing her of doing.

"Well, she did rent a car," said the hotel manager as he tapped quickly on the keypad. "You can check with the doorman and see if it was delivered to her. Maybe she's just outside or in the side foyer waiting for it." He hoped this new information would send this group away without contacting the police. He didn't want anyone or anything tarnishing the reputation of his hotel. If the police did get involved, he would make sure all parties were added to his list of 'undesirables' and let other high caliber hotel managers know about them. He was no stranger to making it a problem for certain types of low clientele to obtain a good hotel room.

"Rafe, what are you doing?" Eden asked in desperation as a nervous sweat beaded on her upper lip. "Please, please!" She closed her eyes and rubbed her temples in frustration, and her hands shook with anxiety. She looked desperately at Jake. "I want my baby back now!"

Stepping in and taking Eden's trembling hands, Julia Hawthorn looked into her inconsolable eyes. "Listen, Eden. Let's stay calm and notify the police, just to be on the safe side," said the tall silver-haired woman with Mediterranean blue eyes in her lilting English boarding school accent. She had known Rafe since their school days in New York and knew at times she could get an idea in her head and follow it stubbornly.

Now, it looked like her friend was in trouble, and Julia was not sure how to help her, or even if she should. Taking Bronte from her mother really was unforgivable. Eden was almost inconsolable.

This whole trip had been Jake and Eden's idea, and Julia thought, after all this time, Rafe could hold it together for two weeks. Apparently, a week was all Rafe could manage. They had barely seen Eden since she left Rafe eight months ago. All of them thought this would be a turning point for Rafe and Eden to start being, at the very least, more civil for Bronte's sake.

Julia looked at the hotel manager and sighed. "In the meantime, we need to check to see if the car she rented is still here or not, and search the hotel." She signaled to the office manager to make the call to the police and saw that he was hesitant.

"Make the call," demanded Jake at the hotel manager's hesitation. "We should start with her room. There may be some clue about where she's going. You'll get us the key, of course, and contact the doorman to find out about the rental car," he stated to the hotel manager.

Sensing there would be no way to quell this drama unless he agreed to at least some of their terms, the manager looked over at his clerk.

"Howard, use your key and take these people up to Ms. Salvaggio's suite so they can have a look inside." He picked up the phone and started dialing as Howard nodded, then led the group away. "Yes, Mr. Anthony? Mr. Ellis here. I need you to send a couple of security guards to the front desk right away.

There may be an occurrence involving the police happening, and I need to make sure the hotel is not involved publically in any kind of scandal." He paused listening to the voice from his phone. "Yes, I'll give them all the details when they arrive. Thank you." The manager terminated the call and sighed, then dialed again. "Yes, this is the front desk. Did a rental car for Ms. Salvaggio arrive? Oh, I see. Call me back and let me know. Thank you."

4

RAFE SALVAGGIO CARRIED Bronte into a quiet sitting area and unloaded her and Bronte's bags onto one of the couches. She released Bronte who proceeded to attempt to toddle by holding herself up on furniture and bounced from couch to chair to table and back happily.

Rafe sat down, pulled out some toys, and then placed them where Bronte could get them. She then watched as the little ball of energy played and fought sleep. She looked at Bronte's shining golden brown eyes and could not help but think about Eden. When she first met Eden, her eyes amazed her, and when she could bring herself to look into them now, they still did.

Once again, Rafe thought about when she met Eden. It seemed her mind was torturing her a lot with memories of her past. At least this was a pleasant memory if it didn't lead to other darker ones. Rafe forced herself to focus on what was important. Only good memories were important right now.

The day they met, she had been on a business appointment to assess a property for restoration. She met her client Mr. Riton at his office to pick up blueprints and go over the scope of work.

When Rafe walked into Mr. Riton's offices, she was greeted by a person she thought could have only come from a renaissance painting. She took in the shine of her golden blonde hair and the hint of pink on her cheeks complementing her red bow shaped lips. Her eyes were a shining light brown with shots of gold that seemed to swirl and could change shape with her mood. She had found out about her beautiful eyes later when they began spending time together.

The blonde's voice was low and soft when she called to let her boss know Rafe was there. Rafe didn't notice the inexpensive, ill-fitting clothes or the lack of makeup or the well-worn flats—she only noticed the way she walked with ease and the way she held her head when she was talking on the phone.

Mr. Riton came out of his office excited about their meeting. "Ah, Ms. Salvaggio. Let's go to the conference room," he suggested then looked at his assistant. "Eden, will you get the blueprints delivered this morning and bring them to the conference room."

"Of course," said Eden and left her desk.

Rafe could not help but look back over her shoulder at Eden as Mr. Riton led her to the conference room for their meeting.

"I'm very excited to get this project started." Mr. Riton smiled with enthusiasm. "The house was my grandmothers, and it's deteriorated over the years. But since I finally bought out everyone, I can start putting money into getting it back to its former glory." Eden walked in with the large set of blueprints. "Thank you, Eden," said Mr. Riton. Rafe stood up to take the blueprints and spread them on the table. "I'm sorry," said Mr. Riton. "Ms. Salvaggio, this is my assistant Eden Kingsley."

Rafe looked into her eyes and smiled. "*Il paradiso terrestre, l'Eden,*"[22] she said involuntarily. "It is a pleasure to meet you," said Rafe recovering and held out her hand.

"What?" Eden stammered shyly. "Oh, it's a pleasure to meet you too," she said as she shook Rafe's hand.

It seemed to Rafe that Eden didn't look at her again the rest of the meeting. She knew the beautiful woman had not understood her outburst in Italian and was thankful she had not embarrassed herself more. Rafe knew she should have been paying more attention to her client, but she couldn't keep from sneaking looks at the woman as she took notes for her boss, tucking her hair behind her ear whenever it fell forward.

After the meeting, Mr. Riton invited Rafe to an event he was hosting, and they said their goodbyes. Rafe had no idea if she would ever see the beautiful assistant again. She thought she would just be a woman whose image she now had in her mind and could be used in a fantasy painting to be put into one of her restorations.

A week later, Rafe stepped into the reception area of the event venue and saw Eden standing across the room. She walked straight to her as if pulled there by an invisible force.

---

[22] The earthly paradise, Eden

She knew immediately she wanted her. She knew immediately this woman was probably straight.

She resolved she would have her if she could, and if she couldn't, then she would just have to live with the disappointment and keep her in her mind's eye. She also resolved that she would paint her portrait if she had the chance.

As she stood there next to Eden and people approached, Eden softly told her a little about each person she knew. She said very little other than things about work, but her presence was noted and felt by many. People talked about her and praised her. Eden had worked for her boss, Mr. Riton, for the past year while going to college, and all of them were wondering if she would stay after her graduation next year or if she would be stolen away by a bigger company. Rafe was surprised to learn she was still in college. She quickly calculated their estimated age difference and was sure their possible seven-year age gap was another reason she should probably stay at arm's length from this beautiful woman.

A French actor told her how Eden helped him write out his script phonically so he could sound more American. A writer praised her help with the notes she gave him in negotiating for a director who would follow his vision. Others talked about her like she was the real company and how her boss would be nowhere without her. Eden was praised for her insight, compassion, ability to mediate, and her positive presence.

Later in the evening, Rafe was in the lounge going through all the business cards she had been handed and sorting them by business potential and throwing away several she had bent the corners on denoting they were clear invitations for something other than business.

At the same time, she was discussing the large painting of a landscape that was the focus of the room. It was obviously an early example of mass production artwork and was clearly meant to have a portrait painted on it at some point. The gentleman suggested they commission themselves to be put in, and Rafe laughed at what was undoubtedly a joke and an attempt at a pickup line. It was then she turned her head and saw Eden. When Eden revealed she couldn't find her ride home, Rafe immediately volunteered.

Somehow, she convinced Eden to have brunch, and as she got to know her more, she wanted her more. Her resolve to live with disappointment didn't last long—as was usual.

Rafe was clearly torturing herself, but she truly enjoyed the woman's company. Eden opened up and told her so much about herself, it was as though Rafe had known her forever, and she was instantly comfortable with her. It seemed like Eden lived such a good, sweet life, and because of that, she thought life was always good.

Seeing the world from Eden's perspective left Rafe in awe. She knew Eden wasn't innocent, but she was naïve in a lot of ways, and Rafe found it very endearing. It made her want to be with her all the time, to be inside the positive world she lived in. She found the goal of having her took a back seat to a new goal of just being in her presence whenever possible. After meeting often, over about three months, Eden agreed to sit for a painting. Rafe was ecstatic. It took a month to complete, but it was worth it to spend so much time in her company.

Rafe did everything she could to keep from torturing herself while still trying to be irresistible to Eden. The day Rafe began working on the painting, Eden asked her about being gay. She was a little afraid it would mean the end before it got started. So, for the entire month, she touched Eden as little as possible, stayed away from too much conversation that might lead to sexual suggestions, and never had more than two glasses of wine. She resolved again not to go after her aggressively and to take her time to see if, at the very least, they could be friends. They seemed to work through the time well together, and the painting was completed.

Rafe almost didn't invite Eden to the party she was going to with her friends. It was at a mansion, in the hills, owned by someone Abby had interviewed. Abby had been invited and was told to bring all of her friends. The owner of the mansion had a lot of art, and Abby arranged it so they could reveal the painting of Eden at the party. Rafe knew it would be like throwing Eden to the wolves and warned her, but she still agreed to go. Eden was very shy and quiet about the attention, but she handled herself well.

After the party, they went to Eden's apartment, and they were discussing her friends. It looked as though Eden had gone into her own world, so Rafe leaned in to see if she was okay, and the next thing she knew, they were kissing.

They were kissing, and Rafe wanted more. She loved the taste of her and the softness of her lips. She loved the feel of her body under her hands.

She wanted her.

She forced herself to stop and pull away. She was breaking her own rules about going slow with this person and might just be losing a friend. She had to leave and not come back for a while.

On her way home, she resolved not to call her. She would not call her, and she could only hope Eden would call.

She did.

When Eden called, Rafe was so surprised she was actually nervous. She had not been nervous about a woman in a very long time. She was worried because she didn't know if Eden wanted to meet to talk about things and still be friends, or if Eden wanted to tell her they needed to go their separate ways.

The door opened, and her heart was already beating fast. When Eden touched her face and then kissed her again, she was both surprised and immediately drawn to her. She saw Eden's invitation shining like a bright light from her eyes meant just for her. She accepted the invitation gladly and passionately.

Rafe remembered her mother talking about her father and the immediate, unmistakable knowledge what she felt was love. Her mother had said, at first she hadn't known what the feeling was, but when she realized it was love and found he felt the same, she knew they were meant to be together.

The same thing happened to Rafe. One day, after they had been together for several months, she saw Eden waiting for her and their eyes locked. The same feeling welled up in her from the first night they were together. That night Eden told her she was in love with her and then proceeded to show her how much. It was then she knew it was love she felt, and it took over her life.

She never thought things would end with Eden. But she knew she had no one to blame but herself for what had happened. Now the light in Eden's eyes that used to shine for her was gone, and her world was very dim without it.

Rafe took a deep breath and rubbed her temples to stifle the pain in her head and the ache in her heart. She smiled sadly as Bronte reached for her toy and went bounding across to the chair again, not realizing she had taken three steps without holding on.

"We'll just wait here for a while where it's quiet," she told the toddler and then took out her mobile phone and dialed her travel service. "Hello, this is Rafaella Salvaggio. I need to change my flight from Ontario to LAX for later tonight or the first one going out in the morning. Right. Is that the earliest you can find? Fine," she said checking the time on the phone. "Book it. Yes, I have a car scheduled for me at LAX. Can you let them know my new flight information? Okay. Thank you." She hung up wishing there was a flight out tonight since she already checked out of the hotel. As soon as Eden was back from dinner, she would head to the airport and hang out in the club lounge or maybe one of the bars.

Rafe got up and crawled around with Bronte for a while. When the baby was playing happily with her toys, Rafe took some hotel stationary and pen from a courtesy shelf. While Bronte played, Rafe began to write.

Writing letters that would never be sent had always been a kind of self-therapy for her since she was young. As she wrote, she couldn't help but think of all the people she had lost in her life and fought the despair threatening to take control of her.

She looked at Bronte and thought of her childhood friends Gabri and Brettito. She hoped Bronte would have friends like them, friends who would be there to go on adventures with her and help her when she was going through hardships in her life. Friends like Gabri and Brettito who were there for Rafe when her mother died and would be there for each other just as she and Gabri had been there for one another when Brettito died.

Brettito was the sensitive boy while Gabri was the more outgoing and extroverted performer. Rafe was the friend who balanced and led the group. She made Brettito feel brave and made Gabri feel challenged and alive. Both boys were amazed at how different Rafe was from the other girls and were in awe of the adventures she could think up and take them on.

Gabri and Brettito were both infatuated with Rafe, and they both thought they wanted to marry her someday. They both called Rafe their wild angel teasingly because she was named after the angel Rafael and because her mother called Rafe her 'wild child.'

Brettito knew Rafe was fascinated by the *zingari*[23] kids and what they could teach them about their secret *poteri mistici*.[24] Brettito wanted to help Rafe finish the adventure they had planned before her mother had died by going to the zingari kids to try and convince them to teach them *la magia zingari*.[25]

---

[23] Gypsy

[24] Mystical powers

[25] The gypsy magic

He thought maybe he and Rafe could run away together with them too, and Rafe could be happy again.

While he was secretly trying to talk with the zingari to get information to impress Rafe, and following them all over Florence for months, he didn't know the zingari he had fallen in with were using him to get into places so they could steal things.

Memories flashed through Rafe's mind of when the three of them, Brettito, Gabri and herself, had skipped school one day and went to a festival in their neighborhood. While Rafe and Gabri went to get street food, Brettito, because he was so big for his age, was holding them a place to watch one of the shows. The zingari kids saw Brettito and convinced him to go into the *Tabacchi*[26] with them, and they stole some cigarettes.

At the time, there was a lot of civil unrest, and the *polizia militare*[27] were there making sure nothing illegal happened at the festival. In the chaos, before it was known the disturbance was just a case of petty theft, the polizia shot at Brettito and the zingari. Brettito was hit with one of the six shots fired. He bled out and died on the dirty street in front of the Tabacchi before help could get to him.

That day played itself out again in Rafe's mind as she wrote. When she and Gabri went looking for Brettito, the owner of the Tabacchi tried to keep them away because he knew all three of them. But despite his efforts, Rafe and Gabri saw the ambulance speed away with Brettito's body.

---

[26] Tobacco Shop
[27] Military Police

Rafe looked around her and realized she was standing in a large pool of blood that seemed to fill the street. It was blood belonging to Brettito. She fell to her knees and then lay prostrate in the bloody street inconsolable. Gabri and the Tabacchi owner pulled Rafe out of the street and tried to clean off the blood covering her as best they could as she fell apart.

They called her father and Brettito's family. When Rafe's father got there, he thought she had been shot or injured and rushed her to the hospital. The blood from Rafe's clothes and hands had transferred, covering almost every part of her bare skin including her face and hair. Once Rafe was finally taken home, she got very sick and didn't leave her home for almost two weeks except to go to Brettito's funeral.

Rafe was allowed to go to the funeral, but her father kept her well away from Brettito's family because Brettito's mother blamed Rafe for what had happened. His mother found Brettito's notebook in his room. In it, he had detailed his plan and what he was doing with the zingari. He wrote in the notebook he was doing it for Rafe because he thought he was in love with her even though they were not yet thirteen. Brettito's mother told everyone who would listen, if it were not for Rafe, he would still be alive.

Rafe's only consoling moments were with Gabri, who stole Brettito's notebook so they could see exactly what he was doing. They found out the zingari kids told him they would tell him all their *mistici segreti,* but in the end, they knew the zingari were just using him. They both thought if he had not kept it a secret, they could have helped and he would still be there with them. It was soon after his death when Rafe and her father moved to Milan and then less than a year later, to America.

It was hard for Rafe to think about Brettito without feeling the pain and guilt she felt over his death. She had always felt responsible for him and the way he died. She had resolved never to lose control as she did that day in the street again. Lately, she felt like her control was slipping, and she had to fight hard not to spiral into despair over all the people she had lost.

5

EDEN KINGSLEY WAS let inside the luxury hotel suite once occupied by Rafe Salvaggio by the hotel clerk Howard. Immediately, she and her fiancé Jake, along with Abby and Julia, began desperately searching for clues they hoped would tell them where to find Rafe and her missing baby.

Abby took in the opulence of the room and looked at Julia, her expression a cross between jealousy and being miffed. "How the hell did she get a room like this? Look at this place! It's bigger than my apartment!" She walked into the living room and stopped. "No the fuck way! A balcony! She got a suite with a balcony!"

"Actually, there are two balconies in this suite. One in the living room and one in the bedroom up the spiral staircase," Howard informed them.

"The spiral staircase? Julia, this place has a spiral staircase!" Abby repeated resentfully as they went up the spiral staircase to the bedroom. "I didn't even know they had rooms like this!"

Julia shook her head at Abby's antics. "Abby, you couldn't afford this room. It probably costs more for a week here than a month at your apartment."

"The rooms on this level are for our Gold Club guests," explained Howard.

"Well, how the hell did she get to be in this Gold Club?" asked Abby. "Better question—why didn't she tell me, or even invite me to stay with her? My room is a friggin' closet compared to this!"

Julia headed toward the night table to see if she could find a clue about where Rafe might have gone. "She travels so much for her company. She's probably a member of a lot of hotel clubs. As far as why she didn't ask you to stay in her room," she rolled her eyes, "well, you'll have to ask her about her reasons." Finding nothing, she grabbed Abby and directed her into the stairway to go back down to the living area of the hotel room.

"Oh, I'll be asking her all right," Abby affirmed as she was pushed out of the room and made her way down the stairs. She straightened her skewed shirt and looked up to see Jake entering from the balcony. "So, did you see the balcony? Yeah, there is one up in the bedroom too."

"We didn't find any clues up there. What about you?" asked Julia with concern.

"Nope, just a big ole bathroom, a bed big enough for ten people and a huge balcony!" complained Abby. "I can't believe this place!"

"No clues," said Jake with a frown, "but it looks like she had a toy store dumped in there too. No wonder Bronte always wanted to go with her."

"We have an outside provider who offers a variety of children's packages for our clientele with children. I believe Ms. Salvaggio requested the 'Toddler Mania' package. It's one of the many perks of the Gold Club," expounded Howard trying to be helpful.

"Well, it's just more proof she thinks being a parent is more about playing and buying things than having quality time and being there when times are hard," complained Jake as he crossed his arms.

"I don't know about that," offered Abby backing off her complaining about her friend since someone else was jumping on the wagon. It was okay for her but not for anyone else. "I just think, you know, she hadn't seen Bronte for so long she just went a little overboard. You guys should make sure they get to see each other more."

"Yeah, I don't think so," grunted Jake. "Like I told her yesterday, she needs to move on and not make things harder for Bronte to settle into a normal life."

"What?" Abby screeched. "Oh, no you," she started to say as she tried to go after Jake. She was held back by Julia who had grabbed the waist of Abby's skirt.

Julia was showing more control than Abby but was still clearly shocked by Jakes words. "I think we all need to calm down, and I can't believe Eden would agree with you, Jake," she said calmly, though the steel in her eyes was showing.

Jake looked at the two women and shook his head. They were as bad as Rafe. He couldn't wait until he married Eden and they took Bronte and moved far away from these people. He knew someday Eden would be grateful he rescued her and her child from the clutches of an immoral lifestyle and the people like Rafe and her friends who tried to keep her tied to it by using the innocence of a child as a tool. He turned to go find Eden, leaving the women and their excuses for Rafe behind him.

Julia looked at Abby with concern, and they followed Jake to find Eden. She was almost sorry she held Abby back, but she didn't want to compound the problem at hand.

Eden circled the large suite for what seemed like the tenth time. She rubbed her arms to soothe the pain from the pins and needles caused by her anxiety threatening to bring their pain to her.

"There's nothing here. Nothing!" Close to tears, she looked at Jake and the girls. "She could be anywhere by now!" Jake went to her and put his arms around her to give her some small comfort.

"Let's not lose hope. We should search the hotel," suggested Julia wringing her hands with worry.

Eden, feeling suffocated and angry, pushed Jake away. Being touched while on the verge of an anxiety attack only made her feel worse. "This hotel is huge! Where the heck do we start?"

"Yeah, uh, we can split up," suggested Abby. "Eden, you and Jake look on all the floors and the roof. Julia, look in the parking lots and see if you can find Rafe's rental car. Ask the manager what kind it is. I'll search the bars, the shops, and the lobbies."

Jake looked at Eden then at Howard, the hotel clerk. "You come with us in case we need any doors unlocked. Come on, Eden. We'll find Bronte if she's here, and that woman better not have the baby in a bar."

Anxiety built inside her as her heart pounded, and she began to shake in fear. Eden looked at Jake horrified.

"If she's here? If she's here! And if she's not, we're just wasting more time. Rafe, why?"

She began to collapse and reached for the bed, but Jake intervened and took her into his arms. Between not knowing where Rafe and Bronte were and Jake smothering her when she kept telling him she needed space because of her anxiety, it was finally too much. Her tears released in a storm as her body shook with grief.

"Let's get started," encouraged Abby. "The manager has called the police, and as long as we're looking, we aren't wasting time. Let's go," she said as she looked at Julia worriedly.

"I need to stay and make sure everything's in order here and lock up," said Howard as they walked to the door. "Can I meet you at your room, Ms. Kingsley?"

"That'll be fine," Jake answered for Eden. They made their way out of the room, and Jake gently took Eden's arm and pulled her along. "Let's go check with our friends. Maybe she's been seen by one of them, and if not, we can ask them to help."

Abby gave Julia a look of annoyance. "What the fuck? Like we're not her friends?"

"Calm down. He's just trying to give her some hope," conceded Julia. "I'll head downstairs, but I'm not going to start talking to everyone until we know for sure she's not here. We need to know the facts before we start talking to people. We don't want to make things harder than they already are for Rafe."

"Oh, right. That's for me, huh? You think I'm gonna say something to make the situation harder for both Eden and Rafe. Well, thanks a lot for the show of confidence." Abby pouted.

"It's not that, Abby," she tried to explain. "This isn't about your issues." She knew once Abby even thought she was offended there was no stopping the escalation of temper that would come out. "Listen, let's just focus on finding Rafe. I'll meet you later."

Abby watched Julia head down the hallway, and she was tempted to go after her and put in her thoughts about Julia and her issues. She heard the door to the room click closed, and she turned and saw Howard coming toward her.

"I'm glad you're still here," he said. "The manager just called to let me know about the rental car. Apparently, Ms. Salvaggio did leave for a short while, but then she returned. She's somewhere in the hotel, after all. The manager alerted security but decided not to call the police yet. So your idea of checking all the public spaces is probably the best. I'm sure they're just waiting somewhere."

"I knew Rafe wouldn't do what Jake thought she did. She wouldn't hurt them like he keeps saying. Thanks, I'm on it!" Abby ran down the hallway heading for the closest elevator.

6

THE HUMMING FROM the heating system in the old hotel made a soft whirring sound when it clicked on to regulate the temperature. Rafe stopped writing to wad up the paper she had used to calm herself unsuccessfully and find direction. Absently, she discarded it amongst the pile of toys. She used to be able to write to her mother and work out problems for herself, but lately, it hadn't worked. Now when she tried to think about her mother, there was pain instead of comfort.

She missed her mother and her father deeply and wished they were here to help her deal with the mess she had made of her life.

Rafe took out the book of poetry that had belonged to her father from her shoulder bag. She carried the book with her now whenever she traveled and took comfort in the memories of him reading to her when she was young. She missed talking and laughing with him in Italian. There were not many people around her anymore she could speak with in her childhood language.

She had been seriously considering moving back to Italy if there was really nothing left for her here. Since the death of her father and after her break up with Eden, Gabri kept encouraging Rafe, whenever they spoke, to come back home. Even after finalizing all the work involved for sale of her business Rafe felt like she couldn't leave. Not with the adoption of Bronte still unresolved. When she got a call from a head hunter about a possible job opportunity she decided to accept the position. She hoped it would fulfill the dual purpose of keeping her busy and allowing her time with Bronte, if it was permitted by Eden and Jake. She had not told Gabri about the possibility of losing Bronte yet. She could not bear the pain of confessing her failure.

Bronte was fighting sleep as she played, determined to stay awake even though soon, her body would take control and take the rest it needed for her to dream and grow. Now she was looking at the picture of the reindeer and babbling about what she saw.

Rafe picked her up and lay back on the couch with her and the photo. "Hey, B Girl, did you have fun petting the reindeer? Yeah? Well, it looks like you're getting sleepy. Here, let me put the picture with your toys, and I'll read you my father's favorite poem." She began to read softly, speaking to the baby in Italian, and within minutes, they were both asleep.

7

EDEN KINGSLEY AND Jake Thompson had searched through all the floors in the hotel including the roof and still no Rafe. They made their way back down to the lobby hoping to see Abby or Julia and to see if they had any news. Jake was angry because the hotel clerk was nowhere to be found so they couldn't look inside anyone's room. He kept telling Eden he was sure one of Rafe's friends was probably hiding the baby in their room.

They made it to the main floor of the hotel and were just outside the hotel bar where Jake searched the crowd while Eden paced and worried.

"Where are they?" she asked desperately. "We've been searching the hotel for an hour. Where are the police? Where are Abby and Julia?"

"I'm sure they're still looking," answered Jake. "This is a big place. It'll take some time."

"I'm so lost," Eden sobbed as she rubbed her arms trying to ease the pain brought on by her anxiety.

Jake led her to a chair then rubbed Eden's shoulder reassuringly as she sat down and wiped her tears.

"She knows what she's doing," he said angrily. "She knows you have chronic anxiety, and she's doing this to cause you pain. She's doing it to try to control you again because she's not getting her way."

"What if I never see her again?" she asked terrified of never seeing Bronte again. "Rafe could be anywhere." The thought Rafe would do this to her was a devastating blow. It was so unreal. She felt as if it just couldn't be happening, but it was—it was.

Jake shook his head in frustration. "She has the money to take her away if she has her in custody. Plus you never got Bronte's passport from Rafe. Now you know why I've been warning you about her," he said and hoped it would not be too late to get Bronte back.

"What am I going to do?" she asked in anguish. Eden knew Rafe was angry with her. She had made so many excuses for Bronte not being able to visit Rafe over the last eight months.

But she was afraid.

Jake had told her horror stories about what could happen if they let her take Bronte, and now, it seemed like he was right. All the stories about children taken away, out of the country and never found, spun in her mind. The father of her baby was in Italy. Rafe was his friend. If she took Bronte there, her mind reeled. She couldn't process the thought Rafe would take her away to Italy, and she would never see her baby again. Jake constantly and relentlessly reminded her of those terrifying facts.

Eden's anxiety level had risen, and she was very close to being in a debilitating panic. If she didn't get answers soon, if she did not get her baby back soon, she knew all of her anger would shrink into nothing and the panic growing inside would overwhelm her. Then she would shut down.

Last night, she could see how angry Rafe was with both her and Jake. They had not told Rafe they were having their own little birthday party for Bronte, and everyone was there, all of her and Rafe's friends and all of Jakes friends. Jake thought it would be best they not invite Rafe because some of the people were his friends and they might be uncomfortable with 'the situation' as he called it.

Rafe just happened to be having her dinner and saw them. When she realized what was happening Eden could tell it was all Rafe could do to control herself. Then Jake just had to push her more by announcing their plans to marry and move away. If Jake had let her invite Rafe, maybe this would not be happening.

Being in Rafe's room had only brought on more despair. She was reminded of her wealth and her career sending her all over the world and of what she could offer Bronte. Rafe's scent in the room reminded her of what they had together, a time that seemed so long ago.

Life with Rafe, for the longest time, seemed so good, like they were going to be okay and start their family.

Then it happened.

She knew Rafe had been unhappy for a while, but she never talked about it. Eden was unhappy herself because of the mounting stress and lack of control over her inability to conceive. She felt it was all her fault and took a lot of the anger at herself out on Rafe. She even had the nerve to tell Rafe all she ever did was throw money at the problem, even if it hurt her and made her feel like a breeder cow.

Not even the therapy she had insisted on back then had helped her sort through her anxieties. Then Rafe accused her of changing her mind and not wanting a family. She couldn't deny it. She had been having doubts and feelings of insecurity. On top of her insecurities, she had been feeling like maybe she should be having a baby with a man and not Rafe. It was something she could not bring herself to tell Rafe at the time.

Then Rafe had to bring her friend from Italy home and ask him to be their donor without even talking to her about it. She kept seeing the two of them together.

Rafe and Gabri were like two beautiful dark-haired angels visiting the poor mortals of earth. They would smile down at her, and she felt so overwhelmed at the sight of them. They made everything around them seem insignificant because they were so striking. She could barely utter a word as she watched them speak with each other in a language she couldn't understand and hold each other close.

Eden knew they were not lovers, but they had a closeness that made her jealous. She watched them as they sat close and talked about who knows what. According to Rafe, it was about everything from their childhood to her father who was sick. She also said she told him about their relationship and desire to have a family.

It was just like Rafe to be out working and make some big decision and then come home and announce her plans. She could be so filled with self-interest and so thoughtless. Of course, Rafe had to leave for another work trip to Milan, which left everything up in the air.

Then Rafe's father died, and they had to go to New York for the funeral. Rafe was so caught up in everything with the funeral arrangements and the sale of her father's apartment, Eden felt like an outcast and a stranger. Rafe had everyone she knew surrounding her, and Eden tried to be congenial, but dealing with strangers was hard for her, and she felt like she should just stay out of the way.

Even when they were alone with each other, Eden couldn't push through the doubts she was having and the anger at Rafe for not talking to her first about Gabri. At that moment, they seemed very far apart. She wanted to be there for Rafe, but with everything going on and her own anxiety beginning to overcome her, she decided just to go home.

After she got home, Eden finally calmed herself and thought about what Rafe had done, and why she wanted Gabri to be their donor. She admitted to herself Rafe did it out of love and not just self-interest and felt terrible for feeling angry with her. That night, she did a test and saw she was ovulating, so the next day, she went and withdrew from the sperm bank and did an insemination on her own. She hoped it would be the perfect surprise for Rafe if it worked, and they would be happy with each other again.

A few days later, she went to the front door and was so happy to see it was a flower delivery. She thought Rafe was trying to say everything would be all right before coming home. But after reading the card, her world came crumbling down.

The flowers were not for her.

They were for Rafe. From someone who 'had a wonderful evening, my darling,' and she knew.

Rafe had cheated on her.

Later, in the middle of Rafe denying and then finally admitting what she had done, and then trying to apologize, Eden moved out. A short time after leaving Rafe, she found out she was pregnant. The last insemination treatment she had done on herself while Rafe was in New York had worked. Eden felt simultaneously terrified and happy. She wanted to be a mother but never thought she would be doing something so big on her own.

Rafe found out about the pregnancy when Eden was about four months along. Eden hadn't told Rafe because she was still so angry with her at first, then she wanted to wait to make sure she was not going to miscarry, then... she really had no excuse except it would be hard to face Rafe because she had waited so long.

When everything was finally out, Eden was glad Rafe knew. Rafe bent over backward for her, especially when she had to move back in with her because of some complications with the pregnancy.

But in the end, it just was not enough.

The damage was done.

The trust was not there anymore, and she began to feel like her life was in crisis. She was contemplating spending her life with someone she couldn't trust, and then there was the overwhelming responsibility of a child bearing down on her. Complicating it all were the feelings she was having about needing to be in a relationship with a man she was trying to deal with and understand. She did the only thing she could think of at the time. She left Rafe again a few months after Bronte was born and struggled to make a good life.

Now Jake was a fixture in her life, and it seemed like she was in another whirlwind. Joining her past life with Rafe and her present life with Jake was becoming nothing less than a complete disaster. She just didn't know how to find a place where all three of them could make things work so Bronte would have the best of both their worlds. Now Rafe was proving Jake right and breaking her heart all over again.

"We'll find her," said Jake taking her hand as he saw the worry on Eden's face. "And when we do, we'll make sure she never sees Bronte again. Bronte needs a father. Eden, I want to be her father. She deserves a normal family."

"We will find her," growled Eden, "and when we do, I swear, I'll kill Rafe! All I want is my baby back!" She leaned into Jake and cried into his shoulder again not knowing what else to do.

Jake held Eden and knew this time Rafe had gone too far, and his plan to marry Eden and take Bronte far away from the influence of Rafe and those friends was going to work out. Rafe was doing so many things to make Eden angry he was sure there was no way she would allow the adoption to go through. He held her tighter as she cried and knew if Rafe had left with Bronte, then he would have all the ammunition he needed to take both Eden and Bronte away for good.

Jake couldn't wait to get away from all of these people Eden called her friends, people who defended Rafe every time she did something to hurt Eden. This was exactly what he warned Eden about and why he wanted to keep both Eden and Bronte away from her. Rafe was so cocky and full of herself. She was always trying to undermine him and show him up with her money and connections. But he would always have the upper hand because Eden and Bronte belonged with him. He knew he could give them a better life than Rafe could ever give them. He would save both Eden and Bronte from Rafe and her ilk and all the pain and damage they were causing.

Eden's mobile phone rang, and she answered it quickly. "Rafe?" she answered hopefully. "Oh, Abby, where are you?" she asked disappointed.

"Eden, you need to meet me at the front desk," said Abby through the phone.

"What is it? Did you find her? I'm going to strangle her!"

"Just meet me at the front desk," she answered and ended the call.

8

ABIGALE VAN FALKOV, or Abby as her friends called her, waited happily for Eden at the front desk. She was happy because she had found Rafe and everything would be good again. She and Rafe went back a long way and the past eight months had been hard on Rafe.

They met three months after Rafe moved to Los Angeles over eight years ago. Abby had cornered her at a lesbian club and started interrogating her about her work and personal life. Rafe had laughed at Abby as the questions shot out from her enthusiastically and rapidly.

Abby told her all about herself and her job as a reporter for a small publication and she did freelance work for a few others. Abby was impressed by Rafe's company and wanted to do an article. Rafe told her, in a smooth sexy Italian accent, anyone who could make her laugh so much, she would like to work with. So, she gave her the interview.

They ended up dating for a few months, and Abby found out Rafe could turn her accent on and off at will. It was only a short time later when Rafe broke up with her. Rafe gave her a line about knowing 'her true love was out there somewhere' and they should 'just be friends' because they both needed to 'focus on being in a good place' so when their true loves came, they would be ready.

Needless to say, it didn't go over well with Abby. She was very angry with Rafe for a long time after that night because it looked to her like Rafe was just out dating a lot of women. But, eventually, she realized Rafe was right. They were better off friends. It had taken a lot of emotional work on Abby's part, but they remained friends since then.

Rafe did more interviews it helped her out a lot when she needed local interest pieces. The best thing Rafe did though was to introduce Abby to her cousin, Letty Carver, the actress. It did wonders for getting back into her good graces again. Abby had come a long way with her writing and her personal life. Since then, she spent a lot of time with Rafe whenever she was in town.

Rafe began seeing Eden a couple of years after they had dated. Eden was very shy and didn't talk much, but Abby did enough talking for the both of them. Abby had spent a lot of time with Eden when she was trying to get pregnant because Rafe was gone a lot for work. She even consoled Eden when she left Rafe because of the affair. Abby had been disappointed in Rafe but not surprised she had an affair. Rafe had this way about her and it made people want her. She could just look at someone and smile in her 'wildling' way, and she got what she wanted. Abby managed not to tell Eden her thoughts about it all because they would have just upset her more at the time.

Right now, she was relieved that Rafe had not taken Bronte as they all had thought. She looked up and saw Eden and Jake walking quickly toward her. Neither one looked happy. She knew she would have to do some pre-damage control to de-escalate the situation.

Eden made her way through the hotel with Jake close on her heels. She was angry Abby had not answered her questions. Jake was insisting they were probably protecting Rafe again.

The only thing she knew at the moment was Rafe would definitely need protection when Eden found her for taking her baby.

Rushing up to Abby at the front desk, Eden grabbed her by the shoulders. "Where is she? What's happening?"

"Eden, I think you need to calm down. I know where she is, and I'll take you to her, but you have to calm down." She calmly shrugged out of Eden's grip and crossed her arms.

"Tell us where she is," demanded Jake. "That woman has put Eden through hell, and I'm going to make sure she pays!"

Abby turned her attention to Jake. "You just need to stay here," she said tapping him on his broad chest. She turned to Eden and sighed. "Calm down now. Everything's okay. I promise," she said and waited for her to calm down. "Now come on, just you," she said to Eden then she glared at Jake.

Eden took a deep breath and looked at Jake. She held her hand up as he started to speak. "It's okay, Jake. I think you should stay here. I'll be back." Abby took her arm and steered her away from the front desk.

Abby led Eden down a short hallway and turned into an alcove that had been turned into a seating area with couches and tables. Eden thought she saw movement and tried to rush in, but Abby held onto Eden's arm keeping her from running forward.

"Look, they're asleep. They just fell asleep. Nothing terrible happened," she whispered.

Eden took in the scene and saw Rafe and Bronte really were asleep. Rafe was holding a small book balanced on the couch beside her. Bronte's toys were on the floor and table along with a Polaroid photo.

"They're here," Eden whispered holding back tears of relief.

"Come on. Let's wake up Rafe and try not to wake up the baby."

Swallowing back tears, Eden nodded. "Okay."

She walked quietly over to Rafe, and the baby then knelt down next to the couch and lightly touched Rafe's arm. Eden gently lifted the book from Rafe's hand and was surprised to see Rafe was still wearing the gold ring matching the one she had taken off months ago. That ring had been replaced with the engagement ring from Jake she now wore on her hand.

"Rafe. Rafe, wake up," she whispered gently.

Rafe opened her eyes slowly and seemed to have forgotten where she was laying. She felt the weight of Bronte on her and looked at Eden.

"Oh, *ciao*,"[28] she mumbled then cleared her throat. "Hi. I guess you're back from dinner. I tried your room, but you weren't back yet." She started to lift Bronte and Eden stood up to help.

"Yeah, I'm back." She smiled, and her senses reeled as she caught Rafe's familiar scent. It had been so long since she was this close to the woman who was her first love, but her body remembered and reacted even though she fought against it.

Rafe sat up carefully as Eden lifted Bronte and held her close and then kissed the baby's sleeping face. She wiped her

---

[28] Hello

hand across her eyes as Eden gently sat down with Bronte. She looked at the table and picked up the photo.

"Hey, we went to the petting zoo and saw a reindeer, look." Rafe handed Eden the picture of her and Bronte with the reindeer.

Eden looked at the photo and smiled. "It's nice. It looks like it was fun." She tried to hand picture back to Rafe.

"Yeah, it was our adventure. You keep it, for Bronte. Just in case, you know, it's our last." Rafe looked into Eden's eyes and could see she had been crying. Rafe knew Eden had thought the worst. She had to look away as the pain and guilt of what she had almost done ran through her. She swallowed and forced herself to look back at Eden. "I know you still hate me for... everything. I just wish you had talked to me. But we just can't seem to hear each other right now. I hope you don't change your mind about the adoption."

Breaking Rafe's pain filled gaze, Eden looked down. "Rafe..." She sighed sadly, remembering last night as Jake smiled triumphantly and Rafe stormed out of the restaurant.

Rafe took a deep breath and looked down at the time on her phone. "Well, I have to go. I have a plane to catch." She picked up the phone, her book, cashmere jacket, and bag and then made her way past Abby and out of the room as Eden held Bronte close and watched her go.

Abby watched as one friend left in pain and the other collapsed back into the couch in relief.

"I'll go tell the manager everything's okay."

Eden nodded as Abby left and put the sleeping Bronte on the couch before she began gathering the toys and putting them in the diaper bag.

As she cleaned the area, she found several wadded up pieces of hotel stationery that had fallen onto the floor. She smoothed them out and saw they were in Rafe's handwriting. She began to read.

***

Mama,

I've done something tonight that until hours ago seemed unthinkable. I've just said what may be my final goodbye to the last piece of my life, my daughter Bronte.

So much has happened, and I've lost so much, but I never thought things would come to this end. I lost you so long ago, but the pain is still with me. I've lost so much time with Bronte we will never get back; we are still almost strangers to each other. I lost Papa who I loved so much and was really the only one who could accept me fully and without judgment, though our relationship was turbulent for a long time. I lost a good friend, Brettito, in a way it still haunts me as much as the way I lost you. I didn't get to say goodbye to him or tell him how much it meant he was my friend at a time in my life where I seemed to be drowning. I've lost Eden, the person I loved the most in this world, who now can't love me anymore. I hurt her, and now she wants to live a different life, one free of me. I hope she finds happiness. So many people gone suddenly who I didn't get to say goodbye too.

I ask myself, did I drive her to this because of what I did to her or did she ever really love me? I don't feel like I will ever find the kind of love I had for her again. I don't know if I want to find it. It's just another opportunity for me to lose something.

Now, tonight, I may be losing this beautiful creation Eden and I craved and planned together for so long. The worst part about it is the feeling of helplessness. The last time I felt like this was when Papa died. I feel like I am gripped so tightly by my own fear, pain, and feeling of being lost and out of control of things in my life.

I am haunted by the possibility Bronte will grow up and I won't be able to share even the smallest part of her life. I have a heart connection with her that defies even my understanding. Bronte is Eden's child, but she is a reflection of me too, and her life and future matter to me.

What will Eden tell Bronte about me in the future? I don't want to be just a 'checkbook' as she calls me. Someone who sends money or gifts, who is called a friend of the family, or a godmother. I am Bronte's mother no matter what Eden and her new fiancé Jake tell everyone.

Yes, Mamma, it's true. They are telling their 'friends' I am just some random friend of Eden's. I guess they really are going to block the adoption and cut me out of their life and Bronte's future. I wish you were here to tell me what to do. I wish I knew what else to do besides throwing my checkbook at the problem and prove Eden's accusations to be true. I can't even talk with her anymore without someone accusing me of bullying her or manipulating her.

I really hate to lose or give up, but I am at my wit's end. I don't want to hurt Bronte, so maybe the best thing is just to walk away. It's just so hard to know what to do. Will it be like Jake says 'Bronte can't miss what she never had'? How will she feel if she ever found out I was supposed to be her mother? Will she feel like I betrayed her by not being there? What do I say to Gabri if he asks about the baby he helped us make? Have I betrayed him too? Will I always be the betrayer?

I just hope if Eden dissolves the adoption petition, and I don't get to become Bronte's other parent, she finds the compassion to at least let Bronte know who I am as a person, and about Gabri.

I wish I could be there as our daughter grows and help her be sure of her place in the world. There was no one in my life I could talk to about my feelings, no mother to help me through my high school nightmares. No woman's sympathetic ear to listen to my dilemma about how to handle coming out and who I should date and how to handle my feelings about being attracted to girls when we moved to America and I could barely speak English. I still remember the words you gave me and wonder how different things would have been if you were here to actually say them, and I could look in your eyes and ask you questions. I really wanted to be that person for Bronte, her mentor and her mother, along with Eden, so no matter who she loves or what happens in her life, she will know she can always be herself and be confident she is supported.

It's so clear what Eden and Jake are planning. Tomorrow, I will be starting a new life, one with not a single person in it I love.

My life is so fucking out of control. I'm not sure how to start living again.

~Rafe

***

Eden finished reading the letter and wiped away her tears. She remembered this old habit of Rafe's well. Every time Rafe had a problem she had to work through, she would either draw in her notebook or write to her mom. It was something she said her father started her doing when she was twelve so she could both work through her problems and manage her grief for the loss of her mother. In her letters, she just wrote her feelings in a raw way with little editing just to get the words on paper. There was not always eloquence, but there was always a lot of emotion and questions. It was the same with this letter.

Eden leaned forward to hold her head in her hands. "Oh, Rafe," she whispered to herself.

She realized she had made her first mistakes with Bronte already. She was sorry she had not told her new friends exactly who Rafe was. She didn't think about how much it would hurt Rafe. She wasn't thinking. She knew Bronte needed Rafe in her life. She folded the letter and put it in her pocket. She knew it would be a fight with Jake, but she had to go through with the adoption.

It was just the right thing to do.

9

JULIA HAWTHORN MADE her way through the hotel looking for any sign of Rafe and Bronte. She could not believe the first time they all got together after Eden and Rafe's break up Rafe was doing something so crackbrained. It seemed, for a while, Rafe had dropped off the planet, and Eden had gone to a side of the planet they rarely visited. In a way, she understood why Rafe would be upset, but it was still no excuse for taking Bronte off to parts unknown.

Rafe had come into Julia's life when they were both fourteen. Both of them had just moved to America, and their father's enrolled them in private school in New York. It was there she met Rafe. She remembered Rafe telling her, in her heavily accented English, she was the first silver-haired blue-eyed American she had ever met and had been fascinated with her hair and how blue her eyes were.

Julia was an angry fourteen-year-old and didn't want to be in America away from all her friends left behind in England. Rafe matched her in her hatred of the situation they had been thrown into by their parents.

Julia's father, Ian Hawthorn, an international financial broker, had accepted a position in England when Julia was four years old. Julia had been going to her boarding school as a day pupil since the age of six then went as a boarder from age seven only having summers and holidays at home, or where ever her family was at the time.

The girls from the boarding school had become her family and lifeline for her since her parents were either working or fulfilling other social obligations. Leaving her friends was devastating, and for a long time, she hated her parents for taking her away from the life she knew.

The girls at their new school in New York were relentless in teasing Julia about her English accent. They were always telling her she was not really an American and she should go back to England where she could be understood. She was glad it was not a boarding school, and she could go home at the end of the day.

Julia had a difficult time adjusting. One day, a few months after school had started, she was sitting alone in the corridor. She looked up and saw an olive skinned, dark haired girl, completely disgracing her school uniform. Her tie wasn't done, her shirt was misbuttoned, and flapping out of her skirt, and her school jacket was being used as a book bag. The girl was walking confidently toward the exit before she stopped and stared at Julia for a moment. Julia then became self-conscious.

Julia was angry with the girl for looking at her and asked her what she was doing. The girl said she needed an adventure, so she was leaving. Then she invited Julia along. It was then Julia found out it was Rafe's first day in the school. Julia was impressed and decided she liked the dark-haired girl and the way she thought.

That was the day they began their tumultuous friendship. Soon, their adventures became competitions and sometimes, they became dangerous—though they had been lucky they always managed to pull through without much of a scratch.

Their friendship became more entwined when they realized they had another thing in common—they were both gay. Rafe was much more aware of herself where that was concerned than Julia. Once Julia became aware she was gay, and announced it at dinner, her mother was incandescent. She was so lit up with anger she could have powered a New York power grid. There was no more mucking about with Rafe until Julia's father intervened. For some reason, he had come to like Rafe, despite anything negative Julia's mother had to say about her. Since Julia's father first met Rafe at the age of fourteen, he had come to adore her, though Julia had no idea why.

To Julia's disappointment, she and Rafe decided a long time ago they were better off as friends, and it was probably why they still liked each other. They were both very strong willed and clashed most of the time though somehow stayed friends, even after Rafe was sent off to a different school a year before they were to graduate together.

Now Julia worked for her father in the California division of his international brokerage firm. When Julia found out Rafe had moved to California, she called her with the hope of adding her accounts to their business. Rafe was busy setting up her new offices, but Julia was persistent, and eventually, Rafe found the time and gave them a meeting. Between Julia and her father, Ian, they convinced Rafe to open accounts with them, and they have taken care of her personal and business financial services since then.

They also renewed their friendship. Julia found Rafe had not changed much when they started going out to clubs having adventures again. Every weekend was a party, and it seemed like Rafe could find women anywhere she went. Sometimes, Rafe would be gone for weeks. Then, when anyone asked, she would just smile and maybe wink before changing the subject. It drove Julia mad. She didn't know how she did it but knew it had to have something to do with the accent she could turn on and off at will—when she was sober, anyway. When Rafe was into her pints, buzzed from liquor, the accent came out regardless.

A couple of years later, Rafe met Eden. It seemed like everything had just stopped, and Rafe had become someone new. She settled down and talked about starting a family. It was shocking. Rafe was with Eden for over four years, and things were good until she fell into an old temptation while in New York.

Now Rafe seemed to be behaving erratically and thoughtlessly, which was completely out of character from anything she had ever done before. Julia could understand the old Rafe, and even the newly formed Rafe with Eden, but this strangely erratic Rafe was something new having combined with her old danger-seeking behavior. The idea she would actually take things to this level was even more shocking.

Julia looked over and saw Rafe outside the hotel entrance. She was putting on her coat and waiting for the valet. She stepped outside to confront her. "Rafe! Where the bloody hell have you been?" she asked frantically. "It's almost midnight! Where's Bronte? Eden is looking everywhere and literally worried sick!"

"Calm down, Julia," said Rafe with a frown. "Eden has her baby."

"What the hell were you thinking?" she demanded. "Last night, you stormed out of your daughter's birthday party and today, you took the baby without telling anyone! Rafe, you can't keep doing things like this!"

Rafe looked at Julia holding in her anger as the valet pulled up with her car. She needed to get away from everything. Going home early seemed like the best thing to do since she didn't think she could look at Eden anymore for a while. This whole trip had been a bad idea, and she didn't even know why Eden had invited her unless it was to rub Jake and their plans in her face.

"Fuck off, Julia! You have no idea what's going on!"

"I know Eden has been crazy sick with worry, and Jake is telling me they're planning to move. Are you trying to push them away?"

"I don't have to try," she said through clenched teeth. "Open your fucking eyes! They're going to do whatever they want despite anything I do," Rafe said angrily. "For your information, I wasn't even invited to the fucking party! So it looks to me like there won't be an adoption either!"

She opened her car door and looked over at the friend who she felt was betraying her by helping Eden and Jake.

"Stay the fuck out of my life, Julia! All of you just stay the fuck away from me!" She got in her car angrily, slammed the door, threw it in gear, and left them all to their happy fucking lives together.

Julia stood stunned at Rafe's revelation as she watched her drive away. She went back inside and saw Abby at the front desk talking to the manager. She made her way to Abby as she finished her conversation.

"Have you seen Eden?"

"Yeah, she has Bronte," Abby said with a relieved smile. "I think Jake may be with his friends and Hunter."

"We need to talk to Eden about Rafe," Julia declared. "I know Rafe may still be mad at Eden for the whole break up situation, but Eden's not being very fair when it comes to the baby. Rafe was furious when she left."

"Well, can you blame her? This whole trip has been fucked up, and it's not even over yet," Abby squeaked.

"I think we should try to catch up with Eden and have a talk," said Julia as she nodded toward Eden.

They caught up with Eden who was carrying Bronte and her bag through the hotel toward the elevators.

"Eden," Abby called out. "Wait for us."

Eden stopped, and as she looked at them, she could see the concern on their faces. "I was just taking Bronte up to bed."

"In case you don't know, Rafe was very angry when she left," Julia informed her. "Why would she want to leave a week early?"

"You're not still upset with her, are you? They were just asleep," Abby reminded her, worried Eden and Rafe would continue not to get along.

Julia looked at Eden as she shifted the sleeping Bronte and remembered what Rafe had told her.

"Eden, did you not invite Rafe to Bronte's birthday party? I thought it was one of the main reasons we were here."

Eden looked up at Julia and could not hide the guilt she felt as she blushed red. She sat down in a hallway chair because Bronte was getting heavy in her arms and the guilt she was feeling was weighing heavily on her.

"It was," she said quickly. "Jake, we, we just thought she wouldn't want to be there with all of Jake's friends there, and we thought maybe she had her own plans."

"What the hell?" Abby screeched out then spoke quietly so she wouldn't make a scene. "You didn't invite her?" she asked harshly and sat down next to her. "We were there, and we're Rafe's friends too!"

"How could you put us in this position Eden?" Julia asked in dismay. "How could you not even tell Rafe your plans? I knew there had to be more to her walking out than your engagement announcement," said Julia as she crossed her arms. "No wonder she was so angry and demanded we all stay out of her life."

"Why would you think she wouldn't want to be there?" asked Abby as Eden cringed from both of their barrages of questions and accusations.

"Are you going to leave and not allow the adoption?" Julia asked, and they both looked at Eden for an answer.

"No," she stammered. "I mean yes, I'm still allowing the adoption."

"Well, I think you should tell Rafe, don't you?" asked Julia.

"Yeah, and you should probably stop making excuses for her not being able to see Bronte," added Abby. "Then maybe things like last night won't happen again." She looked at Eden. Eden couldn't meet their eyes, and Abby could not hold back her thoughts. "I know you told her Bronte would be with Jake's son Hunter in the nursery room tonight. Then when we were looking for her, you told us the babysitter had been dismissed from your room. I'll bet when she saw no one was there she decided she should be able to spend time with her."

Eden finally looked at them in shame. "Jake just thought it would be better if Bronte wasn't with the bigger kids, so we changed our plans. We didn't lie to her. We just changed our minds," Eden tried to explain weakly.

"So, you didn't offer Rafe the option of taking her when you knew she wanted to spend time with her?" Julia shook her head in disbelief. "That's just awful, Eden. How could you do that to her? Why did you invite her here if you weren't planning to include her?"

"You better do something about how you handle Rafe's time with Bronte," said Abby sadly. "She loves her, and you always make promises to Rafe you never keep."

"No wonder she thinks you're leaving, and she won't get to adopt," said Julia flailing her arms in frustration at Eden. "What are you going to do about this?"

"You're right," said Eden anxiously, already on edge from arguing with Jake about Rafe and the adoption. "I'm going to fix it, I promise." She put her hand in her pocket and felt Rafe's letter. "I'll make sure she knows," she swallowed, "as soon as we get home."

10

RAFE SALVAGGIO FINALLY felt like the world was a beautiful place, and today was especially good because she was able to spend the entire day with Bronte. She didn't know exactly what happened, but when Eden had come home from Canada, she suddenly gave her more time with Bronte. Eden even made a point to tell her the adoption was still happening.

Whatever the reason, she was not going to waste the time she could be with Bronte wondering about it. Maybe Eden would just tell her eventually why she changed her mind. Now she and Bronte were enjoying some relaxing pool time before it was time for Bronte to leave.

The other big change in her life was Julia had moved into the guest bedroom. Not long after Eden delivered her news about Bronte and left, Julia knocked on her door. She had come to Rafe desperate for a place to go. Her apartment building had been bought by a conglomerate planning to tear it down to create retail space and luxury apartments. Even though Julia could have afforded the new apartments, she decided she didn't like the company buying the property and, until she could find a new home, needed somewhere temporary to stay.

At first, Rafe was against Julia moving in because she was still angry with her for everything that had happened in Canada. After Eden had picked up Bronte, Julia and Rafe had a few drinks. Julia explained and agreed Rafe was right—she had no idea what had been happening in Canada. Then she proceeded to get Rafe drunk and kept arguing her case for being temporary roommates until Rafe gave in and agreed.

The next day, Julia was very proud of herself, and Rafe decided maybe it would be okay for Julia to stay for a while, even if the only reason she agreed was because she was drunk. Rafe had a lot of time on her hands now the sale of her business had finalized, and she had finished helping with the projects she stayed on to help complete. So, over the last week, she helped Julia move out of her apartment and into the guest room and hoped they could stay on each other's good side until Julia moved out.

Julia carried a cold mixed drink as she walked outside where Rafe was in the pool playing with Bronte. She sat on one of the cushioned lounge chairs and watched Rafe push Bronte around in her swim ring and play.

She was glad Rafe had been in a good sense of humor and actually let her rent out the guest room. She had planned to ask when Rafe was relaxed on vacation, but then all hell broke loose. Julia had talked to her father, Ian Hawthorn, about Rafe before they left for Canada. They handle most of Rafe's personal and business financial and investments accounts, and there was always something going on involving Rafe's accounts. It was then she had the idea to ask Rafe if she could move in for a while.

For some reason, Julia's father adored Rafe. Whenever Rafe came in for a meeting or a review, her father tried to fly in to be there for the meeting. Julia was not sure if it was because of her money, her looks, or the way they seemed to get along on the many topics they discussed and debated.

The office was always on high alert when Rafe called or came by, and with the latest financial event of the sale of her architecture restoration business, there had been even more to do. The work on that would probably go on well into the next several years with payout schedules for the buyout and investment schedules. Julia was also sure soon they would be dealing with the financial matters around the death of Rafe's father, the sale of his real estate business, and the income from the investment properties Rafe had inherited. Rafe had already transferred a few financial accounts not required to go through probate.

It seemed like whenever Rafe called, there was a lot of work to push through. It was really quite annoying to Julia. She could never figure out where Rafe found the time to create all the work she did for the brokerage office, but since she was living with her now, she may just get a clue.

She had been both pleasantly surprised and shocked Rafe said yes to temporarily renting out her spare room, even if she was a bit into her pints when she agreed. She knew Rafe had been feeling betrayed by her for taking Eden's side about what happened in Canada. Julia had to convince her it wasn't a complete fact. It was just she really didn't know what was going on at the time. None of them did.

Julia thought maybe the reason Rafe had agreed was she was lonely and wanted company after living alone since Eden had moved out eight months ago. It was probably hard to come home to an empty house when she came back from her business trips.

Julia was happy to oblige. Who wouldn't like living in a great immaculately restored oversized bungalow style home with a heated pool, hot tub, gourmet kitchen and a maid who came twice a week? In her book, she had hit the jackpot and was going to make sure she didn't overstay her welcome, though she would not say no to staying on permanently.

Rafe bought the sprawling property on a double sized lot before she fully moved to California after seeing it in person only once. She knew it would be a lot of work to restore and fix up, but it was what she did for a living and what she loved to do. She did a lot of research, and though the house was not eligible for any historical recognition, she thought it had a lot of potential. She decided, since she was going to live in the home, she would restore it but add a lot of modern updates behind the walls and create a large modern gourmet kitchen.

Over her first year in the house, Rafe gutted the place and painstakingly restored it incorporating a modern lifestyle using warm contemporary interiors while keeping all of the original stained glass windows, ornate woodwork, and built in cabinetry with leaded glass. She also completely transformed the outside area restoring the wraparound porch to the house, adding a pool and an outside entertainment area with a covered deck and a patio outside the kitchen.

For the den, she found and refinished a very large partner's desk she had shared with Eden when she moved in with her. Throughout the house, Rafe had the walls and display spaces covered with art and ceramics she had collected from all over the world from her travels, including her Italian glass. She even converted the third bedroom into an art gallery.

Just off the dining room was the neatly organized modern gourmet kitchen with a large professional gas stove and special countertops. Rafe had them made with a mix of concrete with a special combination of several colors and accented with dark wood.

Off the kitchen and dining room side of the house was a large door opening up the entire backside of the house to the outdoors. Another door led from the kitchen to a small covered and enclosed porch on the side of the house Rafe converted to a studio space. She moved all the things from her office studio into the space after the sale of her business.

The living room featured a large ornate fireplace mantle surrounding a fireplace. The master bedroom was large and open with French doors leading onto the patio and a large en suite with a large old-fashioned claw-footed tub and separate shower.

The second level of the house had been completely redone from the rough attic space it was, too. Rafe did not do anything to it until Eden moved in, and then she transformed it for her into a state of the art media room. They used the space for game nights and movie nights, and Eden used to use it a lot to hold intimate private screenings for clients at her old job.

Rafe had to lift the entire roof so she would have eight-foot ceilings. She also reinforced it several ways because she was worried about earthquakes. Julia thought she went over the top on the whole earthquake preparation, but when Rafe had something in her mind, she sometimes went overboard. She even had a horde of food, water, and supplies socked away.

Outside, the lot was professionally landscaped, and there was a two-car garage with a workshop filled with Rafe's tools. There was also a large heated pool with a deck and lights and a large deck area next to the garage for additional lounging Rafe used when she was having parties.

Julia took a sip of her drink thankful for her good fortune Rafe was her friend. As she watched Rafe with Bronte, it was hard to reconcile the brooding and sometimes danger seeking Rafe she knew from childhood to the Rafe she saw now, who was patient and careful as she played with the little girl.

"So, when is Eden coming to get her?" she asked as she relaxed.

Rafe looked up from Bronte to Julia and saw she was dressed up for an evening out.

"Actually, she should be here in about an hour." She turned her attention back to Bronte. "We have plenty of time to play, don't we, B Girl?" she asked Bronte as she pushed her around the pool in her swim ring.

"Have you thought about coming out with me tonight? You do need to get out. It's time," declared Julia.

"I've thought about it," Rafe answered with a nod, "and you're right."

"Wonderful! I'm sure I can help you find someone to take home tonight!"

Rafe smiled at Julia. "I don't think I'm going to need your help in that area."

"Really?" Julia inquired with a chuckle. "It has been a while, are you sure? It seems to me like you'd want a sure thing, having gone so long without sex."

"Don't you know?" Rafe laughed. "Abby said everyone has been counting the days waiting for me to be back on the market since Eden moved out. So they'll all just be lined up for me to choose from." She grinned mischievously.

"Well, that is something," she said sarcastically, then sipped her drink. "You should probably take your ring off," she said and watched Rafe look at the gold ring on her finger. "It has been a while since Eden left." She took a drink and thought about the ring. "I guess you could leave it on and we could bank on sympathy if necessary." She grinned as Rafe looked at her with a frown. "Oh, and your birthday is coming up. We can use it as a ploy if we need to!" She winked and grinned mischievously. "I got the reminder about it from the girls at work. Why they know your birthday is beyond me," she said wryly.

"Well..." Rafe laughed ignoring Julia's comment about her ring. She knew, technically, it had been almost a year, but she wasn't sure if she was ready to take it off yet. "They have to know it, don't they? It's used a lot for my retirement accounts, investment accounts, and other paperwork."

"Oh, yeah," said Julia sullenly. "Let's not talk about work. Anyway, we should plan something big for your birthday."

"Yeah, I don't know," said Rafe hesitantly. "I don't have much to celebrate this year. It'll be my first birthday without the company I built with my father and without..." She looked at Julia and shook her head then looked at her ring again. "Eden," she finished, thinking about her father and Eden. "Maybe I'll just spend this one alone."

"Oh, no, not with me around," said Julia firmly. "We'll do something!"

"Don't worry about it, Julia," said Rafe as she gave Bronte a turn around the pool. "Plus, I start my new job on Monday, so I have a new job to look forward to focusing on."

"Hmm, yes, well, we shall see," conceded Julia for now, knowing if Rafe was left alone and in a mood, it usually led to no good. She didn't have to be alone—just in a mood for trouble. In Julia's experience, Rafe would either disappear from the world for weeks or months at a time, or sudden chaos would happen. Fortunately, Rafe had been too busy with the work of selling her business for either of these things to happen, barring the Canada incident. So, hopefully, this new job would work in much the same capacity and keep her in check. "Okay then. What do you say we make this evening more interesting since you're apparently a sought after prize? We shall see just how sought after you are."

"What do you have in mind?" asked Rafe as she looked suspiciously at Julia.

"We'll make it a competition." She smiled as she mused mischievously. "We'll each sit on either side of the bar and wait. Then, whenever one of us gets a number, we will send the other a drink."

"So, you plan on getting drunk without spending any money? I think you're exploiting me again." Rafe smiled at the offended look on Julia's face.

"My!" Julia laughed already a little tipsy. "You're very sure of yourself, aren't you? Okay then, a drink for every two numbers we get, and we can put a limit on it."

"What are the limits?"

"Up to say, four drinks, and then after, we have one hour to get someone to take home. Sound good?"

Rafe looked seriously at Julia. "I'll take your hour, but I really don't think I'll need that long."

Smiling and pleased with herself Julia leaned back in the recliner. "Brilliant! It's a wager," she said proudly, her mission to get Rafe out of the house accomplished.

Carrying Bronte out of the pool, Rafe smiled at Julia who sat her drink on the table beside her recliner and smiled in personal triumph. Rafe put the baby on the other recliner and got a towel around herself and one around the baby.

"Come on, B Girl. Let's get you all dry. Mommy will be here soon, and Mama has got to get ready for a big night reminding Zia Julia how things are done, yes she does."

Entering through the side gate, Eden smiled when she saw Rafe and Bronte together. She had made it to the pool area just in time to overhear Rafe talking to Bronte.

"Hi there, baby," she cooed as she walked up and kissed Bronte. "You have a big night tonight?" she asked as she looked up at Rafe curiously. "What's up?"

Julia looked at Rafe and could see the tension run through her body. She knew Rafe was unhappy about Eden coming early and was worried things would go back to the way they were when Eden and Jake would make excuses for her not to be able to see Bronte.

"Rafe and I are going out on the town tonight," she offered and picked up her drink to take a sip.

"Oh," replied Eden as she tried to look unconcerned about the two of them hanging out.

"You're early again," Rafe pointed out trying to contain her annoyance.

"I know, sorry," Eden answered and could feel Rafe's disapproval. "We're going out with Jake's parents tonight, and I just wanted to make sure I could get Bronte ready in time," she explained. "I didn't think you'd mind."

Rafe looked at Eden and frowned for a moment then forced a smile to her face.

"You know, Eden, it just happens, today I don't mind. Julia was just telling me it was time for me to get out there again, and I agree. I'll tell you what, why don't you take Bronte and get her changed so you can take her to dinner, and I'll start getting myself ready for my little adventure tonight," she said as she handed Bronte to Eden. She turned around and gave Julia a high five as she made her way into the house.

Julia laughed and looked at Eden with a crooked smile. "I can't wait until Abby hears." She laughed again at the thought. She looked at Eden and made a note to discuss her choice in fashion. Her skirt and blouse looked like it belonged on an aged crone. She laughed again at her clever observation. It was going to be a great night.

Eden looked at Julia's crooked smile, and dread ran through her at the thought of what those two were planning for tonight. Since Julia had become single again, Abby said she was out at the clubs all the time. Over the years, Rafe and Julia had done some crazy things, and now that they were both single, she wondered how far they would push things. Pushing away and denying the slight sting of jealousy they might actually get together, she followed Rafe inside. She took Bronte to the couch to start taking off the baby's wet bathing suit to get her a bath and dressed for the evening.

Rafe headed to the kitchen and made herself a glass of water. She went back to the living room and watched Eden deftly get Bronte out of her swimming suit.

"What time are you bringing her back in the morning?"

"I'll have her back at seven in the morning," said Eden as she tried not to look at Rafe's more than half-naked body in the towel she knew covered her black bikini. She pulled an outfit out of Bronte's overnight bag. "I have to go into the office early and meet with one of the writers."

"Okay," said Rafe as she bent over Bronte. "*Addio, piccola,*"[29] she said and gave Bronte a small kiss. "*Mamma si vedrà al mattino.*"[30] Rafe raised her eyebrows as she saw Eden looking at her. Eden looked away quickly, and Rafe walked to her bedroom.

---

[29] Goodbye little one
[30] Mamma will see you in the morning.

11

JAYNE EDEN KINGSLEY was her parents' only surviving child and grew up in a very religious rural community on a small farm outside of Hartford, Iowa. Her father, Joseph Kingsley, was lord and master of his domain and expected his wife and children to jump at his command. Her mother, Margaret, or Maggie as her father called her, still lived in the same house. Maggie refused to see Eden, even after her husband had died of heart failure because she felt she had to respect her husband's wishes in order to see him again in the hereafter.

Eden had an older brother, Joe Jr., who died in a farming accident, but she was too young to remember him or what had happened. Her parents never spoke of him but kept his picture on the mantle in the living room. Eden knew from a young age she was not the child her father wanted because she was a girl. The death of her brother only enhanced the feeling.

Her father would always find some fault with her and would disregard what she wanted or what she said and would dictate what would happen in his house without thought of the feelings of others. The biggest issue he had was dealing with her chronic anxiety. He had no time or patience for it, and only grudgingly helped his wife take her to the doctor or the church when necessary. He thought his wife was too indulgent of Eden, and after she had left home, he was sure he was proven right.

Eden had dealt with chronic anxiety problems for as long as she could remember. Though her parents tried to pray the anxiety problems away, they remained with her. She remembered staying at home sick and in pain just wanting to lay in her room in the dark. Her parents would always invite people from church over, or her father would come in and carry her out to the truck, and take her to the church. They would all gather around her, lay their hands on her, and then start to pray and sing and sometimes cry. Eden remembered crying harder than any of them did as she wished they would all just go away and leave her alone.

Later, the church people would see her in town somewhere or at church again. They would corner her and want to touch her again or insist she talk to them and tell everyone how God had helped her through them—testify. She was so shy she would shut down. Then those 'good Christian people' would get angry with her when she couldn't say the things they expected on demand. When she finally could get something out, she would end up feeling so guilty about lying to them about God by saying what they did had helped, and she would end up getting sick again. Soon, she started just telling her parents she was sick almost every Sunday or anytime she had to deal with people who would possibly want to touch her or force her to talk to them.

School was hard for Eden too, mostly because of her shyness and the fact she didn't like to be touched. She didn't think she had dealt with anymore teasing or bullying than most other kids had because she lived in a small town and all the mothers were at the school always watching. While grade school was mostly a blur, high school seemed to drag on forever, and she found herself more and more out of place.

She was required to join a sport so she joined the cross-country team because she could run alone most of the time. It also gave her a good excuse to leave the house early in the morning. Running actually helped a lot with her anxiety. Being out alone early in the morning on a dirt road with nothing around but fields and the sky brought her peace she couldn't explain. At that time in her life, she felt she would have died without it.

It seemed like, as she got older, there was more tension at home, especially with her father. More tension meant she was sick more. Being sick and having to go to the doctor or the hospital compounded the tension, and the cycle never seemed to stop.

Since she stayed home a lot, she watched a ton movies and read loads of books. Her mother got them a secret movie rental card, and sometimes, they watched old movies together. Soon, Eden was sneaking movies into the house even her mother would not approve of if she knew. She also bought subscriptions to magazines about the movie industry she kept hidden in her locker at school because nothing could ever be hidden for long at home.

She was fascinated by what it took to make a movie. She didn't want to be a movie star, though. She knew she could never be in the spotlight. She wanted to be part of the process and work with the creative people who gave the stars the opportunity to shine. She wanted to be part of Hollywood even if it was just in a small way.

Because her anxiety had kept her from many social situations, her parents directed most of her life until she was older. Once she had additional freedom, she went to work figuring out her own voice to decide what she wanted to do with her life. It was during that time she made the decision to leave home as soon as she could to be in the movie industry somehow. After high school, she attended community college for one year and then moved to California when she was awarded a scholarship to USC. She thought it was one of the bravest things she had ever done when she moved away from home to attend college.

Getting the scholarship was her ticket out of small-town living and the chance to fulfill her dream. The scholarship paid for everything including room and board off campus. She worked for a while at the school and at different jobs in the evenings, and some days when she didn't have class, to cover all her extras until she landed a much better paying internship.

After moving away from the farm in Iowa, Eden found many of her anxiety symptoms were a lot less severe. She was sick less, she used her inhaler less, she didn't get migraines as often, she rarely broke out into hives so bad she had to go to the hospital, and she felt like a weight had been lifted from her. But she was still very shy and didn't date a lot. She used the excuse she had to keep up her grades and work if she didn't want to have to go back home. She worked hard and obtained her Bachelor of Fine Arts, Writing for Screen & Television.

The year before she graduated, she met Rafe, and being with her was another big change in her life. Eden never questioned or thought about her sexuality, and never thought of herself as *straight* or not, until she met and began her relationship with Rafe. It was just not something ever discussed in her small community when she was growing up, so it was a new concept for her personally. She knew about gay people from television, movies, and the news, but it wasn't something she had ever directly dealt with in her hometown.

When her parents found out she was in a 'sinful' relationship with a woman, they disowned her and made sure she was formally excommunicated from their church. She actually got an official letter from the pastor informing her of the fact she was no longer welcome along with all the biblical and moral reasons. It was heartbreaking because she had known him and everyone in the church all her life. She never thought she would be so totally abandoned by an entire community of people and family. She went through so many emotions from anger to humiliation until, finally, she actually began to feel empathy for them because they had somehow lost what she felt was the truth of what love was all about. She knew she loved Rafe, and it was something she knew was right in her soul.

It had been a very tough time for Eden, but she had Rafe and many other people around to help her through everything including her anxiety attacks that would overwhelm her after arguing with her father. Rafe was always so calm and supportive. She never pushed or pressured her about what she should do. Rafe listened and would sometimes just hold Eden's hand until she could calm herself enough to think things through. Rafe was always good and respectful about the fact she needed to not be touched when she was having anxiety problems.

When Eden made her decision to be with Rafe, she had more of a problem being estranged from her parents than the church. She didn't agree with most of the church's doctrine, though some of it was still hard for her to push away even after so many years. Then she agreed to move in with Rafe, and it seemed, after a while, most of the anxiety issues that had plagued her for so long completely disappeared. It was as if she had transformed into a different person.

Rafe's touch became a huge calming influence the few times she would have issues, and to Eden, it was an amazing thing to have happen. There were times back then when she would come home from dealing with certain people she had to work with who were overbearing, and she would just shut down. Sometimes, it meant she had to take the entire weekend to regroup. When Rafe got home, she would somehow make everything else melt away. When it was really bad, Rafe would just do something like make tea or get her a blanket and wait for her to come around, even if it meant missing doing things with her friends. When they first moved in together, Eden wondered why Rafe put up with her. She was sure Rafe would get tired of dealing with her and become angry like her father and others, but she never did when it came to her anxiety. She would just rub her back or neck and say something like 'I'm here if you need me, bella,' and wait for her to come around looking for comfort in her arms.

Eden pulled her thoughts out of the past and away from Rafe. She was doing fine now. She really loved her current job at Ascesis Studios as a Script Development Executive. She felt like she was working in an industry she had always been drawn to, and the company was great. She was doing a job she felt she was good at, and though it was high stress at times, she found over the years, being part of the process of getting a script to film was almost second nature to her. She was described by people as very sensitive and intuitive, and this helped her understand people and their needs. It also helped when she worked with writer and producer relationships in pairing them and resolving conflicts.

As Eden drove from Rafe's house toward the restaurant, she wished some of her work skills would translate over and help with her personal life. But it seemed like it never did. She worried Julia moving in with Rafe would be trouble. Since they were actually hanging out as well as living together, she felt she had more reason to worry. Both women were beautiful, strong-willed, and used to having their way, and could mean fireworks in the worse way. Eden couldn't believe it when she first heard they had moved in together. The last she knew, they hated each other because of what happened in Canada. She didn't know what had changed, but it must have been humbling for Julia to ask Rafe if she could move in with her.

"Oh, Rafe." She sighed to herself because she was thinking about her again. She shook the image of Rafe forcing a smile out of her head. It was clear Rafe was unhappy.

She was trying so hard to get along with Rafe and keep her promise to the girls and to herself about Bronte. It was not easy. Jake was dead set against it after what had happened in Canada. He didn't care if Abby said it was all a misunderstanding. He even said he didn't believe it. He still thought Rafe purposely took Bronte to upset her and everyone else, and to make a scene. At this point, Eden felt like she was walking on a tightrope and balancing the anger of Jake on one side and Rafe's anger on the other.

Looking in her rearview mirror, Eden smiled at Bronte as she babbled in her car seat. Rafe was right about her friend Gabri, though. He definitely helped them make a very beautiful little girl.

Eden pulled into the restaurant where she was meeting Jake and his family. She took a moment to take some calming breaths to prepare to deal with new people. She told Jake she was not ready to announce their engagement to anyone, but he told everyone in Canada anyway. Now he insisted they tell his parents their news. She unloaded Bronte and went inside. She was feeling anxious about meeting Jake's parents. It felt strange to be meeting them for the first time and being introduced as his fiancée. She was very nervous because she had no idea what he told them about her and Bronte, and of course, Rafe.

Jake waved from across the crowded restaurant, and Eden made her way to their table.

"Hello, my two beautiful girls," said Jake then kissed Bronte on her cheek and Eden on the lips. He turned to the table and smiled. "Mom, Dad, this is Eden and her daughter, Bronte," he announced proudly. He helped Eden get Bronte into a highchair next to Hunter's chair as everyone said hello and complimented Bronte.

They were finally settled and ordered their dinners when Jake tapped his water glass with his knife to get their attention.

"Mom, Dad, I would just like to announce Eden and I are engaged and plan to marry very soon." He smiled formally while Eden blushed uncomfortable with the attention.

"Oh, I'm so happy for you, Jakie," said Mrs. Thompson, Jake's doting mother, "and you too, Ellen. Jakie is such a sweetheart."

"Eden," Eden corrected her softly.

"Oh, yes, Eden. Such an unusual name," Mrs. Thompson simpered. "From the bible, I guess."

"Well, Jake my boy, I can see now why you've been asking me to help you find a job back home." Mr. Thompson laughed as he leered at Eden. "You'll be the envy of every boy in town." He gave Jake a knowing wink.

Eden looked over at Jake with surprise at this news. "What? Jake, what's he talking about?" she asked trying to be private.

"You know." Jake smiled and tried to wave away her concern. "It's what we've been talking about. I just thought I'd get a head start so we can hit the ground running."

The waiter brought their food, interrupting Eden's chance to respond. When everyone had their plates, Mr. Thompson led the table in a prayer that seemed a little too loud and a little long to Eden. Finally, he finished, and everyone called out *amen,* grabbed their cutlery and began banging away at their food. Eden grabbed her water glass and gulped down some water to quench her throat because it seemed to suddenly go dry. She wished she could just have one or two sips of a good red wine to help her relax, but there would never be alcohol of any kind at this table—or any other—in her life again. Jake and his family didn't drink and didn't allow alcohol under their roofs.

"Evelyn," said Mrs. Thompson suddenly startling Eden, but she took no notice. "Did Jake tell you about my gallbladder? I had to have it removed because I was in so much pain," the thin, sickly woman said as she ate. "I thought I was going to die, but after they operated, I felt better. I had to wear a catheter and bag for a month, and it seemed like forever."

"Yes, Mother," said Mr. Thompson thickly with his mouth half full as he patted her hand, "but you got through it like a trooper."

Eden just looked at her and then at Jake, not sure what to say or if she should correct her again about her name.

"Uh, no." She forced herself to speak softly and shook her head. "He didn't tell me about your illness, Mrs. Thompson."

"Well, when you move close to us, we'll have lots of time to get to know each other." The thin woman smiled tolerantly at Eden. "You'll just love our little community."

Unsettled, Eden looked at Jake. She felt like her lungs were being crushed, so she took a shallow breath to try to control her anxiety. She forced her words, but they came out soft.

"I'm sorry, your community?"

"Yes," Mrs. Thompson nodded. "You'll love our little town, and you'll want to be put on our church rolls. I'm in charge of the registry and can introduce you to everyone," she said self-importantly. "We'll be joining you and Jake at church this Sunday too," she informed her.

"Church?" said Eden quietly and a cold sweat broke out on the back of her neck at the thought of dealing with people she didn't know who would want her to talk with them and hug or touch her. She knew it wouldn't be like when she was younger, but it still made her very uncomfortable. She had told Jake she didn't want to go to church and the reasons why. So she wasn't sure why he would tell his parents she would be there. She hoped it was just a misunderstanding, so she decided to let it go for now. "Well, I'm sure your town is nice, but Jake and I are still discussing where we'll be. I have a great job here, and Bronte's other mother is here."

"Other what?" Mrs. Thompson asked, confused. "It seems like these kids today have two of everything, and now two mothers. That's just silly." She gave a short laugh shooting a small fleck of potato out onto her liver-colored lips.

Jake could see Eden was getting upset with where the conversation was going so he changed the subject.

"So, Dad, did you take Mom to Disney Land yet?"

"Oh, no." Mrs. Thompson laughed. "He tried to get me to go, but you know with my IBS, I can't go places like that." She leaned over and whispered loudly to Eden across the table. "The restrooms are just too far apart, and these days, when I have to go, well, I have to go!" She laughed crudely.

Eden was at a complete loss about what to do with the inappropriate information she was being subjected to. Jake looked at her and shrugged then ate his food without helping the situation. Since she didn't know how to respond to Jake's mother, she turned her attention to helping Bronte and put some green beans on her plate.

"Your daughter is lovely," said Mr. Thompson through a mouth full of food. "She must take after her father," he observed because of the baby's swarthy skin and dark hair in contrast to Eden's light skin and blonde hair. "So, where did you say her father was from, Jakie?"

"Bronte's father is from Italy, Dad," answered Jake as he cut into his steak scraping the plate with his knife.

"And he doesn't want to see his child? It seems sad such a sweet little girl doesn't know her father," he said sympathetically. "But Jake is a great dad! Isn't he, Hunter?" The little boy nodded, smiled, and kept eating his chicken strip. "Yes, Jake's right. A little girl needs her father, and you've made a good choice in having Jake adopt your daughter, young lady," he said while brandishing his fork at Eden then stabbing his thick steak and taking a huge bite.

Eden's face flushed red, and she bit her tongue forcing herself to breathe, angry she couldn't say what she was thinking at that moment. They were very presumptuous because she hadn't agreed Jake would be anything other than a step-father. If they married. She thought she made it clear after Canada Rafe was going to be Bronte's second parent no matter what.

She calmed herself and looked at Jake—who she couldn't believe wasn't saying anything.

"Her father was a sperm donor," she said firmly. "He gave Rafe and me a gift so we could start a family. We have every intention of introducing her to him. He's Rafe's childhood friend," she informed them but felt they were ignoring her. "Jake, didn't you tell them about Rafe?"

"Oh, he told us some silly thing," tutted Mrs. Thompson, "but the baby won't have to worry about him or this Cahfay person after you marry Jake and he adopts her. She can grow up in a nice normal family," she assured her.

"Rafe. It's an R, not a C," said Eden softly feeling like she had to defend Rafe. "Her full name is Rafaella. Some of her co-workers have Americanized it and pronounce it Raif if it makes it easier, though I prefer Rafe." She pronounced Rafe's name clearly as Rah-fā. "It's the Italian pronunciation." She looked at the thin woman who was shoving a large piece of baked potato into her mouth. "And my name is Eden, as in the Garden of Eden, like you said, from the bible." When they all just sat there, chewing their food not saying anything, she felt like she needed to make them aware Rafe was a big part of Bronte's life. "Bronte was swimming with her today. It's amazing to see them together because they look so much alike. I think Rafe looks more like Bronte's mother than I do. Rafe is very good with her," she said and felt her anxiety calm as she talked about Rafe.

The thin woman did not even look at or acknowledge Eden. She looked at the plate in front of Bronte.

"Do you think green beans are a good idea to give the baby? When I gave them to Jake as a baby, he would get the most awful diarrhea."

"Geraldine!" Mr. Thompson guffawed. "Jake was just trying to let you know he was a meat and potato man. Right, son?"

Jake shrugged then leaned back in his chair. "Mom, I'm hoping you can help Eden with the wedding details since her mother may not be able to help her. I'm sure Eden will try to reconcile, and I'm sure, when her mother finds out she's getting married to me, she'll want to be there. Isn't that right, hon?"

"Oh, you poor thing," Mrs. Thomson simpered before Eden could reply. "It must be hard to be estranged from your family. We'll set everything right for the wedding," she assured her.

Taking a breath and blowing it out of her puffed cheeks Eden looked angrily at Jake. "I don't know if that's possible," she said softly as the calm she thought she had found vanished.

"Well, we can only try," said Mrs. Thompson as she scraped her baked potato. "You know, before I went gluten-free, I thought I would die," she said forlornly, "but now I only have diarrhea when my IBS acts up," she said cheered by the thought.

"Hey, Hunter," Jake said enthusiastically to the boy across the table, "are you excited about having Bronte as your little sister?"

"Yeah!" said the little brown haired boy with a smile. "I love Bronte!"

Jake smiled and patted Eden's hand. "We're going to be a great family," he said proudly.

After they had finished dinner and then had to sit through the story about Mrs. Thompson varicose veins, they all made their way to their cars and went their separate ways for the evening.

12

EDEN KINGSLEY WAS angry. She was angry at Jake and everything that happened at dinner, including the fact Jake was pushing her about moving again after they got married. It was a discussion they had not finished, and they were at odds about. She could not believe he had the gall to inform his parents they were moving and already had his father find him a job. She was also upset he hadn't acknowledged Rafe was going to be Bronte's mother to his parents. That was a discussion they did have, and it felt like he was disregarding her decision.

Moving away from everything and everyone she knew was something Eden didn't know if she could do. Rebuilding her life after moving away from home when she was young had been very hard for her. It was not just learning a new city and a new job. It was the process of working through her anxieties around new people and places. There was dealing with the loneliness before she could work up the nerve to deal with meeting new people, then find people who would give her a chance to work through her shyness, and it all took time and effort. More than that, sometimes it was overwhelmingly stressful, and she didn't know if she was ready to go through it again.

She felt lucky because school had given her something to focus on, so she didn't have to worry much about friends. Then her job did the same thing. When she met Rafe, it was like a set of friends was already built in, and she felt lucky after their break up, they could all still be friends. But she didn't feel the same about Jake's friends. It seemed harder with them for some reason. Maybe it was because, with Rafe, she didn't have to meet all her friends right away like she did with Jake. With Rafe, things like meeting friends seemed to go a lot slower. Right now, though, she could feel everything closing in on her, and it was not a pleasant feeling.

When Eden got to the apartment, she put Bronte to bed in her room and then went into her and Jake's bedroom. She walked into her closet and pulled out a small shoebox hidden behind her purses, and then took it to the bed. She sat down and opened the box, taking out a folded but crumpled piece of paper. She held it to her nose and smelled the familiar scent of the person who wrote the words on the paper, and it calmed her. She unfolded it and read the words inside, sighing. When she was finished, she folded the paper back up and put it back in the box. After putting the box in its hidden place in the closet, she waited for Jake to get home after taking Hunter to his mother.

When Jake got home, she barely allowed him to walk in the door. "What was all that tonight, Jake? You know I haven't agreed to move. I have too many things to consider—my job, Rafe, and all of my friends. I don't know if I want to go back to the Midwest, and I certainly don't think marrying you is going to change my mother."

"Calm down, Eden," said Jake as he sat down and started taking off his shoes. "I was just making inquiries. It's good to have options."

"It didn't sound like you were making inquiries. It sounded like he had a job lined up for you," she said anxiously feeling those familiar pins and needles rush over her skin.

"Eden, listen," he said calmly as he undid his pants and leaned back, "it's just an option."

"I love my job, Jake, and if you think I'm just going to stay home and be a mother and housewife in some small backwater town... no way!" She scoffed at the idea. One of her biggest fears was she would be living the life of her mother where her father dominated everything in her life. Her mother was confined to a very small world by her father, and it was not the way Eden ever wanted to live. Eden didn't know how her mother stayed with him and still let him have hold of her after his death. "Oh, and I also told you I'm not going to your church."

"It's one Sunday," he said getting frustrated with her being so unreasonable. "It won't kill you."

Eden just looked at him and could not believe what he had said. She couldn't understand why he would want to make her do something she told him she didn't want to do—and he already promised she wouldn't have to do. She walked out of the room and into the kitchen to get away from him. Picking up Bronte's backpack, she began to clean it out. She worked between the kitchen and the laundry room making sure there were clean clothes and supplies in the pack getting it ready to go to Rafe's tomorrow morning.

Lately, she felt like Jake had been treating her just like her father had. She didn't know how she could stay with Jake unless things changed. On top of everything, it seemed like she had gone back in time and all her anxiety issues were taking over her life again. She had already been to the hospital three times for cortisone shots when she had broken out in hives. Her migraines and light sensitivity had started giving her problems again, and she seemed to always be on the verge of a sore throat or getting a fever blister.

The doctor suggested her stress level with work and being a new mother and starting a new relationship were too much. Jake thought it meant she should quit her job, and they should move away. Eden felt like no one was really listening to her. It felt like they were trying to say she couldn't have the things she had worked hard to have like her dream career. Or the things she wanted like a life living where she felt good for the first time in her life. And it felt like they were saying she had to break her promise to Rafe and couldn't have Rafe as part of her family if Eden was to marry Jake.

Eden looked up and saw Jake walk into the kitchen. He leaned against the counter. "I like living here. I love my job, Jake. I'm not ready to just give everything up and move away."

"I don't understand," said Jake. "You quit your job for Rafe."

"No, it's not the same," she insisted as she stood across from him trying to control the pain from the pins and needles racing over her skin because of the confrontation. "That was a decision we made together and the final decision was mine to make! I wanted to stay home and get my body ready to have a baby and not be under the stress of work. Plus, we were lucky we could afford me not working when I was with Rafe."

"Oh, so now you think I don't make enough money?" he said angrily.

"No," Eden sighed annoyed he was doing the same things her father had done by putting words in her mouth instead of listening. "That's not what I said. I just mean you and I both need to work since we've moved into this new place. I don't want to argue about money again."

"Well," said Jake changing gears, "it's Rafe's fault you can't go home and see your mother. I thought I could help with reconnecting to your mother and your roots."

Eden just looked at Jake in disbelief this issue was coming up again. Her mother's decision had nothing to do with Rafe. Her mother didn't even know Rafe.

"My mother's problem is with me," she said angrily. "I told you she's hanging onto my father's rejection of my relationship with Rafe. Rafe will still be in our life, just as your ex-wife is still in our life. And you know, you really should make sure your mother can remember my name, and Rafe's too!"

"Oh, please. She just met you," he rebuked not liking her criticism of his mother. "Even Rafe pronounces your name wrong half the time, and she's known you for years."

"She doesn't pronounce my name wrong," Eden sighed and rolled her eyes wary of having this conversation again. "It's just how my name would be said in Italian."

Even though Eden tried to reassure Jake he had nothing to worry about, Jake seemed to be jealous of everything Rafe ever did and picked on anything he could to make her look less. One thing was the way she sometimes talked when she slipped into her Italian accent. Eden happened to like the way Rafe pronounced her name and found it endearing. Rafe pronounced her letter 'E's like 'A's so Eden came out as 'Adan' when she slipped into Italian. No one else called her by that pronunciation, so it had made it special when they were together. She was not sure why it made Jake so jealous, but she made sure not to tell him about the other private name Rafe had for her. It was sad she would probably never hear that name from Rafe's lips again.

Jake was convinced helping Eden reconcile with her mother would make moving away easier. He was sure if he could solve Eden's problems with her mother, things would move forward, and she would want to be closer to both of their families finally. Maybe being with her real family and getting away from all the bad influences she's been surrounded with would actually do her some good. He just needed to convince her.

"If I adopt Bronte, you won't have a problem with your mother anymore," he tried to reason with her gently. "Then your mother can still follow your father's wishes and see you too because you won't be with a woman."

"No, Jake," she said upset he would not even try to really understand the situation with her parents and was again pressuring her about adopting Bronte. She zipped up the backpack, sat it on the counter, and headed back into the living room.

"All we have to do is explain how you made a mistake and ask for her forgiveness," Jake said as he followed her trying to sound reasonable. "Let her know about everything we've talked about over the past few months. Tell her you've gone back to men because you realized the few years you were with Rafe couldn't compete with all of the years before you met her when you were with men. It conflicted with everything you knew and all you had been taught. Now you're finally back where you need to be. And now you're with the love of your life—me." He smiled charmingly as he sat back down on the couch.

Shaking her head, Eden was not sure how to respond to what Jake was saying. Being in a relationship with a woman did conflict with what she was taught, and the church had pushed her out. But it wasn't as if she had ever been in a real relationship with a man before Jake. She went out with some guys before she met Rafe and only had sex with two, one from her hometown and one in college. Jake made it sound like she had experiences she just didn't have.

"When you have your mother's forgiveness, she can come to our wedding," Jake continued. "Then we can talk about where we want to live, me adopting Bronte, and if we want Rafe to be part of the life we want to make for ourselves."

Eden felt anxious as Jake again tried to define and box her life into an explanation she didn't know if she was certain of or not. She knew things were more complicated, but she couldn't untangle them enough in her mind at the moment to deny what he was saying.

"Jake, I'm just not sure things are going to be that simple." She sighed as she rubbed her arms to ease the pain and then began to pick up the toys and clutter around the house.

"Things are that simple. All we need is to be around our families and live in a place where our kids can grow up like we did," said Jake earnestly. "It really would be best if we moved close to my parents so we'll have the help from other friends and family. It really won't be so bad."

"I just..." Eden hesitated. "I feel like you're pushing me somewhere I don't want to go," said Eden anxiously, "you're trying to control things, and I don't get to have an opinion."

"You're right," sighed Jake. "I'm acting just like Rafe. I'm sorry. I didn't mean to control you. I just want to make you happy," he said trying to back off the subject.

"Rafe never tried to move me away or keep me from having a job," she said, not understanding how he could compare what he was doing to anything Rafe might have done. "She didn't force me to make the decision to be with her and not my family or friends. She never pressured me like this."

"Oh, so now Rafe is a great person?" he asked sarcastically getting tired of dealing with Eden's stubbornness and anxieties. He never had to deal with someone with so many issues. She just needed to calm down and see reason. "Now that you're seeing her again and dropping off Bronte with her more, she's suddenly golden? I remember all the things you told me she did when you were together. She cheated on you! Humiliated you! Have you forgotten?"

"No, Jake, I haven't forgotten anything," Eden said shakily gripping the toy she held in her hand tightly. She hated he thought he had to remind her again, like she could ever forget it or the pain. "You know, she was hurt too with everything that happened."

"What?" Jake laughed. "Are you defending her now? Don't tell me you're buying into all the crap her friends were saying when we were in Canada about how hurt she is about things and how you have to be more understanding." He laughed and shook his head. "I think we understand her just fine. You know I'm right, and she left early because she was going to take Bronte and was caught or something."

"You don't know that," Eden said shaking her head. "Even if she thought about it, she wouldn't do it because she cares about Bronte and wouldn't hurt her. She left because we threw the engagement and the fact we may move in her face, and we excluded her from Bronte's party."

Jake looked at Eden for a moment and shook his head at the fact she was defending a woman who had been so heartless and thoughtless to her. This was exactly why it was so easy for Rafe to manipulate Eden. She just had too much empathy.

"Rafe put herself in the position she's in," Jake asserted. "We have the right to make plans for our future and be happy even if she's in the room. We don't owe anything to her and don't have to ask her permission to live our life the way we want to live or even where we want to live it."

"But Jake," Eden sighed, "I think you've forgotten I made a promise to her and we made our baby together. I can't take Bronte away from her. I made a commitment."

"A commitment," scoffed Jake. "Rafe never committed herself to you! Even after the marriage equality started here, she didn't marry you."

"Getting married wasn't something either of us wanted," she said and looked down at the toy in her hands wishing he would just listen to her and stop pushing.

"Right, she just expected you to carry a baby for her, for her own ego. It's probably why she refuses to give you Bronte's passport, and she barely pays you any child support!" he yelled angrily because he was losing his patience with her taking Rafe's side all the time suddenly.

Eden stepped back at his unexpected animosity and forced herself to speak. "Rafe pays exactly what I asked her for to help with Bronte," she informed him and put the toy in the toy bin.

She then rubbed the back of her neck feeling the slight sweat emerging. She kept silent about the fact Rafe was really paying much more than she had asked. Rafe had determined there would be more expenses than Eden thought, and she had been right. She also didn't tell him she had never brought up the subject of the passport with Rafe. He was upset she didn't get it when they went to Canada, but it wasn't needed as long as she brought a birth certificate.

"You can't compare our relationships!" she said as her anger finally pushed through.

"You're right," said Jake calmly, trying to de-escalate the conversation. "Our relationships are different. Ours is better. We are going to be a truly committed couple who get married and share a life and a name and know we belong together."

"I don't know," said Eden nervously shaking her head. "I think I might be making a mistake. I've been feeling really pressured, and I don't think we really want the same things." She didn't want to confess, even to herself, she felt like she was back in her father's house and feeling beaten down and sick all the time.

"You're not making a mistake," said Jake on high alert. He couldn't lose her.

Eden slipped off the engagement ring and bravely held it out to him. "I think we should wait on the engagement. We need to be on the same page on a lot of things, and I don't think we're there yet."

"Eden," Jake said sadly as he stood and took her hand and the ring. "Please," he said as he slipped the ring back on Eden's finger. "I'm sorry. I want to marry you and make you happy." He pulled her close and held her. "We shouldn't be fighting. We're the same, you and me." He gave her a small kiss on her forehead. "We both have exes who cheated on us, and we had to find our way out of the pain it caused us. We helped each other, and we have a real connection because we were raised the same way too. Let's just slow down and think about things. We don't have to make up our minds about anything right now," he said and kissed her sweetly on her lips and neck. "We belong together," he said softly. "I love you."

Eden took a calming breath as he rubbed her back to comfort her and held her close. *He's right*, she thought, *we didn't have to make a decision today.* She had to figure out some way he and Rafe could coexist. If she could, she hoped it would help them all get along and cause her less anxiety. She knew it was not going to be an easy job.

She let him kiss her again deeply, and as he held her tightly in his arms, she felt him lifting her skirt as he hardened under his already unfastened pants.

13

RAFE SALVAGGIO AND Julia Hawthorn could see by the crowd outside of *Club La Femme* the place was going to be packed with beautiful women of all kinds. They walked up the sidewalk, taking in the scene, and could feel the vibe of excitement in the air.

Julia was feeling intimidated and a little anxious to begin the night because Rafe walked out of her bedroom looking like dark smoldering sex. There was no doubt about what she wanted, and it showed in everything from her clothes clinging to her in all the right places to the way she walked down the street to the bar. It was as clear as a green light signal Rafe wanted blazing hot, earth-shattering sex.

She looked over her shoulder and was surprised at how calm and composed Rafe seemed to be her first time out after Eden had left. Getting Rafe back to normal was the first step in seeing if she was ready for a new relationship, one she had been hoping for years would be with her. Living with and going out to places with Rafe would remind her of the times they had in their school days. It would also give Rafe the chance to see what it would be like to be in a relationship together. Rafe had always been against the idea, but Julia hoped maybe Rafe would start to see her differently after she finished her self-imposed mourning period for Eden. She planned to get it sorted starting tonight. Once Rafe was back in the dating saddle it would be easier to broach the subject again.

Julia took a deep breath in preparation for the night and the competition about to begin.

"Okay, are you ready?" she asked Rafe over the noise of the hordes of women.

Rafe looked at her with a slight smile, and without a word, she walked into the bar with more sexual confidence oozing from her than Julia had ever witnessed. "Bloody hell," Julia mumbled as she felt her body react to that Salvaggio smile.

Inside the pulsing nightclub, the two women, one dark and one light, surveyed the room. The throb of the music tapped into the erotic energy within all of the women in the bar as they danced and laughed. Rafe soaked in the energy surrounding her and let it top off the natural confidence inside her as she started for the bar with Julia not far behind.

Julia stayed a few steps behind Rafe, giving herself space so she could be sure to be seen walking through the club. As she moved forward, she noticed the path clearing in front of Rafe as she made her way up to the bar. It was as if Rafe had turned something on inside her that worked like a beacon. Julia had always admired the smooth rolling walk Rafe had that screamed confidence while hinting following her would lead to intimate secrets. Several women actually felt the need to sit down as she passed them. It had been a while since Julia had seen Rafe out and single like this, and now she recognized she was up for more of a challenge than she anticipated. It looked like all those years with Eden did nothing to dull Rafe's prowess.

Julia made her way to the opposite end of the bar from Rafe and motioned for the bartender. When she got her drink, she looked across the bar at Rafe who already had a drink in her hand. Rafe looked up at her and lifted her glass in salute. The first brave woman began her way over to Rafe.

"Let the games begin," said Julia softly as she raised her glass to return Rafe's salute.

In the lower part of the club, at a table near the DJ booth, Abby and her friend Erica were drinking beers and admiring the women on the dance floor while simultaneously trying to set up a video shoot. Erica Sunley was rocking a boy cut hairstyle and was the cutest little baby dyke Abby knew. She was also pointing her camera around the club for filler shots then back at Abby.

Abby smiled for the camera. "How's my hair?" she asked Erica who she considered her protégé who she was teaching everything about the lesbian vlogging world. She followed Abby around a lot with a video camera, and they did many projects together.

"Looks great," answered the doe-eyed brunette, Erica. She loved hanging out and doing the crazy projects Abby dreamed up. She still lived with her parents, and since she was only going to school part-time, she was glad she found Abby to work with. After graduation, Erica really wanted to make a name doing independent film projects and a web series.

Looking into the camera, Abby began her one of a kind narration as Erica followed her for the shot.

Abby made it her business to come out to all of the hot spots in town so she could write about them and all of the happenings in town on her blog, and in several other publications, and talk about them on her YouTube channel.

She had worked at several newspapers, magazines, and radio stations but felt trapped by the political correctness of their philosophy. She began writing under a pseudonym in order to write in her 'true voice' and soon became very successful.

"That's it for now," said Abby as she looked around, taking in everything so she could make sure she didn't miss anything, and she could write about it tomorrow on her blog. "Let's get some interviews from some of the girls and then get the show," she told Erica as she looked around for Rafe. "Have you seen Rafe and Julia yet?" When Abby talked to Julia earlier, they had agreed she would try to get Rafe out of the house to join them for drinks, so she was on the lookout for them.

"No." Erica shrugged as she took a swig of her beer and smiled at the girls who began to approach. The camera was like a magnet to some girls. "What's the big deal? You seem jumpy."

Abby flashed a look at Erica and then realized Erica didn't know Rafe like she did. "Let me tell you," she said as she leaned close to Erica, "there are a lot of women on the lookout for her now the word's out she's single."

"Really?" Erica laughed as a bunch of girls joined them at the table.

"Really," said Abby with a sharp nod. "I dated her when she first came to L.A.," she revealed to the table.

"Who?" inquired a blonde girl.

"Rafe Salvaggio," said Erica with a smile.

"Oh, I've heard of her," said another girl. "Isn't she that hot Italian construction woman? I heard she's single now."

Abby gave Erica a knowing look. "That's her," she confirmed. "When I dated her, I was possessed by her wildling ways after I went out with her a couple of times. But she's changed now after being off the market so long."

"Wildling ways? Possessed?" repeated the blonde girl. "What does that mean?"

"Well," said Abby as she revved up to tell a juicy story, "her last name literally means 'wild' so..." She dragged out the word and arched her eyebrows. She failed to mention how Rafe said her mother preferred to call her father her 'wild love.' "I swear, back then, she was a wildling rogue who wanted to possess souls." She loved the shocked faces and the buzz she got from telling her stories about Rafe's wild soul possessing ways.

"Well, I'll keep my eye out for her." The blonde laughed lustily.

"Me too," the other girl said with a matching laugh.

"Well, like I said, she's not like that now," Abby clarified. "She's serious and has a kid, so she can't be that way."

"Oh, too bad." The blonde smiled as she looked at the other girl, not believing Abby at all.

"Hey would you two want to do an interview for our vlog?" asked Erica, not wanting to subject them to Abby much longer.

"Sure," they said in unison, and Erica took them aside to mic them for the shoot.

Abby turned her attention to her friend Jude who had been dancing with a girl out on the edge of the dance floor—if you wanted to call grinding in place dancing. After making out with the girl, Jude got her phone number and then made her way casually back to the table. She looked like a sexy surfer boi with her sun bleached, shoulder length hair and tan skin. Her dark brown eyes made it look like she was shy and all the girls seemed to fall all over her for her looks as well as the fact, to Abby's understanding, she could really satisfy the girls in bed.

She thought Jude was going to settle down after she met her last girlfriend, Chloe, when they moved in next to Rafe three years ago. Abby could not believe how bad Jude fucked up her relationship. She thought they would become a real power couple in the massage business. At least Jude got to stay in the house, but it was about all she was left with after the breakup.

Jude seemed to sabotage every relationship she was in and used the excuses of either the girl would be better off or could do better when things got too serious. But Jude was a great friend and had sat through many uneasy nights over the past few years with Abby after her heart had been broken, and she needed a friend.

"Look. Is that Rafe sitting at the bar?" Abby asked when Jude made it to the table. She pointed across the room to the dark beauty at the bar.

"Yeah, and Julia is at the other end," said Erica as she rejoined the table and looked over to where Abby pointed. "We should go tell them to come over."

"No, you shouldn't," said Jude with a smile as she looked over at them.

"Why not?" asked Erica with a frown of confusion.

Jude laughed at Erica's naivety. "They're working the room."

"What do you mean? They're just sitting there," said Erica as she strained to look at Julia and Rafe.

"Just watch," said Jude knowingly and then leaned back in her chair and took a swig of her beer.

"When I told Julia to convince her to go out, I didn't mean for her to bring her out looking like that!" Abby complained as she looked Rafe over. "Her outfit is making a lot of promises it shouldn't be making."

"She really is looking hot tonight." Jude laughed at Abby's distress at seeing Rafe in dating mode again.

14

RAFE SALVAGGIO LOOKED out over the sea of women and wondered what she was doing in a bar again. She wondered if she would regret going out with Julia tonight and getting sucked into the wager they had made to pick up a date to take home. She knew why she agreed. She did it because she was angry with Eden. No, that was wishful thinking. The truth was she did it because she was still in love with her, and she knew it was a lost cause because Eden was now engaged to get married. Since Eden left, Rafe felt like she was in a cage waiting for Eden to open the door.

Rafe looked down at her scotch, and the image of her father came to mind—his favorite drink was a good well aged single malt scotch. She remembered talking to him about why he never remarried. They were working on a restoration of an old Spanish style horse ranch while Rafe was on a break from school before starting on her doctorate. Rafe was helping to put the finishing touches in the house and had hung up a painting depicting war horses unbridled and abandoned after a battle. Her father looked at the painting as he spoke about her mother.

He said when her mother was with him, it was like he was a tamed wild stallion and she was his world and direction. After she had died, he felt like he was still carrying her with him and he had to keep her there. Then, one day, he remembered he was a wild stallion, and if he were unbridled, he should truly go back to his nature and be free. He knew Mary would approve and she would want him to be happy, and maybe even find love again.

So, he began paying more attention to the women around him who were trying to gain his attention. He hoped he could find love again, but he would be happy with just enjoying life and being free. He never met anyone he felt he truly loved enough to marry, but he did have many caring relationships throughout the rest of his life, and after a while, he was happy again. From that point, her relationship with her father also made a turn for the better.

Rafe looked down at the gold ring on her finger and realized the cage she felt trapped in was similar to her father's feelings. Only she still had to see Eden all the time, so it was harder to break free. Rafe took a sip of her drink and forced herself to push thoughts of Eden out of her mind.

She looked around, and for the first time, she really saw the women around her. They were so full of energy and sexuality. She missed being surrounded by the vibe of desire that could take over a room and be able to be part of it.

She noticed the women who were looking at her. Some looked openly and others from the corner of their eye. She gave a slight smile encouraging to anyone who happened to be looking at her. She recognized her need to feel desired and wanted, the need for touch and passion, did not have to include Eden. She could break out of her cage on her own and be free to find new passions, and maybe even new love. Or maybe just have what her father had and at least have a caring relationship with someone.

Rafe sighed and slowly slipped the gold ring off her finger and felt the sting of sorrow in her heart. She held on to the ring until it was very warm then put it in her left pocket. Like her father, she had nothing to lose anymore. It was possible she had everything to gain by being free again. These women were looking for something, and she knew she had that something. It was time to take her heart out of its bondage.

Lying on the bar beside Rafe's drink was a small stack of cards the bar provided for networking. They were a fun throwback to pre-mobile phone days but were a novelty for the club. The girls came to the club just to collect cards. They had the bar name on one side and a small message on the other that read *Hello, we met at Club La Femme,* with blanks for names and contact information. The cards next to Rafe were filled out with phone numbers on them and were intended for Julia. Julia had sent them over, per their bet, along with two drinks.

As Rafe reached for one of the drinks, a stunning redhead approached her with a smile Rafe recognized well. Rafe looked across the bar at Julia and smiled wickedly. It was time to remind Julia how an overachiever won a bet.

"Hi," said the redhead as she moved in close to Rafe.

Rafe set her burning gaze upon the woman and smiled back. "*Ciao, bella*," Rafe replied in her smooth Italian accent.

"You're Rafe Salvaggio, right?" she asked not waiting for Rafe to answer. "I'm Jillian," she declared and handed Rafe a card with her number. "Here is my number, but if you want, we can get out of here now," she suggested with a blush running from her neck to her cheeks.

Rafe rewarded the woman with a small laugh and a feral smile. "I would like to, Jillian, but I have to stay here for about ten more minutes. Will you wait?"

"Sure, okay," answered Jillian surprised and pleased, loving Rafe's accent. She was deciding how to stay close and also go tell her friends at the same time when Rafe leaned toward her and moved her lips close to her ear.

"Jillian, you don't mind if one more joins us, do you? You see the girl over there?" Rafe asked, her hair brushing Jillian's face as she glanced toward the dance floor. They both saw the beautiful girl with shoulder length black hair wearing a cut-off shirt showing her well-defined abs who danced like she was the only one on the floor. "I'd like you both to come home with me tonight."

Jillian looked over at the girl and then into Rafe's eyes and swallowed hard. "Of course," she whispered hoarsely.

"Why don't you go have a drink with your friends. When you see me leaving, meet me at the door," instructed Rafe with her accented English as she ran her fingers down Jillian's back.

Jillian shivered with excitement at Rafe's touch and soft voice. "Okay," she answered. She slowly turned and walked toward her friends and then stopped and looked back at Rafe, who was still watching her walk away. She felt her knees wavering, so she quickly turned back toward her friends and rushed to their table to sit down.

Rafe watched until Jillian joined her friends. Then she signaled to the pretty bartender. "Please send another drink to the lady along with these two cards," she said and motioned to Julia who was at the other end of the bar flirting. "And close out my tab."

"You've sent her three drinks already. Maybe you should just go talk to her instead of sending her cards," the bartender offered helpfully.

Rafe smiled at her and winked. "Just give them to her, and the drink." The bartender shrugged then took the cards and the fourth drink to Julia.

From their table, the freckle-faced Abby watched Rafe approach the dance floor as the path cleared before her until she reached a girl who was displaying her well-muscled body. She just knew Rafe had turned on her Italian accent and was whispering to the girl. Then somehow, the girl ended up in Rafe's arms.

"Oh, my god, you guys. This is terrible!" said Abby with fear and worry on her face as she watched Rafe run her hands over the girl.

"What?" Jude asked as she looked around to figure out what she was talking about.

"I think the old Rafe is back," she whined. "Look!" She pointed at Rafe dancing slowly with the girl with the abs even though the music was fast.

On the dance floor, Rafe gave the girl a smile promising untamed carnality in the dark. She whispered into the dark haired girl's ear, turning on her Italian accent and pointed toward Jillian. The girl gave a trance-like smile as she nodded to the dark haired and swarthy-skinned beauty with eyes full of promises in front of her. Rafe took the girl by the hand and headed for the door.

"Rafe," said Julia calmly as they met at the door. Julia had a pretty blonde by her side, and she was ready to go home with her.

"Julia," Rafe answered back and gave her a smoldering smile.

"This is Carey," said Julia as she took the blonde's arm showing off to Rafe.

"Nice to meet you, Carey," she said politely. "This is Leslie," she said to them both.

"Shall we go?" asked Julia and started to turn toward the door.

"Just a moment," said Rafe as she turned her head to look back over the room. Jillian appeared in front of Rafe like magic and smiled. Rafe looked at Julia with a gloating smile. "This is Jillian." She winked. "Now we can go." Rafe took both Jillian and Leslie's hands and looked at Julia who just raised her eyebrows before turning and leading them out of the bar.

Abby was watching Rafe and Julia at the door with squinted eyes. "Rafe just walked out of here with two girls. It was a redheaded Amazon and the girl from the dance floor who looked like she was all muscle. Oh, no, no, no!"

"Great," said Jude as she smiled at a girl who had touched her lightly as she walked by her.

"No, not great! You didn't know Rafe before she met Eden. She was," she bit her lip, "she was a wild woman on the prowl. She would just, just fuck you and then drop you. It was like she was insatiable. And, if the old Rafe is back, it means it's really over for her and Eden. I really hoped never to see this wild soul-possessing side of Rafe again."

"Abby, this is no big deal," Jude said as she shook her head. "Besides, Eden is off fucking some guy, so why can't Rafe fuck two girls?"

"Well, what if this is just a phase for Eden? If Rafe regresses into her wildling self, Eden won't have a chance to be with her again. One," she held up a finger, "I don't know if Eden will see her the same if she sees her like this, and two," she held up a second finger, "I don't know if Eden or anyone can stop the crazy wild side of her if Rafe goes all in again."

"Well, it's Eden's own fault," exclaimed Jude with annoyance. "You really can't expect Rafe to wait forever for Eden to get over her man-phase. And what if it isn't a phase? It's been over eight months, and this is the first time Rafe has taken anyone home. Besides, you said Eden is supposed to be engaged to the guy now. Rafe deserves some happiness."

Abby sighed and sat her empty beer bottle on the table. "Yeah, but those girls don't deserve the pain she is going to give them when she forgets all about them in the morning."

"Abby, they're all consenting adults. Just let it go," said Jude as she was pulled to the dance floor by the girl with the light touch.

15

RAFE SALVAGGIO FOUND herself suddenly enjoying her little competition with Julia. When she first met Julia in school, Rafe explained the adventure concept, and she was quick to join her in fun. The trick was to not only go on the adventure but also, never get caught at whatever it was you were doing by anyone in authority.

Tonight, it felt almost like their school days or when she first moved to L.A., and they would go out looking for adventure. This competition was similar, but now they were adults and both single again, they had no one to worry about but each other and the adventure.

Rafe slid out of the car, opening the door for the others, and then led them up to the house. At the door, Rafe motioned the girls inside and stopped Julia. "Julia, wait."

"What is it?" Julia asked anxious to get inside.

Rafe smiled knowingly. "I have another wager for you."

"Another wager?" Julia laughed. "What?"

"Well, you stay out here, and I'll go inside," Rafe explained. "If I can get the girl you brought home to kiss me, then you have to stay out of the house tonight and make me breakfast in the morning."

Julia laughed softly not really believing what she was hearing. "And if she doesn't, what do I win?"

"If she doesn't kiss me and stay the night, I'll buy you the outfit you saw last week, do your laundry," she smiled, "and I'll make you breakfast and serve it to you both, in bed."

"Oh, now she stays the night?" scoffed Julia.

"Yes." She smiled impishly. "I had considered never dating a blonde again," she shrugged and winked, "but then I thought of this bet."

Julia looked at Rafe through squinted eyes considering the bet, then looked through the door at the women who were waiting inside.

"You'd have one of each hair color if you won, a wild ginger to boot." She chuckled along with Rafe. "You do know how to make things interesting, and I really loved that outfit. But where shall I stay, supposing I lose, that is?" asked the fair-haired woman curiously in her lilting English boarding school accent.

Rafe looked at the neighbor's house and saw the light was on. "You can stay with Jude and Stacey. One more thing, if I win, you have to tell everyone we see tomorrow I'm amazing."

Julia laughed. "Okay, you're on. Let's see if you can do it then," she dared her.

Rafe looked over her shoulder at Julia as she walked into the house. "Julia, I'd like French toast with eggs, fruit, and bacon for breakfast," she said in her smooth Italian accent. She knew it would jazz Julia up. Julia hated the fact Rafe could easily slip in and out of her accent and she could not. Rafe figured it was because she spoke and learned English with her mother in addition to school, and Rafe also was fluent in French from a young age, so switching languages and accents was easy for her.

Watching through the window, Julia saw Rafe walk up to all three of the girls and take the hands of her date, Carey. Rafe was talking to her and slowly began running her hand over her shoulders and up her neck to her face where she softly brushed her lips with her fingers. She leaned forward slowly and began kissing the side of her mouth and her chin all the while saying things to her Julia couldn't hear but knew were in Rafe's damn Italian accent. Then she put her lips close to Carey's, and the girl leaned forward, unable to stop herself, and they kissed.

As they kissed, Rafe reached out her hand to Jillian, the redhead who was standing behind Carey and pulled her into the fold. Jillian began to take off Carey's top as Rafe turned to give some attention to Leslie. The orgy began, clothes were removed, and lips, tongues, hands, and fingers were exploring many, many body parts. Julia walked away sadly, exasperated and sexually frustrated at the same time. Rafe had turned back into her old self a little too quickly in Julia's opinion.

16

SITTING ON THE couch in front of the television at the neighbor's house, Julia Hawthorn was drinking wine and watching old black and white horror movies with Stacey. Julia was berating herself because she should have known Rafe would have to go over the top. It was just like in school and the 'adventures' Rafe would invent. The adventures were usually good fun, but sometimes, it felt like they were in a duel to the death to out-do each other. It was both exciting and not just a little bit scary. It was a lot scary sometimes. At least this adventure didn't include heights or breaking and entering. She pushed down her frustration and denied her jealousies foothold in her mind, though it was putting up a good fight.

When Rafe first moved to L.A., they got into all kinds of situations, and Rafe was a challenge to keep up with most of the time. Julia was not sure if Rafe ever actually slept back then.

Julia stopped going on adventures with Rafe for a while when she got involved with Andrea, a woman she thought might be *the one*. Julia was not sure if she was actually really over Andrea yet, but she was working on it in the best way she knew how—other women. When the relationship didn't work out, Rafe was there to help get her out again, and Julia wanted to return the favor and possibly help them both. Her only regret was she underestimated Rafe and her ability to get back on the horse, losing the wager to her.

Julia looked over at Stacey and sighed. "I really appreciate you letting me crash here tonight. Believe me, it wasn't the plan," complained Julia.

"Oh, no problem." The pale freckled woman with the long curly fire red hair laughed. "I still can't believe you guys made such a crazy bet! I mean, is betting a normal lesbian thing? I've heard guys talking about doing that sort of thing but never women," Stacey revealed as she pushed her oversized retro glasses up on her nose. She would put them on over her Irish blue eyes when she took out her contacts for the night.

Since moving into the house, Stacey found out one of her roommates was a gay man and the other, as well as her neighbor, were lesbians. She had received a different kind of education after moving here, one she found very intriguing, but something she just couldn't see for herself. She felt lucky to find such a great place to live and a great bunch of people to hang out with. Over the past year, they had become good friends and hung out a lot.

"I don't think it's something normal. We don't make wagers like that all the time," explained Julia. "But I've found over the years it does make things interesting at times." Julia took the last sip of her wine as the door opened and Stacey's roommates, Jude and Flynn, entered the house along with Jude's date for the evening.

"Hey, Julia. Why are you here?" asked Flynn as he sat down next to her.

"Yeah, didn't I see you leave the bar with someone tonight?" asked Jude with a grin as the quiet girl held onto her belt loops.

"You guys aren't going to believe this! Rafe took Julia's date!" Stacey exclaimed and laughed uproariously.

"What? Julia, what's she talking about?" asked Flynn.

Julia sat her wine glass on the table then rubbed her temples with a sigh, feeling and looking defeated. "Never make a wager with Rafe," she complained. "I know it's her Italian accent she can just turn on and off," she said in frustration. She was jealous she didn't have the same skill of turning her accent on and off at will without sounding ridiculous.

Oh, my god! You mean Rafe has *three* women over there?" shouted Jude and bent over laughing.

Stacey bounced up and down on the couch excitedly and laughed with Jude. "Yes! Oh, my god! Can you believe it?" She looked at them with her glasses making her eyes look huge. "What do you think they're doing over there?"

"Fucking," scoffed Julia disgruntled, and Stacey bounced with laughter along with the others.

"You guys, Abby is going to freak when she finds out about this!" said Jude through her laughter while leading her date, the girl with the soft touch, to her bedroom, leaving the others behind as they laughed and talked over each other about Rafe.

17

IT WAS A beautiful morning, and Rafe Salvaggio was sitting outside at her table on the patio. She was wearing nothing but her robe, freshly showered, reading the financial news on her tablet, and eating the gourmet breakfast Julia had made her per their wager. The evening had been full of pleasure, and the early dawn had brought even more satisfaction in both her need to give pleasure to a woman, or several, and receive some much needed sexual satisfaction for herself. Now she was ravenous and was happy Julia came through on her part of the wager by making a generous breakfast.

Julia came to the table with a fresh pitcher of orange juice. She sat the pitcher of orange juice down on the table and spoke softly to Rafe. "Why did you have to use my room?" she groaned. "Walking in on a bed full of women who weren't there for me was quite a shock."

"I'm sharing my bathroom with all three of them this morning, so I think it's fair," said Rafe with a chuckle and put her tablet down. "No complaining, just breakfast, and don't forget—I'm amazing," she reminded Julia then took a bite of her egg.

"Of course, you shared *your* bathroom. It's three times as big as the one in the guestroom," Julia mumbled under her breath.

There was a knock on the door, and Julia looked up at the clock and then at Rafe, who nodded her head at her to answer the door as if she were a servant. Julia rolled her eyes thinking it must be either the neighbor coming over to snoop or a ride for one of the girls.

Julia answered the door and was surprised to see Eden this early toting the car seat with a sleeping Bronte and her backpack.

"Good morning," Julia whispered. She hesitated a moment, unsure what to do because they had a house full of naked women. "Rafe is outside on the patio. Do you want to take her out there or leave her inside?" she asked as she decided to let Eden enter and quietly helped with Bronte's bag. She certainly could not let Eden go into Rafe's room right now, but she figured the rest would be fine. Hopefully, they could get her out quickly.

"I'll just leave her in her car seat for now and put her over by the patio doors so Rafe can see her," said Eden and took Bronte toward the open patio doors. Julia stopped in the kitchen to bring more food to Rafe. Eden took note of what seemed like Julia's servitude but said nothing as she put Bronte down, unbuckled her from the car seat, and took off her tiny sweater.

"You're early," observed Rafe as she saw Eden in the doorway. "It's only a little after six," she said as she wiped the corner of her mouth and gave Julia a look, her eyes twitching toward the bedroom and back.

"More bacon, Rafe?" asked Julia as she shrugged helplessly and put a fresh plate of bacon on the table. Rafe nodded in defeat knowing there was nothing she could do about anything now. Julia placed two pieces of bacon on her plate without a word.

Rafe's mood shifted to annoyance tinged with a small amount of anger at Eden for, once again, showing up at a different time than she agreed.

"I know, I'm sorry," Eden said as she watched Julia refill Rafe's orange juice glass. "Is this part of your living arrangement, serving her breakfast? It seems a bit demanding."

Julia smiled at Eden. "Believe me, she earned it, and I really don't mind at all. She is *truly* an amazing woman." Julia watched as Rafe tensed and could see her mood change.

Rafe wished she could go rush the girls along or make them stay in the bedroom until Eden left but knew it was probably much too late now.

"I can't believe this," muttered Eden wondering just what all Rafe was demanding of Julia. She put Bronte's sweater in her bag and looked up in time to see a tall, beautiful redhead walk out onto the patio from the direction of Rafe's room carrying her shoes.

Jillian went up to Rafe and kissed her lustily. "You were beautiful this morning." She winked then gave her another quick peck on the lips.

"So were you," Rafe said softly hoping Eden could not hear her. "Uh, I'm sorry, but my daughter got here early, so I'm not going to be able to have you stay for breakfast," she said in her normal volume and nodded toward the baby.

Julia looked at Rafe and frowned. There was no reason Rafe needed to make the girls leave. This was all more of Rafe trying to do what she thought would get back into Eden's good graces, and it was making Julia feel splenetic. Usually, Rafe just did what she wanted everyone else be damned, but she still treated Eden with kid gloves even though they were split. Julia wanted a chance to chat the girls up this morning, and now her opportunity was ruined. It was complete and utter bullocks!

"It's fine," Jillian assured Rafe and looked over at the sleeping baby with a smile. She glanced at Eden briefly then dismissed her and focused on Rafe. "That's not what I'm hungry for. Besides, I already called a cab." She kissed Rafe again and lingered over her. "Mmm, call me anytime," she moaned through the kiss. "I mean anytime." She flashed a smile up at Julia. "I heard what you said, and I agree!"

"Ah, yes," nodded Julia as she chucked down a container of warm syrup on the table in front of Rafe. "She *is* amazing." She was already feeling the stress of losing the bet and having to say her obligatory phrase to everyone she saw, and now the girls were leaving. *Damn Eden*, she thought in frustration. Now not only does she lose the bet but she loses a second chance with the girls. The only positive thing was Rafe still being in a congenial mood.

A car horn honked outside. "There's my cab," said Jillian. She blew another kiss to Rafe and headed toward the patio door. She smiled at Eden as she passed her to go inside and out through the front door to catch the cab waiting for her.

Eden did her best to ignore the stunning redhead and the sting she felt after seeing her kiss Rafe so passionately. She sat out a stuffed animal for when Bronte woke and then took the sippy cup out of the backpack. When she looked up again, she saw a small, disheveled blonde, whose hair was still wet from her shower, amble out onto the patio from the direction of Rafe's room.

Carey stumbled over to Rafe, kissed her soundly, and took a piece of bacon from her plate. "I'll never forget this," she said then peeked at Julia from under her long lashes. "Sorry, Julia."

"It's fine," said Julia as she held her chin up and smiled bravely. "Rafe is amazing."

Carey laughed and nodded in agreement. She exchanged only a brief look at Eden then leaned down and whispered in Rafe's ear. Rafe nodded to her with a smile and gave her a playful smack on her ass. Carey stood and smiled happily. "Well, my ride's here. I've gotta go to work this morning, bye," she said with a wave as she made her way out the back gate where her ride was waiting.

Eden watched the girl leave before looking over at Rafe and Julia with surprise trying to comprehend what was happening. She pushed down a feeling she denied was jealousy. She didn't understand why both women were kissing Rafe or why Julia kept saying Rafe was amazing. Again, she wondered what Julia had to agree to so Rafe would let her move into the house.

Rafe smiled up at Julia, who she could tell was dying to know what Carey had said, and then gave her a sympathetic pat on her hand before taking another bite of bacon. She nodded to her empty plate, and Julia promptly placed two more pieces of bacon in front of her. Rafe forced herself not to laugh. She would save her laughter for after breakfast.

Eden shook her head at the completely surreal situation. She was about to make her way over to talk to Rafe and put the sippy cup on the table when another bleary-eyed girl, who seemed to be wearing only a sports bra for a shirt, walked out onto the patio from the direction of Rafe's bedroom. Eden was stunned and couldn't believe what she was seeing. She was getting a clearer picture in her mind of what was going on, and her hands began to shake with anger.

Leslie made her way out to Rafe, and the black-haired girl gave her a long, deep, wet kiss and a hug. "Rafe, thank you so much. I think, no—I know it was the best sex I've ever had."

Rafe smiled and winked at her as she dabbed the corners of her saliva covered mouth with her napkin. "You're not so bad yourself." Rafe grinned and held up her orange juice in a salute and then took a small sip.

"Well, when you have three girls fucking you, how can it be anything other than good?" Julia forced a laugh trying not to be jealous of all the attention Rafe was getting this morning, and the fact they were all leaving. "Rafe is amazing!" she said in vexation, happy there would not be more people she had to say the phrase to this morning and dropped more eggs on Rafe's plate unceremoniously. Things were not quite working out how she had imagined.

"Good point," agreed Leslie with a grin. "She is amazing," she said and kissed Rafe again. "I threw my shirt away. I guess things got a little out of hand," she laughed and ran her fingers under Rafe's nose and over her lips.

"I guess," said Rafe not missing the scent on Leslie's fingers. She was tempted to reward her aggression with some of her own, but the sight of Eden from the corner of her eye had stopped her.

"By the way," Leslie said sweetly, "I think Carey took home a souvenir. One of your monogrammed washcloths." She smiled down at Rafe. "I may have taken one too." She winked then stood up and took Rafe's orange juice from her. She drank the juice while brazenly showing off her abs and body to Rafe again at the same time.

"I see," said Rafe as she surveyed Leslie's abs and body openly and then looked up at Julia and winked. "I think I'm going to need some cappuccino now, maybe with a little bourbon. It was a long night." She laughed trying to break the sexual tension she was feeling.

Despite her frustration, Julia fought to stifle her laugh as she enjoyed the aggressiveness Leslie was subjecting Rafe to under the circumstances.

Rafe looked at Leslie with a smile. "I'm sorry I can't invite you to stay for breakfast, but my daughter is here early."

"No problem," Leslie said softly and smiled knowing they had appreciated her body. She sat the glass down and ran her hands over Rafe and then under her robe one last time for good measure, showing her own appreciation. "If I stayed, I'd need more than breakfast anyway." She hummed into Rafe's ear and kissed her again. "Bye," she said and pulled herself away slowly. She started to walk past Eden toward the front door but turned back and looked at Eden with a frown. "You're the ex? The one everyone called Salvaggio's Paradise?" she asked because it was the rumor she'd heard from some girl named Abby a few months ago. "The one who left her for a man?" She shook her head in disbelief and continued on her way out.

Eden clenched her fists, and her face turned red as she looked at Julia and then at Rafe who was pulling her robe closed covering her exposed breast. She couldn't keep her silence any longer. "What the heck is this, Rafe? You two have a parade of girls going through the house now?" she said in a low, harsh voice.

"Whoa! None of those girls were mine," said Julia defensively. "Well, one of them was supposed to be mine, but I lost her in a wager," she said weakly, throwing her hands up and walking back into the kitchen to make cappuccino—with bourbon no less.

"Great, Rafe! This is just a great thing to have going on around Bronte," she said as she crossed her arms and tapped her foot. "Is this how you treat women now?"

Rafe looked up from her breakfast at Eden and gave her a seductive smile. She stood up, and her robe opened slightly. She walked over to Eden all the while holding her gaze until she stood very close. She reached out her hand as if to caress Eden's face, but stopped, and instead, she leaned down and picked up the sleeping Bronte from her car seat.

"*Ciao*, B Girl," Rafe whispered to the sleeping baby. "You know what, if Mommy had just shown up at the time she was supposed to instead of an hour early, she wouldn't have had to watch my parade, now would she? It's just a good thing she didn't come any earlier. Yes, it is," she cooed then carried the baby across the patio to the door leading to her room. She went inside and placed Bronte in the crib. She then worked on feeling indifferent to Eden's anger.

Eden looked furiously after Rafe, and as Julia walked back over from the kitchen, she turned her angry gaze upon her.

Julia saw the fire in Eden's eyes and held her hands up in a surrender signal. "You did it to yourself," said Julia. "You did say seven. You know it's true, Eden. They were out before seven." Eden just looked at her angrily. "She didn't treat any of them wrong. As you could see, they were all happy to be with her," she said trying to defend her friend. By the look on Eden's face, she could tell announcing all three women were with Rafe had not helped matters. Julia crossed her arms defensively. In her mind, after eight months apart, Eden had no right to say anything about what Rafe did anymore. "You're with Jake now," she said crossly. "She can do what she wants."

"I know," Eden choked out then shook her head as Rafe's scent lingered. She tried to wrap her head around what she had just witnessed and tried not to let the hurt of seeing other women with Rafe show. She knew Rafe had been with others because of the woman in New York, but it was something she had never seen in person and in what used to be their home. She also tried to block out the fact she saw enough to know Rafe was naked under her robe. The memories of the rest of what her half-open robe was hiding made her mind reel.

"Three?" she demanded. Julia bit her lip to suppress her smile and nodded her head in confirmation. "Just great! Tell her I'll be back no later than two o'clock," she said and stormed out of the house.

After hearing the door slam, Rafe walked back outside and over to the table. "Is she gone?"

"Yeah," said Julia and grinned as Rafe sat back down to finish eating. "Don't let her ruin your morning."

"Too late. Now get my cappuccino," she said, and Julia gave her a smirk.

Julia went inside, returning with the cappuccino and set it in front of Rafe. She joined her at the table and started filling her own plate with food. Her patience level with Eden had grown thin since Canada and all she had found out about what had been happening. It was understandable Eden was upset about what Rafe had done, but punishing her with Bronte was wrong.

"So," said Julia as she put her napkin in her lap. It was time to get Rafe's good mood back. "What was all the whispering about with Carey?"

Raising her eyebrows, Rafe grinned. "She wanted to know if I was the one who left a mark on her."

"Oh, my." Julia covered her food-filled mouth as she laughed. "Was it?" Rafe took a sip of her cappuccino without a word and winked. "It was!" Julia laughed again.

Rafe smiled and nodded her head. She looked at Julia and sighed. "Next time Eden comes early, tell her to come back, or at least warn me," she said annoyed. "The goal is to have fun, not piss off Eden."

"Oh, please." Julia scoffed. "It's not going to hurt her to be a little pissed off," she said as she tucked into her breakfast.

"She already hates me." She sighed and picked up her tablet. "I don't need to give her more reasons to be mad and keep Bronte away."

C. L. CATTANO

"Well," Julia said petulantly, "she can't be mad at you for having a life. She was going to have to see you out dating sooner or later anyway."

"Later would have been better," Rafe muttered as looked to her tablet and rubbed her temples.

"Rafe," Julia said firmly since Rafe's mood was getting melancholy, "you've taken your ring off. You're doing great now. No more depressing wishful thinking about Eden. She's with boring Jake now." She grimaced. "And you have just proven you're still desirable and exciting. Things are going to be great for you."

"I guess," Rafe mumbled as she tried to focus on her reading. "I just don't like seeing myself do these things around her." She shook her head knowing Julia would not understand.

"Well, at least she was dressed in something decent today. Did you see her clothes last night?"

Rafe looked up at her from her tablet with confusion. "What are you talking about?"

"Her outfit last night," Julia said and looked at her with arched brows as if she should know what she was talking about. "She looked like she was wearing the clothes of a hundred-year-old corpse."

"She said she was going to dinner with Jake and his parents, so she was probably dressed for where ever they were going," said Rafe with a frown because she hadn't noticed what Eden was wearing. She didn't want to admit she tried not to look too closely at Eden anymore because it still hurt when she was close to her. It was easier sometimes to just try to block her out because otherwise, everything about her rushed in painfully.

"Uch," Julia groaned. "You didn't spend any time with his friends in Canada. If his parents are anything like them, it will have been a boring night. Did you know Jake never takes off his shirt in public? Can you believe it? So he wears a t-shirt when he swims or is on the beach." They found out about the fashion *faux pas* when they went swimming in the hotel pool. Julia thought Abby was going to have a fashion heart attack with all the ugly swimwear surrounding them. "Oh, and I think the reason they don't drink alcohol is because they wear so much polyester they might combust if they catch on holy fire." She laughed at the absurdity.

"They don't drink? Even wine?" Rafe watched Julia shake her head no. Rafe frowned because she couldn't imagine life without at least wine. It seemed strange to Rafe not to drink wine and to swim with a shirt on since they lived in California with all the sun and wine. "Eden probably still has her glass of red wine after work when she needs it, though. It helps her," she said, certain Eden would not give up something even her doctor said was good for her anxiety in moderation.

"I don't think so," said Julia. "She didn't drink when we were around her," she said before she took a sip of her juice.

Rafe shrugged her shoulders and took a sip of her drink. "Well, wine is the drink of the gods. It's in all the holy books as a sacrament. It's life. It's healthy in moderation, and a good wine will make your friends very happy. Maybe Jake has a problem and can't have alcohol. If so, then Eden is doing the right thing by not drinking."

"Rafe," Julia shook her head, "stop defending them and making excuses for them. I'm not attacking them. I was just making fashion observations that led to other stuff." She pushed her plate back. "I'll do a better job of making sure things like today don't happen again." She grinned. "Especially the 'me making breakfast' part."

"The day isn't over," Rafe reminded her with a smile. "I'm amazing for the rest of the day."

"Yes, you are." Julia laughed. She decided she needed to make up for the Eden fiasco and not be a sore loser. There would be more wagers after all and who knew where they might lead. "The adventurous Rafe Salvaggio is back," she said as she got up and patted Rafe on the back. "It's brilliant! Brilliant! And you *are* amazing!" She laughed. "Wait until Abby finds out." She happily began clearing the table. "Get dressed because as soon as the baby is awake, we're taking you on the walk of champions."

18

RAFE SALVAGGIO WALKED quickly through the halls of the fledgling, but impressive, California Conservatory of Art and Design following the tenacious President Clarice Biggalow, who wanted to introduce Rafe to several staff members. They walked into a large classroom full of students working on some sort of project involving lots of paint on their hands. Clarice led Rafe to one of the tables but made sure she was well clear of the mess and tapped the slight woman who was standing over some students.

"Ms. Salvaggio, I would like you to meet Dr. Greer Noble," said President Biggalow as the woman turned to face them. "Greer is head of our Art Therapy Department. She teaches medical students from every medical field how art can be used in teaching and healing both the physically and mentally challenged. Well, except dentistry possibly, oh, and maybe podiatry, well, she works with most medical fields anyway. Her program covers everything from patients with minor childhood problems to the aged and severely ill and everything in between. I recommend you catch one of her lectures. She is wonderful!"

Greer Noble gave President Biggalow a smile and slight nod and then took in the sight of Ms. Salvaggio and her casual smile. She wanted to reach out and touch her to make sure she was real. She looked at Beth and signed to her. "Wow." Beth signed back, 'gorgeous' and tried to hide her smile.

"Thank you for the wonderful introduction," said Greer in her throaty voice. "It's nice to meet you," she said as she wiped off her paint covered hands. She offered a hand to Ms. Salvaggio, who shook it lightly and then looked to make sure she had no paint transfer. Greer motioned to the woman in brown next to her who had been signing. "This is Beth. She's my ASL interpreter and also my girl Friday for just about everything. You'll probably be seeing a lot of her."

"Greer, this is Ms. Salvaggio," President Biggalow said excitedly. "She will be Dean of the new Department for the Advancement of the Arts as well as teaching introductory and advanced Art History and a few introductory classes on Architectural and Cultural Preservation. She'll be putting together shows, helping with recruiting, and of course, the ever important funding for the art department. Oh, and she'll also serve on the Conservators board for procuring art for our gallery. Dean Salvaggio will be the youngest Dean the school has ever hired, and she has an eye for the exquisite! Her father was the great Ettore Salvaggio. He and Ms. Salvaggio have done a lot for historic preservation all over the world, and he was very generous to the arts. We're so lucky to have Ms. Salvaggio at our institution."

Rafe smiled at the president's praise of her father. He was generous to the arts. He gave because he knew it was what his wife would have loved, and it made him feel close to her when he gave in her name. She turned her head and took in the scenery noting Dr. Greer Noble was as exquisite as a piece of art herself, even with her paint covered hands. She hadn't noticed the fact the doctor was signing to her mousy brown shadow, Beth. Dr. Noble was slight of build, had auburn hair and pale blue eyes that looked like they were filled with humor at the moment.

"It's a pleasure to meet you both," said Rafe cordially. "This looks like an interesting class."

Greer saw how the new Dean Salvaggio looked over her classroom and knew she was one of the doubters. Well, she would just have to learn a lesson.

"You'll get used to it," she said as the humor left her eyes and they hardened with a challenge.

"What?"

Greer smiled up at her. "Everyone telling you how wonderful I am."

"Oh, yes." President Biggalow laughed. "Wonderful! She's also a very gifted artist. But it in no way impacts her effectiveness as an instructor."

Rafe smiled at her boss. "I see," she said and raised her eyebrows as she looked toward Greer and Beth.

"So, *Ms.* Salvaggio, Clarice seems to be excited to have you. What's your background? I have heard of your father, of course," Greer smiled and put her hands on her hips.

Rafe looked Greer over and knew she was challenging her credentials. She was probably one of the people she beat out of the job and was jealous. "I studied Real Estate and Construction Management under my father, of course, and in Italy, I attended *Politecnico di Milano* for my *Dottorato di Ricerca in Conservazione dei Beni Architettonici*, it means Doctorate of Preservation of the Architectural Heritage," she explained turning on her smooth Italian accent. "Then I studied Drexel University PhD Materials Science and Engineering as part of the double doctorate program between the two schools. My passion is Art History," she said as Beth interpreted. "I received double Master Degrees from *Université Pierre-Mendès France, Grenoble II for Histoire de l'art— spécialité Histoire des échanges culturels internationaux et relations* and *Sapiena Universita Di Roma, Italie* for *Scienze storiche. Medioevo, età moderna, età contemporanea — deve rivolgersi ai docenti coordinatori del percorso.*" She paused letting the small woman in brown sign, wondering if she could really interpret what she was saying in French and Italian, but then decided she did not care. They could ask President Biggalow to see her resume.

"It was my business to know as much as possible about the world of historical architecture, materials and design and the art belonging in the historical places we restored and preserved for my company," Rafe said formally. "I'm known more for my restorations, but I am an accomplished artist having created my own art for pleasure and creating many reproductions for our projects in many mediums and have published papers based on several of my projects. Though I don't have a large catalogue of work, as I have had little time over the past few years to indulge in writing papers or creating more art pieces, my art hangs or has been placed in the homes of several Italian government officials as well as the homes of others who appreciate my work. I have also had pieces in several private galleries in different parts of the world." She paused. "Do you have pieces showing anywhere?"

Greer waited for Beth to finish signing her last question then looked up at Rafe. "Not anywhere prestigious, yet—but a few pieces are in the school's gallery and some other places. My primary work is focused on the personal needs of patients not self-congratulations," she signed, and Beth interpreted. "Beth is very talented in her own right and does shows all over the country."

"I look forward to seeing what you both have created," she said and smiled patiently.

"Why Ms. and not Doctor or Maestro?" Greer pressed without the help of Beth.

"Actually, it would be Maestre, because I'm a woman." Rafe gave the doctor her most charming smile and shrugged. "I just never needed to use either title to do my job." She chose to let her interpret it however she wanted. She didn't want to explain some people in the construction and real estate industry were intimidated by her background, and it was just easier not to throw titles around on a construction site.

"Well, we must be off for the rest of our tour," declared President Biggalow as she saw the two women challenging each other and Dr. Noble about to rebut. "Come along, Dean Salvaggio. . Greer, don't forget about Dean Salvaggio's welcome party in two weeks. It will be held at the gallery next Friday evening."

19

EDEN KINGSLEY FELT like life finally seemed to be getting back to normal. She was glad it was Friday, and there was nothing pressing happening over the weekend. Over the past two weeks, she felt like her life with Jake, her job, and even her tense relationship with Rafe was turning around for the better. Jake finally, but grudgingly, relented about Rafe seeing Bronte, and she hoped this meant all the tension between Rafe and Jake would ease and they could all finally get along.

Seeing Rafe dating again was very hard, though. She didn't understand why what Rafe had done had affected her so much. She was pretty sure anyone would have been upset if they found out their ex had taken home three women. Especially if they had to watch as the women came parading out of her room to kiss her in the robe she was clearly naked underneath. Eden gripped the steering wheel of her car tight, and her heart raced as she thought about what she had seen and about Rafe.

Eden met Rafe in the year before she graduated college through her boss at *Cypress Literary Agency* when he wanted to restore the mansion he had inherited from his grandmother. He had contacted Rafe's company, *Eroina Conservazione e Design,* and he was entranced with Rafe immediately upon meeting her. His hopes were in vain, though, because Rafe was always aloof and didn't to respond to any of his not so subtle hints he wanted her.

Eden had never seen anyone so beautiful, and every time Rafe looked at her and smiled, she couldn't speak. Her boss invited Rafe to a big industry party. When she arrived, people actually stopped talking and watched her walk evocatively through the room as if she owned it and everything inside.

Rafe walked up to Eden and whispered in her ear. "You'd think they'd never seen Versace. I hope you'll come to my rescue and keep me company." Eden looked at her and couldn't speak. "I hope you remember me." She smiled and held out her hand.

"Oh, yes, Ms. Salvaggio," Eden stammered and took her hand to shake it focusing on keeping things businesslike to hide her nervousness. "It's nice to see you again."

"Please, just call me Rafe," she said pronouncing her name slowly—Rah-fā—and smiled. "Though the guys on my construction sites call me Rafe," pronouncing it Raif. "It's easier for them when they see it written down." She shrugged and smiled.

"I like the first way you said it, Rafe," she said the name softly and tore her eyes away from the beautiful dark Italian woman with gray-blue eyes looking like sparkling jewels. Eden could feel her shyness gripping her and forced herself to recall she was at a work function and had to pull herself together. She had met some very famous people after all, so being around this woman with her regal beauty shouldn't be difficult.

The rest of the night, Rafe had stayed by Eden's side, and the line of people who came to start a conversation with Rafe was very long. Eden wasn't sure where she had them, but Rafe handed out quite a few business cards, and she was given even more. Eden's boss was very popular for inviting Rafe, and he had reveled in it all. Eden was sure the night would be spun into more than it was by her boss, and Eden had dreaded what she would have to listen to the following day.

Rafe was dazzling and graceful, speaking in a couple of different languages when appropriate, pleasing the people whose native language she knew so fluently. She spoke about many different subjects, and it seemed she was so knowledgeable about every one of them. Eden could only stand there and smile because, a lot of the time, she had no idea what was being talked about, but Rafe made it seem like she was included.

At the end of the night, Eden had been walking through each room looking for her boss because she rode with him, but he was nowhere to be found. Instead, she found Rafe lounging elegantly in a chair near a large painting. She laughed as she talked to the man standing near her. They were discussing the painting, and Rafe was clearly amused at whatever the gentleman was saying. Eden just watched for a moment, and then Rafe turned her head and saw her. She gave Eden a smile that took her breath away as she stood up to greet her. Eden explained, rambling, how she couldn't find her boss, and Rafe immediately offered to give her a ride home.

When they went outside to the valet stand, all of the valets were falling over themselves to get Rafe's car. The lucky winner ran off quickly and came back with a little blue two-seat sports convertible with the top down.

"Here she is, ma'am," said the valet as he got out of the car and another valet opened the passenger door. "Say, we were wondering what year she was," he asked with a grin as if he had not checked the car out thoroughly and already knew the answer.

"Nineteen sixty-nine," said Rafe with a smile as she got in, closed the door, and looked over to see if Eden was in her seat. She revved the engine, popped it in gear, and sped them toward the highway.

Eden had no idea what type of car it was until Rafe told her later it was the car her father brought over with them when they moved to America. It was a 1969 Maserati Ghibli Spyder convertible her father bought before he was married. He loved the car and insisted Rafe take it to California to save it from New York weather. Rafe's father said it was the first moving piece of art he owned, and he made sure it was well taken care of at all times. Rafe rarely drove it but thought it would be fun to take out since it was going to be a nice evening. She had planned to drive it to Ocean Park and then run it down One Highway to Malibu and back, but since she had driven Eden home, she said she would just take it back to the warehouse after dropping her off.

Their ride home was quiet, other than the sound of the revving engine. Rafe was first to break the silence when they were at a stop light.

"You're very beautiful. Has anyone ever painted you?" she asked over the sound of the engine.

In the dark, Eden blushed, and the heat of embarrassment warmed her.

"No," she answered shyly and pulled her hair back so she could hold it in a ponytail when they were on the highway.

Rafe just smiled and nodded, and there was silence under the sound of the engine once again. When they got to Eden's apartment, Rafe parked the car, cut the engine, and then turned to Eden.

"I really appreciate you coming to my rescue tonight. It's always easier to relax when I know someone in the room."

Eden shifted in the seat and flushed red again. "I just stood there and didn't say much of anything," she insisted as she noticed Rafe's hair, though it looked wild, was still hanging beautifully down onto her shoulders while her own was a tangled wreck.

Rafe smiled and chuckled. "Well, thank you for standing there." She looked over at Eden's apartment building then back at Eden. "How would you like me to buy you brunch tomorrow? I know a good place, and maybe I'll let you talk a little." She grinned. "It'll be a thank you brunch for having my back tonight."

Eden was not sure what to do. She knew Rafe was important to her boss, and he would be upset if Rafe was insulted. She didn't think Rafe would be upset if she refused, but her boss might. She was definitely intrigued with Rafe. She was divinely beautiful, very smart, knew many people, and ran her own company. She happened to shift in her seat, looked down, and noticed Rafe had been driving without her shoes on. Her expensive designer shoes were lying in the floorboard halfway under the seat.

Eden had no idea why Rafe wanted to spend time with her—she was just an assistant for a small literary agency and still in college. Was she just being nice or did she really want to be her friend? It was obvious she was rich and had no problem talking to people and making friends. So Eden wasn't sure why she was being so nice.

Rafe waited for her to answer and could see something was on Eden's mind. "Listen, you don't have to go. I really just thought it would be fun. You did something nice for me, and I appreciate it. I thought we could talk and get to know each other. You didn't get to do much talking tonight so, I owe you." She smiled playfully again.

"Oh, no," Eden started hesitantly, "I'd like to go. I was just wondering why you were acting so nice. Really, I literally didn't do anything," she said as she continued to wring her hands nervously.

"Oh, well," said Rafe with an easy smile, "I can answer why I'm being nice. I think you're smart and kind. You didn't get pulled into any dull conversations. You knew a lot of the people there and were kind enough, the times you did talk, to tell me who they were. Oh, and Serge said you were the reason his script had been produced. And at least three people told me your boss would have gone out of business if you hadn't started working there." She paused and nodded. "Yes, and as I said, you're very beautiful." Rafe watched as Eden swallowed nervously. "Oh," Rafe said and bit her lip. "I'm sorry. Would you rather go with a group or something? I was thinking we could have a more casual conversation with just us, but if you want to invite someone else, I understand. So there you go," she said. "Does my answer help you with your decision?"

It did help Eden with her decision. This person just gave her a choice about how they could spend their time together. She seemed kind before she even knew her.

"I think casual, with just the two of us would be nice," she said amazed at how easily she had agreed. She met Rafe the next day for brunch and great conversation.

Monday morning, Eden's boss acted stranger than normal and asked her about Rafe giving her a ride home. She told him about their Sunday brunch—he told her she was gay. He laughed about it, so she wasn't sure if he was telling her the truth or just being weird because he didn't get into Rafe's pants. She didn't tell him she had plans to meet her again or that they ended up meeting several times over the next three months.

Eden found Rafe easy to talk with and it seemed like they laughed together easily and a lot. She talked to Rafe about everything from her anxiety to what it was like growing up on a farm. She really liked being Rafe's friend. Being with her felt calming and right. She had never those feelings with anyone before, and she liked the feeling.

In return, Rafe showed her around town and took her to some great attractions. She seemed to know she preferred not to deal with crowds. Sometimes, they would walk down the street or through a museum and Eden would be lost in her thoughts. Suddenly, she would feel Rafe's hand on her elbow or on her lower back as she silently guided her around an obstacle or toward something of interest. When Rafe saw she had her attention, she would just smile and point something out or ask her what she thought. Eden had never experienced someone who was happy spending time with her in silence sometimes.

When Eden met Rafe to start the portrait, it was at Rafe's office. The companies building actually had several offices and a warehouse with a parking garage where Rafe stored her father's car and where the employees parked.

In the warehouse section, there was a space for architecture restoration work with tools and machines. There were also a number of other rooms Eden wasn't exactly sure what they were used for and storage spaces.

They took the freight elevator up to the offices, and Rafe led her to what was her private office and studio space. Rafe placed their dinner and a bottle of wine on the table in front of the couch and showed Eden around. Everything was neat, organized, and filled with different paintings and all kinds of art supplies and tools, paint and building material samples and things Eden didn't have names for.

Rafe sat down and started sorting their dinner. Eden sat down beside her and was nervous because this was the first place they had been together not a public space. The memory of her boss and his idiotic laughter about Rafe being gay was going through her mind.

"Are you gay?" she blurted and saw the surprise on Rafe's face. "Oh, I'm so sorry! I didn't mean for it to come out that way. Just someone said you were and..." she forced herself to stop talking.

Rafe laughed and took a sip of the wine she had just poured. She smiled slyly and winked at Eden. "Yes, I am. I thought you knew. Does it bother you?"

Eden took a large drink of her wine. She had no idea how to react appropriately. Why would she think she knew? She knew there were many gay people in California, and she had met several gay men, but she had never met a gay woman—she knew of anyway. She hadn't really paid attention.

"Uhmm, no, no. I—" She cut herself off again. She had no idea what to say.

"Don't worry," said Rafe as she filled their plates with Indian food. "I'm just like everyone else, except I'm attracted to women. Oh, and you're safe. I wouldn't want you to think you're here because I expect anything from you. I really do want to paint you. I think you have a classic beauty and it needs to be celebrated on canvas," she said cheerfully being overly dramatic hoping to put her at ease.

Eden picked up her plate, took a bite of food, and then looked up slightly from her plate.

"It's fine," she said. "I think I'm straight."

Rafe laughed. "You *think* you're straight?"

Eden nodded and could not help but laugh with her. "Well, I never really thought about it. I've always dated boys so..." She shrugged and took another bite of her food.

"Boys? No men?" teased Rafe as she ate her food.

"You know what I mean," said Eden shyly.

"Oh, I know." Rafe smiled, and Eden could feel the heat on her face. "I tried a boy once, and it just didn't 'do it' for me, you know? So we didn't get past second base."

"Well, I did get past second base, and now that I really think about it—it wasn't really so great," Eden confessed. "But he was young. I'd dated more in college, and it was better." She shrugged trying not to think about what her parents would say if they knew she had sex outside of marriage. "Maybe I just haven't met the right guy. I'm mostly focused on school," Eden declared and was amazed she felt comfortable enough to talk to this woman about so many very personal things.

"And now?" asked Rafe then took a drink of her wine.

"Mmm..." Eden breathed as she swallowed her food. "Nothing, I mean no one, really. There is this one guy, though, Jeffery. He's from my hometown in Hartford, Iowa. He's going to school here in California too. When I go out, it's usually with him. But I haven't been out a lot lately. Work and school," she reminded her.

"I see," said Rafe raising one eyebrow as she put her plate down. "Well, I'm finished here, so I'll get things ready to paint your portrait. Maybe, when I'm finished, the painting will help you find a date." She laughed as she went to get her paints set up and put a large canvas on the easel. She looked over at Eden and smiled. "I have an idea for a painting in mind." She hesitated as she thought about her idea. "I'll start with rough-ins, and you can decide how much you want to model for it."

"How much I want to model?" she asked as Rafe led her to where she wanted her to stand and posed her. "I thought this was a portrait."

"Oh, it will be," Rafe assured her. "Hold this," she said and handed her an apple. "It'll be you in a scene."

"Holding an apple?"

"*Mela.*"

"What?"

"*Mela,*" said Rafe. "It's Italian for apple. Say it."

"*Mela,*" Eden repeated.

"Very good." Rafe smiled. "It'll get you in the right frame of mind for posing. Think about all the models in the past artists said to them '*tenere questa mela in tuo mano*' or 'keep this apple in your hand.' You'll be in good company." She smiled and then headed back to the canvas.

Eden laughed. "Okay, but what does this have to do with how much I'll want to model?"

"Oh," Rafe said from behind the canvas. "Well, I'd like to do a nude."

"What?" Eden said shocked and turned red. "I'm not posing nude."

"Okay. It's no big deal. I can paint from my imagination." Rafe chuckled playfully. "But if you want me to get it right. You know, for dates..." her voice trailed off.

"I'm not posing nude," Eden reaffirmed and smiled at Rafe's laughter from behind the canvas. "Are you just messing with me because I asked if you were gay?"

"No." Rafe laughed mischievously. "Of course not," she said but kept chuckling as she painted.

It took a little over a month to finish the painting. Eden kept her word and did not pose completely nude. But after Rafe explained her vision for the painting, she did let Rafe convince her to dress in more revealing clothes, and for the rest, Rafe was forced to use her imagination.

Over the three months they had known each other, and then the month Rafe was painting her portrait, Eden became more drawn to Rafe each day she saw her. She found herself thinking about her often and couldn't wait to see her again. Once she got over her shyness, Eden found she had started to notice more and more about Rafe. She noticed her when she touched her to shake her hand, to move her back into her pose for her portrait, when she put her hand on her shoulder or back to get her attention, or ushered her in the direction of something she wanted to show her.

The entire month she was posing for the painting Eden noticed Rafe hadn't touched her as often as she had before, and she never touched her accidentally. When she did touch her, there was a clear reason. Eden did not know why, but she began putting herself in positions and situations where Rafe would have to touch her. It was like a game sometimes. Rafe seemed always to find a way not to touch her like by using the end of a paintbrush to direct her or doing a pose and asking her to copy it. But just as many times, Eden won, and Rafe had no choice and would finally have to touch her. Eden wasn't sure why at the time, but winning a touch from Rafe made her day, and she felt good for days afterward.

When Rafe's smile became more familiar, other features caught her attention—the tone of her arms, her knee revealed through the hole in her old jeans as she sat down on the couch, the agility of her hands as she mixed paint and held her paint brush. The day she looked up and caught sight of Rafe's cleavage, she went home and had a panic attack. "I'm just spending too much time with her," she told herself. "Maybe I should stop hanging out with her." She didn't, though.

When the painting was finished, she found herself agreeing to go to a dinner party with Rafe and her friends. Normally, as she told Rafe, she would beg off anything to do with groups of new people if it was not work related. "Don't worry, I'll protect you," joked Rafe, and she did.

Eden was very quiet because of a mix of her anxiety and her shyness. She felt like she was a bright shade of red the entire night. Rafe's friends were very nice to her, but they almost immediately wanted to know everything about her and had many risqué comments about the painting. They good-naturedly teased Rafe about 'having a new girl' or 'if she had recruited the straight girl' and many other quips Rafe laughed off. Rafe made it clear Eden was just another friend. No one believed it, and Eden was surprised she felt hurt at being called just another friend.

Reluctantly, Rafe left her with a woman named Abby for a while to take care of some things. Eden assured Rafe she would be fine with her. Abby was a friend of Rafe's, and Eden had been listening to her talk most of the night. Abby was a fount of information about everyone there including Rafe. While Rafe was gone, Abby informed Eden a little about Rafe's history and told her to be careful if she really was dating her.

"She has this, this way about her," Abby said. "Women just fall for her, and Rafe will have her way," she snapped her fingers, "and then it's over. And what's worse, no one ever says anything about it. They just keep trying to catch her eye."

It became obvious quite quickly, Abby had been one of those girls, and she was hurt. Abby may not have realized it, but Eden could see it clearly. Abby kept talking, and Eden would contribute a word or two every once in a while, and both of them were happy with the arrangement. It was the beginning of their friendship, and the night Abby became protective of Eden.

Later when Rafe drove Eden back to her apartment, and they were having a glass of wine on her couch looking out at the city lights lighting up the night.

"Your friends were nice," Eden said, "but they were really going on a lot about us being together. Are they always so, involved?"

Rafe laughed softly. "They were just jealous I brought a beautiful woman to the party. And they *think* they're always involved."

"Hmm," was all Eden had said as her thoughts pulled her in many different directions. She was hurt Rafe said she was 'just' a friend—but why it should bother her? She didn't know. She had definitely seen in Rafe what Abby talked about and felt entranced herself. She couldn't stop thinking about Rafe.

Looking at her made her want to touch her. She could smell her perfume, and it was good—more than good.

Then she was pulled back to her roots—her belief system— her parents. But, as she looked at Rafe, she had an overwhelming feeling she had to know things. How it felt to kiss her. How it felt to have her kiss back. She looked up from her glass, and Rafe had leaned in close to her.

"You okay?" she asked softly.

Eden felt Rafe's breath on her face and could smell her sweet perfume mingled with the scent of her skin. Her mind shut down and her body reacted. She fell forward letting her emotions lead her into Rafe's lips. She felt Rafe's lips press against hers. Their mouths opened, and she noticed how sweet Rafe tasted. Then Eden lost herself.

Rafe finally pulled away and stood up. "I think I should go," she said in a quavering sexy voice. "Just so you know, I didn't plan this but," she smiled sensuously, "I'm not sorry." She found her shoes and put them on. "I hope this doesn't change things. Your painting is finished, and I was hoping to have a real unveiling party with people both of us know." Rafe looked at her, but she just looked back without a word because she didn't know what to say. "Okay," Rafe paused. "Bye," she whispered and walked out of the apartment.

Eden waited a week before calling Rafe. It was the longest wait she had ever had to live through because of the turmoil she went through in making her decision. She could not stop thinking about the kiss she had savored. She hoped Rafe would call her, and when she didn't call, she knew she would have to work up her nerve.

When she opened the door and saw Rafe's smile, her heart surged in her chest, and her body surged toward Rafe's lips. Rafe took control of her body, and she felt like she had lost her mind because of the things she did to her. It was the night she learned what it was to have a woman love her and how to love a woman in return. The night she was born into an entirely new world. It was the night she became 'Salvaggio's Paradise' and knew soon after, she was lost to Rafe and deeply in love with her.

She had always thought it was crazy when people said they felt so strong about someone after being with them one time, but after their weekend it felt like she had been with her a thousand times, and she wanted more, needed more. It was not long before she had to tell her out loud how she felt in her heart. She felt like she would burst, but she forced herself to wait until she graduated college and then all bets were off. As soon as her parents were on a plane back home, she met Rafe. While making love in the night, she told Rafe she was in love with her. It was crazy and scary, and it was right.

20

TAKING A DEEP breath to clear her mind Eden Kingsley brought herself back into the reality of the present. The best thing right now was they were getting along for Bronte. She was keeping her promise to Abby and Julia, and to herself, to make sure Rafe got to see Bronte a lot more, no matter what Jake thought about anything.

Jake just had to try to understand how things had to be and accept Rafe as part of Bronte's life. She just didn't think he understood everything they had gone through to make Bronte possible, and then all the things they had to go through to just be able to get along after they broke up—and until recently, they were losing the battle to get along.

After *it* happened—the affair—and Rafe finally came home from New York, Rafe did everything to try to win Eden back. Rafe sent gifts, love notes, and apologized many times. But Eden was heartbroken, and she was still emotionally confused about their relationship and her feeling she should be with a man. On top of all those feelings, Eden was also still so very angry with Rafe, and she felt betrayed and humiliated.

In her effort to try to move on from Rafe and figure out what she wanted, she went on a date with one of the writers she had met through a screenwriters networking conference where she was looking for a job and trying to meet people in the industry. During the conference lunch, she was sitting alone at a table, and a woman sat next to her and smiled.

"Aren't you Eden Kingsley?" she asked as she opened her boxed lunch.

"Yes." Eden smiled gearing up to network. "Do I know you?"

"Oh," she laughed, "probably not. I've heard a lot about you from some people you worked with doing some freelance work. I'm Regan Chadwick," she said and held out her hand.

Eden took her hand. "It's nice to meet you, Regan," she said, and they spent the rest of lunch talking about their work and their lives.

After the conference, Regan caught up with Eden again. "Hey, Eden," she called, and Eden stopped and turned to her. "Hi," Regan panted catching her breath. "Listen, I was wondering, since you're single now, and so am I, maybe we could go out."

"Oh," said Eden in surprise. She hesitated, unsure if she wanted to start dating anyone let alone another woman after Rafe.

"It's just a date." Regan smiled encouragingly as she saw Eden's hesitation. She had been very taken with Eden's beauty, and after talking with her, she couldn't stop thinking about her.

Eden looked at her anxiously and decided she seemed like a nice woman and maybe she would be the one who helped her get over Rafe. Maybe getting out there again would help her move on.

"Sure." She smiled anxiously.

"Great! How about Friday, and I'll pick you up."

"That sounds fine." Eden nodded, and they exchanged information.

They went out a couple of times and ended up sleeping together, but afterward, instead of feeling better, Eden seemed to feel worse. It was not that the sex was bad, but the feeling she had when she was with Rafe just was not there.

Then in February, Eden found out she was pregnant and broke it off with Regan. She didn't think to continue an affair she didn't feel good about, especially since she was pregnant, was a wise thing to do. Eden didn't tell Regan the true reason she was breaking it off, but in the end, Regan was very understanding when Eden told her she wanted to end things.

Eden didn't tell Rafe she was pregnant when she found out in February. She didn't get to tell her at all. She meant to, but she kept putting it off. She was still angry with Rafe, and her excuse at first was she wanted to make sure she didn't miscarry. But even after she knew things were good, she still didn't say anything because she was anxious about what Rafe would do when she found out she had not told her about the last insemination, either.

Rafe found out Eden was pregnant in April from a stranger. She had been meeting a new client who wanted to start building an authentic Tuscan Villa in the hills of California with some of their new wealth.

They were discussing the client's plans when Rafe found out he had hired a freelance script developer to help with his project, and the Studio ended up hiring her. 'She was a very sweet woman who was also very smart,' he told her. Rafe said she knew a person who did something similar.

In the end, the client revealed the person was Eden Kingsley and she was also about to become a single mother and they hoped the father would help her out. At the time, Eden had told them the father was out of the picture. Rafe was stunned and angry but managed to make it through the meeting and set up times to go through blueprints and material samples and even go check out the land to be developed. Eventually, she helped the client get the home of his dreams built.

The next day, Rafe knocked on the door of Eden's small studio apartment. Eden opened the door but left the chain on to see what Rafe wanted. She was not expecting her to come over and had just gotten out of the shower. Rafe asked if she could come in because she needed to talk. Eden relented and let her inside.

Eden was wearing a thick robe. Unless you were looking for it, her pregnancy was hidden. She anxiously stood back away from Rafe as she looked at Eden intently with those steely gray-blue eyes and could tell by her hurt look Rafe knew she was pregnant.

Rafe approached her and gently touched her stomach through her robe and then kissed her on the forehead. Eden saw the tears brimming Rafe tried to hide and hold back. It was difficult to watch because it seemed like Rafe never cried.

"Congratulations," Rafe said softly. She turned, took flowers and a bear out of the gift bag she was holding, and put them on the small end table. Then she left quickly.

By the next day, Eden had figured out how Rafe found out about the pregnancy. She went to lunch with Abby and told her Rafe found out she was pregnant.

"Did you tell her you used, you know, *the sperm*?" asked Abby worriedly.

"No," Eden answered apprehensively. "I didn't really get a chance to say anything. Like I said, she just congratulated me, kissed my forehead, left the gifts, and walked out."

"Well," Abby hesitated, "don't you think she has the right to know? I mean she's part of this too."

Tears fell from Eden's eyes as she looked anxiously at Abby. "I messed up so bad, Abby. I really thought we were good when I did the insemination, and now," she stopped and wiped her tears away. "Yes, you're right. She has the right to know. I should have told her when I found out. I just," she stammered, "I just couldn't talk to her."

"Well, you're going to have to find a way to talk to her now. You can't just let this go. It isn't fair for either of you and certainly not fair to the baby you're about to have."

"I will," she said as she pulled herself together. "I'll tell her tonight."

Eden went to Rafe's house, the large bungalow style home she had painstakingly restored, and hesitantly knocked on the door holding a bottle of wine and a stuffed baby lamb.

When Rafe answered the door, she was in her painting clothes, old faded jeans with holes in the knees, and a denim shirt with the sleeves cut off at the shoulders and was holding a glass of scotch. She had been painting in the small studio she had set up on the covered porch off the kitchen. Eden thought she looked so beautiful yet so sad.

Rafe just looked at her and pushed her dark curls from her eyes as she turned around to walk back to her studio. Eden nervously followed her through the familiar house where she used to live and had felt so loved.

Eden could see Rafe was painting a portrait of her mother and father from a photo taken when they first met. It looked like she was still dealing with her grief over her father's death. It was just after his funeral Eden had come home and decided to do the insemination.

"You look a lot like your dad when he was young," Eden observed as Rafe sat down and took a sip of her drink. Rafe didn't acknowledge or look up at her. "The painting looks really good. You're so talented. I could never understand why you didn't paint more," said Eden remembering how Rafe talked about the art lessons her mother had given her.

When Rafe finally looked up at her, Eden looked into her eyes, saw the misery behind them, and knew there was probably a spark of anger not far below. It was the reason for her silence.

Eden sighed and handed Rafe the bag with the gifts inside. Rafe took out the wine and then the lamb and looked up at Eden uneasily. "I'm so sorry you had to find out the way you did," Eden said softly. "I know I should have told you sooner."

Rafe just looked at her, so she continued.

"While," she cleared her throat, "while you were in New York, I found out I was ovulating. I wanted to surprise you," she said softly. "It's our baby," she said, and a tear slipped down her cheek.

Rafe's eyes softened, as she understood what Eden was telling her. She looked away trying to find words to respond and then looked back at her. "Will you come home?" she asked softly.

Eden's heart beat hard against her chest. She was torn between wanting to comfort Rafe, hold her, and stay with her and the anger she felt at her for what she had done, for cheating. She also knew she still wasn't sure if she could go back into a relationship with Rafe or any other woman. Her time with Regan had not helped her figure it out at all. She just couldn't give herself or Rafe any false hope, so she knew what she had to do.

"No," she said softly. "Rafe, I," she hesitated, "I just can't come back right now."

Rafe looked up at her, and Eden could tell she was working hard to control herself. "Will you," she started, "will I get to be part of its life?"

"Yes," Eden promised immediately. "Yes, this is your baby too. It's still our baby, Rafe, no matter what."

Over the next three months, Eden did her best to include Rafe in everything with the pregnancy from appointments to picking a name when they found out they were having a girl. Eden had always loved the name Bronte, and Rafe wanted to give the baby her mother's middle name, so they decided to name her Bronte Lijia.

They discussed Rafe's second parent adoption, and Eden agreed it was the best thing for Bronte. They even agreed they would make sure the baby had dual citizenship in Italy either through Rafe or Gabri. Rafe wanted to make sure Bronte could take advantage of being part of the EU when she was older. Eden just wanted to get along even if in the future they were not together as a couple.

Then she had a scare and some complications with the pregnancy, and the doctor ordered her to bed rest. Rafe begged her to move back in so she could take care of her, and Eden finally relented. Rafe was on top of everything from helping her move back into getting out of her lease.

Rafe was so good to her and so gentle and patient with all of her needs, including sex. Eden couldn't help but show her affection for all she was doing for her. She knew, at the time, Rafe couldn't have been happier or more excited about the baby. Eden didn't know for a while, but Rafe was contemplating selling her business, looking for something to do that allowed her to travel less, stay home more for her and the baby.

After Bronte was born, it seemed like Eden could find nothing but fault in Rafe. It seemed like everything Rafe did was wrong. Eden complained about everything from how she spent money to sometimes Rafe's very presence. Eden began to have issues again with her anxiety and overcome with emotions and feelings, making Eden doubt her relationship with Rafe all over. She was feeling more and more like she should be in a relationship with a man. Rafe knew something was wrong because she had been refusing sex and being close. Eden finally worked up the nerve and confessed her feelings to Rafe so she wouldn't have to lie to her anymore.

In her frustration after Eden's confession, Rafe told her to go figure out her feelings and made her move into the guest room. Eden hoped it meant Rafe understood she just needed time, and no matter what, they could get along for Bronte.

Eden met Jake when Bronte was about three months old while out running errands. He was out with his son Hunter, and he sweetly helped her load her groceries into the car. She agreed to meet him for drinks, and they ended up having sex on their third date. She had no expectations of sex with him being like sex with Rafe, and it wasn't.

Because of her expectations for sex being different with a man, she did find satisfaction, up to a point, and it was no better or worse than the other experiences she'd had with men when she was younger. It was just familiar. He kept telling her he loved her, he was a great listener, and Eden told him all about her problems with Rafe and how they were living in separate bedrooms. Plus, she didn't know if she even wanted to feel with anyone the way she had felt with Rafe again.

Eden knew Rafe had figured out she was seeing someone, and when Rafe met Jake, she immediately didn't like him. Eden brushed it off to jealousy and hoped Rafe and Jake could get along someday.

Rafe had gone on a business trip to New York and then to Italy to take care of selling her business. Jake asked Eden to move in with him. She decided, with Jake's encouragement, it was time for her to get out of Rafe's house, so she accepted Jake's offer and was out of the house before Rafe returned.

Eden knew everyone was angry with her because they were not shy about telling her. They also told her Rafe had been angry and upset when she came home and found her gone. Oddly, Rafe never confronted her about it, and Eden was surprised but relieved. She hoped Rafe was letting her go down the path she needed to go down, and they could stay cordial for

Bronte. But soon, they were arguing about Rafe getting time with Bronte. Eden was able to save her friendship with Abby, but she was still working on getting back just a thread of something to help her and Rafe get along for Bronte's sake.

It seemed like Jake felt the same way about Rafe as Rafe did about him. Eden knew part of it was her fault for all the complaining she did about Rafe. Then life just happened, and it seemed like they were always busy and had something going on. Suddenly, Rafe was becoming less of a presence in their life.

Rafe would call, and they would try to make time for her to spend with Bronte, but it didn't always work out. She knew she should have been more on top of making sure Rafe got her time with Bronte, but she and Jake were talking about getting married and Jake possibly adopting Bronte.

She could never tell Rafe they were thinking about moving because it was just a discussion. Rafe was already angry, and Jake claimed Rafe was making threats. He had even been telling Eden every chance he got Rafe was going to make their life hard. She thought Rafe really was going to prove Jake right when she couldn't find her and Bronte in Canada.

It was then she realized just how much what she and Jake had done had hurt Rafe and would hurt Bronte in the future. She always knew Rafe would be part of Bronte's life no matter what because it was what she had promised her. So now, she was really focusing on making sure Rafe got to see Bronte, even if it caused problems with Jake.

Eden wasn't sure what she would do if Jake continued to push her toward moving away. Jake was pushing her more and more about it and about being Bronte's father. She just hoped she wouldn't regret taking back the ring and not postponing the engagement. She was feeling very anxious about the direction the relationship was going. She was at a loss at what to do about it and make Jake understand, even if they got married, Rafe was going to be Bronte's parent no matter where they went if they decided to move.

Eden refocused her mind onto work as she parked her car and headed for her building. She smiled as she thought of all the things she was accomplishing at work. She had signed several great writers with promising scripts she actually felt good about pitching and had built some great interest in several projects her company wanted to produce. She was finally back doing what she loved and working for a great company.

As she walked into her building, she waved hello to the receptionist who was already on the phone and started to go straight to her office when the receptionist waved her over and put her hand over the phone.

"You've got flowers," she said in a singsong voice and indicated the vase of flowers on the counter.

"Thank you," Eden said and smiled as she picked up the vase and took the flowers into her office. She put them on her credenza and pulled out the card. They were from Jake, and the card said he was sorry and he loved her. She smelled the flowers, and the scent calmed her. She loved the smell of lilac. She had planted lilacs at Rafe's house after she moved in and loved smelling their scent while sitting outside at night.

Eden sat down at her desk covered with mail and notes from the weekend. There was a thick manila envelope marked, *'Personal and Confidential' for Jayne Eden Kingsley*. She frowned because not many people used her full name.

Worried it would be something upsetting from her mother or from Rafe's lawyer, she sat it aside next to a stack of scripts for later. She scanned through the rest of the mail and found nothing urgent. Then she looked at the manila envelope again. She sighed and used her envelope opener to open the thick package deciding to get it over with instead of prolonging the inevitable. She looked at the first page and saw it had no name or return address.

It read: Ms. Kingsley, I am sorry to be the bearer of bad news, but things aren't always what they seem. I think this information may save you from any surprises that may be in store for you. Consider this a favor from a friend who has been where you are now and who wasn't so lucky. Good luck to you.

Eden looked at the note again with confusion then set it aside to look at the pages underneath. She began to read and scan the pages quickly, her expression getting more concerned and confused with every page. "What the heck is going on?"

21

EDEN KINGSLEY HAD come home early to the apartment she shared with Jake. The manila envelope she brought from her office was clutched under her arm. Someone had sent her an envelope full of information and photos anonymously. It looked like they were trying to threaten, incriminate, or blackmail her and Jake. She had been tempted to call Jake and the police, but she decided to take the time to calm down first.

Once she had calmed down and read the note again, it was clear the information was meant for her specifically, but she wasn't sure yet what it all meant. There was no actual demand for money or anything in the note. Just a strange warning there may be 'surprises' in store for her. She was worried maybe someone was threatening to do something to Jake or his son, and she wasn't sure what to do. She didn't know of anyone who would want to hurt her or Jake. Neither of them had money someone could extort or secrets worthy of blackmail—at least none she knew of, anyway.

She sat down on the couch, opened the thick envelope, and pulled out the contents. There was a stack of photos and papers she spread out over the coffee table. Most of the photos were of Jake with different women. It looked like they may have been people he dated over the years. There were also photos with Jake's son Hunter and Jake's parents and other people Eden didn't recognize. She sat the pictures aside and looked at the stack of papers.

As she shuffled through them, she found photocopies of difficult to read news articles, address book pages and printouts of web pages, lists of names and pamphlets. There were also several pages of what looked like financial account information and institutions where Jake had money. Eden began to wonder if Jake was doing something illegal at his company but could not imagine the possibility.

She put down the papers and read the cover note again.

Ms. Kingsley, I am sorry to be the bearer of bad news, but things aren't always what they seem. I think this information may save you from any surprises that may be in store for you. Consider this a favor from a friend who has been where you are now, and who wasn't so lucky. Good luck to you.

Things aren't always what they seem, kept running through Eden's mind. She picked up the photos and looked through them again. The more she looked at them, the more a few of them started to look familiar. Taking a few of the photos with her, she got up and walked around the apartment looking at all the pictures hanging on the walls. She held two of them to the framed picture on the wall in the hallway. The framed picture had the images in the two photos she was holding merged together so they made a very convincing original of Jake and his ex-wife. At least Jake said she was his ex-wife. Eden had never actually met her. Jake said he had to hang the picture up for Hunter so when he came over, he could have a family photo with his mom. Eden never thought anything about it even though there were no photos of Rafe in the house. She looked at the photos again against each other and realized she really didn't know which one was the original.

She took the framed photo off the wall and went back to the couch. As she looked through the photos again, she saw there were a lot of other photos in the envelope with the same picture of Jake coupled with other women next to him.

"What is this?" she questioned under her breath shakily. "Why?" she said softly. She didn't understand why someone was putting his picture with different women. Were they trying to accuse him of having an affair? Why would they send so many photos?

She picked up more pictures from the stack and found some showing Hunter being held by different women or standing with other children. She took them around the house and found pictures on display where it looked like Jake's son had been cut out from the photos in her hand and placed on a new background or added into a new photo. She shook her head in confusion and went back to the coffee table where she put the pictures back in the pile and sat on the couch.

She looked through the photos again and saw there were also photos of Jake's parents with Hunter and with other children. Eden wondered how many women Jake had introduced to them or if those photos were even real. She shuffled through the photos and saw photos of other elderly people with Hunter, and she suddenly wondered if the people she met were even really his parents. She started to panic again, so she closed her eyes and focused on breathing.

She sat for a while trying to calm herself and focus, attempting to contemplate exactly what was happening. All she understood at the moment was it was possible all of the pictures in the apartment were fakes.

As she flipped through the photos again, she noticed on the back of them were names and dates, but she had no idea why they were important. She stopped when she noticed something else. It was a mark she had seen before from Jakes business cards. In the corner on the back of the photos was the company logo from the firm where Jake worked. All of the photos were printed from one of their machines.

She slowly sat the photos aside and began reading the photocopied and printed pages as well as the other information included in the envelope again. As she read, her face went pale, and she began to shake with fear, as she finally began to understand what it all meant.

A wave of sickness flowed through her, and she broke out in a nervous sweat along her brow. She shakily wiped the moisture from her temple as she rubbed her head as it began to ache.

"He's a graphic designer," she mumbled to herself. "Oh, my god, I think I'm in trouble," she said, finally realizing what the information was about and beginning to comprehend the threat. She pulled out more papers to read, and she couldn't stop shaking. She could not believe this was happening.

22

RAFE SALVAGGIO WAS having a busy Friday night in the school's art gallery, as she should because she was the guest of honor. The event was not only a welcome celebration but also a time to introduce her to the staff, financial contributors, and big wigs in the community. The crowded gallery was filled with conversation, and Rafe had just shaken the hand of the last person who had been in another small line of people wanting to meet her. President Biggalow stood beside her and stopped people who she thought Rafe needed to meet as they walked by.

"Well, Ms. Salvaggio, it looks like you're quite the success," said President Biggalow as she beamed with pride. "From all of the people here who already know of you and your work, I am positive you'll be a great asset."

"Thank you, President Biggalow," said Rafe, amused she was obsessed with saying her last name. Rafe thought maybe she liked associating her with her father, and it was fine with her.

"Clarice, please," she insisted. "Well, I have obligations to which I must attend. I'll see you again later."

"Of course," said Rafe, who watched her walk away and began to scan the room for anyone she missed talking with.

"I hear you've had a busy week," said a halting voice from someone behind her.

"Dr. Nobel, good to see you with clean hands," said Rafe humorously when she saw who was speaking.

"I'm sorry I can't say the same for you," said Greer not reading the humor in Rafe's remark.

"Excuse me?" Rafe was confused by her antagonism.

"I just found out you're booking a show for Dr. Thomas Leriche. How could you agree to do an installation for him?" she demanded.

"What do you mean? His work aligns with yours. I would have thought you, of all people, would appreciate acknowledgment of the service and accomplishments of your work."

Beth signed Rafe's answer to Greer, and when she was done, Greer shook her head and scowled. "Our work does not in fact align," she signed as her eyes flashed with anger and Beth interpreted. "Dr. Leriche is a con man and a cancer to the work I'm trying to accomplish. You should rethink your decision to install the work he plans to provide."

"I've looked at the work, and it's incredible. Why should I rethink the exhibit?"

"None of his work was obtained ethically, and I can prove most, if not all of it, was coerced from a few of his select patients," Beth interpreted for Greer. "One of whom is not mentally ill as claimed but is paid by Dr. Leriche to create pieces to fit his agenda. Dr. Leriche is misrepresenting the works as well as the effectiveness and results of art therapy for personal gain and notoriety."

"Dr. Noble, again, the board and I have listened to Dr. Leriche's presentation and have viewed the pieces to be installed. It made sense," Rafe said firmly. "But if you can prove the allegations you've made, you deserve the chance to be heard. I'll send you a copy of the presentation and the slides, and you can present your case to the board next week. I'll wait to make my final decision then. I'm surprised you weren't at the presentation since you're so adamant it's unethical."

"I was in session at the time, but I thought, because of your reputation, you would be able to see through his con. I guess your reputation was inflated."

"I can assure you my reputation was made by hard work and attention to the most finite of details in my preservations and reproductions of historically significant architecture and design. It was not made by my knowledge of medical and art therapy methods. That is where your reputation is made. I suggest next time something affecting your work and reputation comes before the board you reschedule your sessions and attend the meeting. It was nice to talk with you again. I'll see you at the board meeting next week," finished Rafe before she calmly turned and walked away.

23

IT WAS LATE, and Stacey Randall walked into the living room from the kitchen where she had been working on her latest creation, an alien mask for a small budget sci-fi film. She loved her job doing makeup and creating different looks for movie characters with everything from normal makeup to prosthetics and molded masks. The fiery redhead joined her roommates, Jude and Flynn, in the living room. They had cut their Friday evenings short for a variety of reasons and were just chilling out for the night. Jude was talking animatedly about her latest dramatic encounter to Flynn. Stacey sat down on the arm of the couch next to Jude to enjoy the story.

"And then I told her if you can't take the heat, get your hands out from between my legs." Jude laughed crudely.

"Oh, that had to make her mad," Stacey said, laughing too.

"Yeah, she got up and left," Jude said as she nodded and smirked. She looked up as she heard a knock on the front door.

"I'll get it," offered Flynn and made his way to the door. "Hey, Eden, come in."

Eden held a sleeping Bronte as she followed Flynn into the house and into Jude's living room. "Hey, guys. Sorry to bother you. I came to see if Rafe could take Bronte for the night, but she's not home yet."

"She has a gallery party at the school tonight," said Jude as she moved over to give Eden a place to sit.

"Yeah, she looked *really* good when she left too," gushed Stacey as she fanned herself with her hand. "Oh, sorry, Eden," she offered as she saw Eden shift uncomfortably.

"It's okay. I'm sure she did look nice," Eden said quickly. Then in a hesitant voice, she asked, "Did she mention when she would be back?"

"No, she didn't," Jude answered. "You can stay here and wait for her if you want."

"It would be nice, thanks," Eden said as she laid the sleeping Bronte on the couch beside her.

24

RAFE SALVAGGIO WALKED from her car and into her home where she immediately removed her shoes and threw her bag and keys on the entry table. She had a long day, made longer by the welcome party she felt was really an interrogation party. She knew there had been a lot of competition for her job, but she hadn't realized just how much of the competition was from within the school.

Then, to top things off, she had been accused of not doing her job by an art therapy teacher of all things. She only listened to the proposal by Dr. Leriche with the hope Dr. Noble would see it as a goodwill gesture. Now it turned out she had something against the doctor, and Rafe felt no remorse at handing off the responsibility for Dr. Leriche's selection into Dr. Nobel's hands.

She sighed heavily with exhaustion, and the thought of a nice hot shower was beginning to brighten her mood when the doorbell rang.

"Great," she moaned thinking Jude was probably calling to 'borrow' more beer. She opened the door and was surprised to find Eden holding a sleeping Bronte. "Eden? What's wrong?" Her mind rushed to the thought Bronte might be sick.

"Nothing's wrong," she said as she shifted nervously. The girls were right, she noticed—Rafe was beautiful tonight. "I was just hoping you could take Bronte tonight instead of in the morning."

Shocked and a little bit hesitant, Rafe opened the door wider so Eden could come in the house. "Yes. I mean, are you sure? Come in."

"I'm sure," confirmed Eden as she carried Bronte back toward Rafe's bedroom with Rafe not far behind. "I've been picking her up early lately, and I just thought you'd like it if you had a little more time with her." Eden hesitated at Rafe's bedroom door and then walked quickly into the once familiar room. She was immediately inundated with the scent and memories of her time there with Rafe. She laid Bronte down in her crib gently and stood back as Rafe leaned over the crib to look at the baby.

"Thank you," whispered Rafe. She stroked Bronte's head as she lay sleeping.

"I have to go into work extra early in the morning," explained Eden nervously because she felt she had to lie to Rafe. "I had to schedule a Saturday meeting because it was the only time everyone was free."

"Okay. I have to go to the office tomorrow too. I think Bronte will have fun going with me," she said as she smiled at Eden. She was excited this was happening and didn't want to do anything to make Eden change her mind or be upset with her again.

"I'm sure she'll have a great time," she said and looked everywhere but into Rafe's eyes, grateful she didn't question her excuse for bringing the baby over. "You look nice," she said softly.

"I had to go to an event for my new job," said Rafe as she smiled. "They have more of a dress code than I ever did with my company," she said with humor.

Rafe could see Eden was anxious, and it looked like she was having a hard time with her anxiety. She could see the dark circles under her eyes and places on her arms where it looked like there were fingernail indentions and reddened scratches made from when she was in pain.

"Are you okay?" she asked with concern because she had not seen those marks for a long time.

"I'm fine," Eden said quickly not wanting to involve Rafe in her problems. "Well, I have to go," she announced and then hurried out of the room.

Rafe made sure Bronte was tucked in well, and then she went quietly out of the room after Eden. When she got to the living room, she saw Eden had gone. She was surprised there were no last minute instructions. "Well, there's a first," she said as she shrugged and went to make sure the front door was locked.

Driving away from Rafe's house, Eden felt a sense of relief. She knew Bronte would be safe with Rafe. No matter what, she had always been able to count on Rafe to be there.

Eden knew she couldn't go back to her home with Jake because of what she had found out today. She verified her doubts by looking online and making some phone calls. What she found shocked her and rocked her to her foundations. She didn't want to believe it, but it was all right there in front of her, and she knew there was no choice but to believe. It took her a while to pull herself together so she could function. At first, she thought about confronting Jake, but she knew her anxiety would prevent her from thinking clearly. Eden decided the best thing to do was to take Bronte and leave immediately.

It was not Jake someone was threatening. Jake was the threat she was being warned about.

Eden pulled into a hotel and turned off her engine. She shook with fear and dug her fingernails into her skin trying to ease the pain where it felt like hives wanted to break through. She took a deep breath to calm herself. She didn't know what else to do except try to stay away from him. She got out of her car and made her way into the hotel lobby to check in for the night.

25

EDEN KINGSLEY HOPED she would find a long-term solution to her need for a place to live soon. She had been sleeping at different hotels around the city for over a week afraid to stay in the same one too long so Jake wouldn't find her easily. She didn't want to confront him or let it slip she had the information about him someone had left her anonymously. Fear and anxiety had taken over her mind, and it was not letting go. She felt it was best she just avoid him until she had her emotions under control and could think clearly. She made sure to avoid running into anyone she knew and took great pains to keep Jake at a distance.

It had taken days, but she finally worked up the nerve to go back to Jake's apartment. She was trying to pack all of her and

Bronte's remaining things as quickly as possible. Almost nothing in the apartment belonged to her so she was hoping she would only have to make two trips to get out everything she owned.

Jake had not even put her name on the lease or utilities. He just announced they were moving and asked only that she pay half of the expenses until they were married. She refused to get a joint bank account, and though Jake was unhappy about it, he conceded to her. She was glad she never told him Rafe was still on her account because she just never seemed to get around to taking her off.

She had hoped to be able to avoid Jake on her last visit to his apartment. Unluckily, Jake had come home early and found her packing the last of her and Bronte's things. She was glad she decided to leave Bronte with Rafe today.

"Where've you been?" demanded Jake when he walked in and saw her packing. "Where are you going, Eden? Back to Rafe?"

"I don't know where I'm going," Eden said as her voice shook. She knew it would be best if she told him as little as possible, but he just kept pressing. "I just know I need to get out of here for a while."

"Why? I thought we had something good. Please stay," he begged and tried to take her in his arms.

Avoiding his embrace and terrified of confronting him with the information she was sent, Eden moved to put more of her things into a suitcase.

"I can't give you a reason right now."

"Is this about moving away? I told you it was only an option. We can talk and work things out," he reasoned sadly. He was hiding his anger at her avoidance. He didn't understand what had happened to cause her sudden need to move out and leave him. He had been doing everything right.

"I just need to do this," she said warily. She looked down and saw the ring on her hand. She slipped if off her finger and put it on the dresser next to her key. "I'm sorry, Jake. I just can't do this. It's over," she said nervously.

"Are you going back to women?" asked Jake as he picked up the ring. "What about us and our connection? What about the family you wanted for Bronte? First, you let Rafe get away with terrifying you at the hotel and then you changed your mind about the adoption. What happened? What did she say to you?"

"She didn't say anything to me. This has nothing to do with Rafe."

"Well, then, what the hell does it have to do with?"

"I just need time," she said and saw it was not enough for him. "This is just going too fast. I'm feeling too much pressure from you. I need time to really think about what I want. You said you didn't have a problem with the way I lived my life, and you have to understand, this is a big change for me."

"So, you're saying I'm right, and you may want to go back to your old life?"

"I don't think it is possible to go back," said Eden sadly as her anxiety built about where she was going to go and what she was going to do. "But I really do need to figure out what kind of life I want."

"I'm warning you, Eden, if you take Bronte back to the life you were living instead of giving her the life she deserves, one with a real family and father, you'll be sorry."

"What do you mean, Jake? Are you threatening me?" Eden asked in shock as the information she had just became more real to her. She wanted to tell him she knew everything but was afraid of what might happen if she did. Instead, she deflected and tried not to let him see her fear. "Bronte is my child and will be Rafe's legally soon like I always agreed. It's her life no matter if I'm with you or not."

"Don't do it, Eden," he begged and tried to give her the ring back.

"It's too late," she said backing away from him and the ring. "Just, please, give me the time and the space I need." Eden walked out of the apartment pulling a suitcase with one hand and carrying the rest of her and Bronte's things in her other arm.

Jake watched Eden walk out the door and then picked up his phone and dialed. "Hey," he said when the call connected. "She's wavering. What should I do next? Yes, get everything ready. We may have to resort to it soon if I can't convince her to come back." He paused and listened. "I'll do everything I can."

26

GATHERED AROUND A table looking out onto the busy street at The Kiki Bistro, Abby Van Falkov and her friends Jude, Erica, Flynn, and Stacey were having coffee and breakfast before heading their separate ways to jobs and appointments. Stacey watched as Rafe walked past the window and into the bistro and then lined up to place her order. She looked over at Jude and nodded her head toward Rafe.

"Eden dropped off Bronte with Rafe late last night again." Everyone looked at her with surprise. "Yeah, I think Rafe is getting really pissed about Eden's erratic schedule. She's picking the baby up early dropping her off at odd hours. She's acting weird in my opinion."

"It is kind of out of character for her," Jude joined into the conversation.

"Well, she has had a lot on her mind, and Rafe does need to help with Bronte too. She should be happy Eden is letting her have her so much," Abby said feeling defensive on Eden's behalf because she knew how Rafe could be at times.

"Oh, I think she's happy about having the baby. She's just worried about Bronte not having a stable schedule," Stacey rationalized.

"Well, I haven't even seen Eden or Jake for a while. Maybe they need more time together." Abby winked crudely.

"Yuck! I don't even want to think about that," exclaimed Jude as she shuddered.

"I know!" Abby laughed.

"He gives me a creepy feeling, and I like men!" added Stacey with a laugh.

"Is it the men or something else?" Erica joked, and everyone at the table laughed.

"Erica! It's the men! You know what I mean, Abby. You date men," Stacey said as she took a bite of her scone.

"Yeah, I used to think that way. I've decided it's just women for me from now on," declared Abby.

"Oh, good! All the men are left for Stacey and me then." Flynn laughed and fist bumped with Stacey.

Jude laughed knowing Abby would probably date a man again if she felt drawn to him. "Good for you, Abby."

"Now I just have to find one." Abby sighed despondently.

"Well, maybe you'll find one tonight. You're all going to be back here for the concert, right?" Stacey asked excitedly.

"Of course, I'll be here. It's Rafe's birthday party," Abby reminded them. "I think Letty got the singer Amanda Hughey because Rafe said she liked her once."

"She's a very hot singer!" Jude winked.

"Yeah, taken," complained Abby with a pout. "I have no luck."

"Well, I'm going to be the first one on the dance floor!" Stacey laughed.

"So, you're saying you'll be drunk before the rest of us?" Jude laughed, and Abby slapped her on her arm and joined in as everyone at the table laughed.

27

LATER IN THE evening, The Kiki Bistro was packed with a mixed crowd excited about the night. Rafe Salvaggio and her group of friends were lucky to have a big table strategically placed close to both the stage and the dance floor. Because of Abby, it seemed like everyone in the place knew Rafe was there for a birthday celebration.

Their table was littered with birthday decorations as well as a few cards and gifts. There seemed to be a constant procession of people approaching the table to give well wishes to Rafe as well as a few birthday propositions. Julia was amazed Rafe had not taken anyone up on their offer and was jealously wondering just what she was waiting for tonight.

Greer Nobel and her interpreter, Beth, made their way through the crowd looking for Rafe. Greer felt Beth tug on her jacket, and she looked where Beth was pointing. Greer spotted Rafe and pulled Beth along with her as she headed toward her target.

"Hello," said Greer interrupting the conversations at the table.

Rafe looked up and gave Greer a warm smile. "Hello, I'm so glad you made it." She nodded toward Beth as she translated to Greer and then motioned for them to sit.

"Thank you for inviting me to your birthday party. We didn't start out on the best of terms," said Greer through Beth.

"Well, your presentation to the board was very impressive. I think we've come up with a solution. Consider this your victory celebration." Rafe smiled as she signaled for a waitress and motioned to her half-empty drink.

"I think I will," Beth translated as Greer signed.

The waitress Rafe signaled made her way to the table with not only the drink she ordered but two more. They had apparently been sent over by a couple of women at the bar.

Abby laughed as the waitress left. "This is great. Free drinks!" She picked one up and took a sip then turned her attention to Greer and Beth. "So, who's this, Rafe?" she asked as she nodded toward the women.

"Oh, I'm sorry," Rafe exclaimed and then addressed everyone at the table. "Abby, everyone, this is Dr. Greer Noble and her interpreter, Beth Westbern. Greer is one of our best professors at the Conservatory. Greer and Beth, this is Julia, Abby, Erica, Stacey, Flynn, and Jude," said Rafe as she pointed at each person.

"It's nice to meet you all," said Beth as Greer smiled and gave a small wave.

"Okay, I get it now," said Julia as the beautiful auburn haired doctor joined them. She now knew what, or rather who, Rafe had been waiting on. She rolled her eyes, and Rafe just gave her a smirk. Once again she contained her jealousy. Her hopes of a possible relationship with Rafe were dashed again, for now. No change in the status quo. She took a large swallow of her drink then looked out on the dance floor determined to find a way to take her mind off things.

Abby leaned in and attempted to whisper to Rafe without success. "Nice. You do work fast." She picked up her drink and looked around the table. "And now it looks like you get drinks and women in twos!" She bent over in laughter at her own joke while the rest of the table groaned. Abby didn't care as long as Rafe was not out using her wildling ways on women.

Rafe gave Abby a half smile of tolerance and turned away from her to cut her from further conversation. She turned her attention back to Greer.

"So what do you think of The Kiki Bistro?"

"I love it. There's so much energy. By the way, remember, I read lips, so I know what Abby said." Greer laughed as Beth relayed her signs.

"Don't worry about her," said Rafe amused Greer caught Abby's comments. "She's only a danger to herself. You should hear some of the things she says on her webcasts."

"I'll have to set aside some time so Beth and I can review them," said Greer as she motioned to Beth.

"I'm sorry," said Rafe embarrassed she forgot Greer was deaf. "I didn't think."

"It's okay, Rafe." Greer smiled. "I know I'm deaf."

"It's funny, but I forget when I'm speaking to you," explained Rafe.

"I think that's a compliment for Beth," voiced Greer and laughed along with Beth.

Rafe looked up and smiled as she saw a familiar face approaching the table. It was the owner of the bistro, and her cousin, Letty.

Letty Carver was Rafe's cousin from her mother's side of the family. They first met when her mother brought Rafe to America for a visit when she was just a baby. When she introduced Letty to Rafe, there was a little confusion.

"This is your *cugina*," Rafe's mother told Letty, meaning this is your cousin. But Letty thought cugina was her name for the longest time. Since then, Letty continued calling her Cugina as a pet name.

They were reintroduced when Rafe moved to America with her father. Letty was a wild child too, and Rafe loved her for it. She was eight years older than Rafe, and she would often stay with her when her father was away for work. She would take Rafe with her to auditions and film shoots all over New York.

Letty got a big break, left New York, and made her way to California. She was successful in the B-movie genre, and some of the films she starred in were now cult classics.

She decided to retire from film while on a high and, with Rafe's help in procuring the building, opened The KiKi Bistro with her husband and chef, Ephraim Holden. The bistro was named after one of the characters Letty played in her most famous movie. The restaurant had grown into a great success with the help from her friends and the community.

Letty finally made it to the table, and Rafe smiled at her. "Hey, how are you? Letty, this is Greer. Greer, this is Letty Carver, the owner of this place."

Letty smiled at Rafe and her date. "Greer, it's nice to meet you," she said warmly. "I am the owner, but more importantly, Rafe is my favorite, and only, *cugina*! Well, none we know of anyway!" She winked. "Who knows how many relatives are hidden somewhere in the provinces of Italy!" She laughed along with Rafe as Beth translated.

"It's nice to meet you," said Greer. "I've seen most of your movies," she said, and her eyes sparkled.

"Another fan," Rafe teased.

"Well, you're the star tonight, birthday girl." Letty laughed. She looked over at Greer. "I'm sorry, but I need to borrow Rafe for a moment if it's okay."

Caught off guard by the sudden change in topic, Greer could only nod her head as Beth translated, "It's fine," and watched as Rafe was dragged away by Letty.

Abby quickly took Rafe's place not wanting to miss her chance at being the first to know everything about the woman Rafe had invited for birthday drinks. "So, what do you teach? Oh, sorry do I talk to you or her?"

Beth laughed and signed what she was saying as she talked to Abby. "Talk to her, and if she has a problem reading your lips or wants me to translate, she'll let me know."

Greer nodded in agreement. "I teach art therapy techniques to doctors and medical students."

"Art therapy? So it's like art to help you get well or cures the crazies with paint?"

"Something like that." Greer laughed, and her pale blue eyes were filled with humor.

"So, you're a doctor? Wow. It seems like Rafe gets all the beautiful, smart girls." Abby laughed jealously.

"I don't understand. Rafe has a doctorate too, so does it mean I get the smart girls too?" Greer chuckled.

"She does?" asked Abby confused because when she interviewed her years ago, when they first met, Rafe never told her she was a doctor. "So, Rafe's a doctor? Doctor Salvaggio? This is too much!"

"Well, she got her PhD in Italy so she probably would use the title of Maestre if she used one. She told me she didn't need the title to do her job." Greer shrugged.

"Maestre Salvaggio? Now I will never look at her the same," said Abby as she shook her head.

"Well, if she didn't tell you, and chooses not to use the title, then you should respect her wishes," Greer instructed her.

"Okay," said Abby filing the information away. "So what do you think of this place. We all hang out here a lot since Rafe's cousin owns it, but I think Rafe owns the building. It's like our family place."

Greer looked around and took in the space. "It's nice." She leaned closer to Abby, "Rafe seems to be very popular." She nodded toward Rafe and Letty at the bar.

"Popular? I guess." Abby shrugged. "What do you mean?"

"Well, I can read lips, and there are a lot of people here talking about her. It's pretty easy to pick out the name Rafe on people's lips," she said with a conspirative smile.

"Really? What are they saying?" She looked over the crowd and conspiracy thoughts ran through her mind. She wondered if she could get her to tell her what everyone was saying so she would have lots to report on her blog.

"Apparently, the story is someone reported Rafe was incredible in bed and is back on the market. But she is almost unattainable. And every one of them is scheming a way to get her to notice them." She watched Abby's eyes widen as Beth interpreted her signing. Greer didn't let her know she and Beth had heard the story not long after meeting the new dean and really, she had seen some more mentions here at the party.

"Hmmm," Abby mused remembering when Julia kept saying Rafe was amazing, "No wonder we keep getting free drinks." She looked at Greer and loaded her next question. "So, you're family?"

"Yes," Greer acknowledged with a laugh, "I'm family."

"What about her," Abby asked nodding toward Beth.

"Straight." Greer grinned.

"Damn." Abby sulked while Greer and Beth laughed.

Rafe approached the table while gracefully fending off several women. "So how are you two getting along?"

"Fine, just fine," said Abby not wanting Rafe to know she had been interrogating her date. "Greer was just telling me about art therapy. I may write about her on my blog."

"Oh, great. It is fascinating, how it really helps people." Rafe turned her attention to Greer. "Would you like to dance?"

Greer smiled and leaned over to Abby, speaking directly into her ear. "It seems like I'd be a fool to refuse." She held out her hand to Rafe. "Of course, I would love to dance." Greer then allowed herself to be led to the dance floor by the woman everyone in the bar seemed to be talking about.

28

RAFE SALVAGGIO LOOKED up from the paperwork she was working on to check on Bronte. She felt bad she had to bring her into the office on such a nice Saturday, but so much was happening and she needed to be here to stay on top of things.

For some reason, Eden said she had to work today too. It was unusual for Eden to work on the weekend and not know about it until the day of, so when she showed up at her door unannounced early this morning, Rafe was actually happy about it because she could spend a whole day with Bronte.

She tossed her pen down and pushed away from her desk. "This can wait," she said to herself.

Making quick work of packing up all of Bronte's things, she put the baby bag under the stroller and got Bronte settled and buckled in.

"Okay, do we have everything? I think we do. Let's get going." She pushed the stroller out of her office and down the corridor toward the exit.

Turning the corner, she saw the door to Greer's classroom was open, so she decided to stop in. As she walked in, Beth signaled to Greer someone was there.

"I didn't mean to bother you," Rafe said as she pushed the stroller into the room, "but I saw the door was open so I just thought I would stop in and say hello." She smiled warmly. "So, hello."

"Hello. It's great to see you," said Greer and then motioned toward the baby in the stroller. "Who is this?" She bent down so Bronte could see her and signed to her as she spoke. "Hello, little one."

"This is my daughter, Bronte." She bent down next to Greer and saw Bronte smiling. "Can you say hi?" she asked the baby and unbuckled the safety strap to take her out of the stroller.

"This is the little girl in the picture on your desk. She's adorable. I didn't know she was your daughter," said Greer.

"Yes, well, she will be officially very soon," she said as she held Bronte and gave her a small kiss. "She's Eden's daughter." Rafe hesitated in saying more. It was hard for her to talk about her situation with Eden, but she liked Greer and wanted to be honest with her. "We made her when we were together."

Looking from Rafe then back at the baby, Greer shook her head in wonder at how alike they looked in their coloring. "You're very surprising, Rafe." She held her paint covered hands up to Bronte and the baby smiled and grabbed her colorful fingers. "Do you like all the colors? Has mommy shown you all the beautiful art she has been filling the school with?"

"I hope she is artistic and creative. Her donor is my friend, who is a brilliant musician, and Eden is a very creative person. I hope by exposing her to art, she will grow to love it like I do."

"Well, has she had her first art lesson yet?"

"She's a little young yet, isn't she? Even most of the great artists didn't start really working as an apprentice until at least six in some cases," said Rafe going into her lecture mode without realizing it. "Earlier, only if they showed signs of natural talent. Some of the chemicals involved with painting and other mediums are quite toxic. My mother started teaching me formally when I was four or five, I think—because I was always getting into her things. She kept the toxic stuff where I couldn't reach it."

Greer laughed. "Rafe, there is no such thing as too young for art." She looked at the pair thoughtfully for a moment. "If you want, I have special paint just for children her age. I can give her an art lesson anytime."

"Really?" Rafe was touched by Greer's offer and was excited about the prospect of Bronte having art lessons. "That would be wonderful. It's more than wonderful. I know we both would love it."

Greer looked at Beth, and they spoke to each other silently with signs, and then Greer turned back to Rafe. "I have time this afternoon if you want to do it today."

Feeling an unexpected surge of excitement about having art lessons for her daughter, Rafe made an excited, happy face at Bronte. "We would like to, wouldn't we, B Girl?" Switching into her planning mode, "What do I need to do?"

Clasping her hands together and catching a wink from Beth from the corner of her eye, Greer answered, "Nothing, I'll bring everything we need. Say about two?"

"Two o'clock is perfect. Eden will be by to pick her up at six-thirty to take her trick-or-treating in her costume, so it gives us plenty of time."

"Oh, well, I don't want to interrupt your plans for the holiday," said Greer.

"No, it's fine," said Rafe and hesitated. "I'm not usually included in Eden's holiday plans. But we have plenty of time to play," she said excited about the art lessons.

"Great! Just give me your address, and I'll see you then."

Rafe let Greer take Bronte and buckle her back into her stroller while she sent her address to Greer's phone. "There, all set. We can't wait. Come on, Bronte. Let's get home and get ready for your first art lesson." Rafe waved goodbye as she wheeled Bronte out of the art classroom.

29

WALKING AS QUICKLY as she could, Eden Kingsley made her way down the sidewalk trying not to run or show the fear coursing through her body. She looked back over her shoulder and could see Jake gaining on her. She rushed toward The KiKi Bistro where she knew her friend Abby sometimes worked on her blog and might be having lunch. She was desperate to make it inside before she had to confront Jake. She knew he wouldn't say or do anything in front of anyone they might know.

It was getting harder for her to avoid him and not let him know about the information she had been given about him. She was close to her goal when she felt Jake's hand as he grabbed her by the arm to stop her and then spun her toward himself.

"Eden, you have to talk to me!" demanded Jake.

"No, I don't, Jake," she shouted back and jerked her arm away. "Just leave me alone."

"I'm not going to leave you alone. You have to listen to reason."

"Reason? Whose reason, Jake? Yours? You think you know all the answers for my life?"

"Yes, I do," he said in frustration. "I thought I was part of the answers for both you and Bronte. I feel like she's my daughter too."

"She's not your daughter! Please, just back off."

"I'm not going to make this easy for you, Eden. You're going to stay with me, and we are going to save your daughter from a life without morals and normal relationships."

"What are you talking about, Jake?" She looked at him expectantly wondering if he was going to say something to further confirm the information she had.

"I'm talking about you and me taking Bronte away from Rafe and your old life and moving to a place where she can have a normal childhood and life. I thought it was why you were with me. I thought it was what you wanted. We talked about all of this."

Eden looked outraged and confused at Jake. She had never agreed or said she wanted any of those things.

"Who are you? You never listened to anything I said. I've never wanted to take Bronte away from Rafe and my home here. I admit, when I thought Rafe had taken her, I said things, things I regret. But I was wrong about her and so were you. I told you, I made a promise to Rafe."

"What about us?" he asked throwing up his arms.

"There is no *us* anymore," she said firmly. "And my daughter will have a life much, much better than your so-called normal life. She'll have a great childhood with people who love her and don't judge her for the people *she* loves." She turned, hoping she had not said too much, and quickly entered the bistro, escaping him.

Letty had watched the argument between Jake and Eden from behind the counter. She motioned to Ephraim, who had started walking to the door concerned, and he gave her a nod indicating he would keep an eye on things. Letty followed Eden when she came inside, and Ephraim kept an eye on Jake.

Jake stood outside for a moment debating on whether or not to follow Eden inside. Then he paced in front of the door for a bit while he made a phone call.

Eden felt the cool air of the bistro wash over her and straightened herself. She looked around and saw Abby sitting at a table near the coffee station, so she made her way over to her.

"Hi, Abby," said Eden as she approached the table.

"Eden!" exclaimed Abby as she jumped up and hugged her. "How've ya been? I haven't seen you since Canada!"

Eden was relieved Abby was happy to see her. "I'm fine," she said with a small smile as they sat down.

"What's going on, Eden?" Letty asked as Eden sat at Abby's table.

Eden looked up and seeing the concern on Letty's face, she looked over and saw Ephraim looking out the window where Jake was leaving angrily. She knew she had no choice now but to tell them what was happening.

"Jake and I broke it off," she announced nervously.

Abby looked from Eden to Letty and back in surprise. "It'll be okay. There'll be others," said Abby sympathetically.

"Thanks, Abby," she said tensely.

Ephraim walked over and sat with them. "He's gone,"

"Good riddance," said Letty. "Eden says they're over."

Taking in the situation, Ephraim knew Eden was in a bad place. "So where are you going to live now?"

"I," she hesitated, "I guess I'll stay in a hotel tonight and start looking for apartments today." She couldn't let them know she had already been living in a hotel for two weeks and hadn't been able to find a place yet. She hoped one of the applications she submitted would be accepted next week. "Guys, please don't tell Rafe what's going on right now. I'll tell her soon."

Letty didn't like what she was hearing at all. "You're taking Bronte to a hotel, on Halloween?"

"What else can I do?" Eden sighed and leaned her head into her hands feeling a headache developing. She hoped it would not turn into a migraine.

"Let her stay with Ephraim and me tonight," suggested Letty. "We can take her trick-or-treating and you can get yourself together and pick her up in the morning, unless you're going to tell Rafe and let her keep Bronte for the night."

"No, I need some time before I tell Rafe. I can't believe this is happening," said Eden trying not to cry. She wished she could tell them everything, but she knew from the information she had read in the envelope it would just cause problems for all of them if she did.

"Why don't you and Bronte come stay with me?" Abby offered. "I mean it's only one night, right? Then you can stay with Bronte. I'd love to snag some candy with you tonight."

"Are you sure? I'd like the help," said Eden relieved to take the offered help.

"I'm sure," Abby insisted happily.

"You know you have to let Rafe know what is going on," said Letty firmly. "We saw how angry he was with you. Rafe needs to know he's not in your and Bronte's life anymore."

If Letty knew how much more of a threat Jake was, Eden knew she would go straight to Rafe.

"I'll tell her, I will," she promised. *It just has to be the right time*, she thought.

"Be sure to bring Bronte by tonight so we can see her costume. Ephraim made a special treat for her," said Letty with an excited smile. She loved spoiling that baby.

"I will," Eden assured her.

"Okay, dinner will be ready at six," said Abby. "Don't be late. You know, I've never had you guys over for dinner. I've got to shop! I need a costume! This'll be great!" she said happily and started out of the bistro before Eden could say anything more to her.

30

RAFE SALVAGGIO MOVED quickly to clear a space for Bronte's art lesson while Bronte played with her toys nearby. She thought they could set up everything under the shade of the deck in her backyard. Looking around at the sound of the gate latch, she saw Greer walk through the gate with a load of paints, loose canvas, and other art supplies.

"Hello, I'm here!" Greer smiled as she spotted Rafe and deposited her supplies on the deck.

"We're ready for you. Where's Beth?" Rafe asked as she looked around for her.

Greer laughed and explained, "I don't need her everywhere I go. Mostly when I am dealing with a crowd or I'm somewhere I need to make sure I know everything said. When it's just one on one, it's easier, and I can read lips or find other ways to communicate." She winked playfully. "So let's get set up."

"Okay, let's start," she said not noticing Greer's wink and picked up the cloth tarp. With Greer's help, she started laying out the art lesson area and covered the deck with the tarp.

Greer unpacked the paints as Rafe carried Bronte over and placed her on the cloth tarp.

"Now these paints are totally safe," Greer explained. "They're food based and all natural. So if she decides she is hungry, she can have dinner and paint at the same time. The best thing is it tastes really good."

Laughing, Rafe pulled a paint cup over and placed it where Bronte could reach it. "I wish I would have known about this and started it when she was even younger."

"I'm glad I was the one who got to tell you about it," said Greer with a smile. "Before she starts, I recommend you strip her down to her diaper and a t-shirt. This will get messy. Here are smocks for us. Some of the colors aren't the best for clothes."

Rafe looked down at what she was wearing. She had changed into her favorite linen shorts and a soft natural cotton blouse when she came home. She looked up at Greer and saw she was in old shorts and a tank top. She was much more appropriately dressed for painting outside.

With a sudden lurch, Rafe stood up and looked down at all the paint, Bronte, and Greer. "Will you watch her for a minute? I think I need to change clothes."

There were absolutely no clothes in her closet Rafe could bear having ruined with paint. She had cleaned out most all of her old paint and work clothes when she sold her business thinking she wouldn't be doing much painting for work anymore.

Digging through her drawers, she opted for last year's swimming suit. She looked at herself in the mirror and noted she had lost some tone over the last year. Her schedule and focus on other things had not included a lot of exercise as it had when she worked in her shop or on construction sites, but she decided she still looked good in the teal bikini.

She threw the painting smock over her bathing suit, grabbed a t-shirt for Bronte, and headed back outside. Greer had Bronte stripped to her diaper, and they were swirling paint on large pieces of loose canvas. She touched Greer on her shoulder to let her know she was back. "I'm back. I didn't have any shorts I could bear to get paint on."

Greer looked up and laughed as she saw Rafe in her smock-covered swimsuit. "I think what you're wearing will work perfectly."

Smiling, Rafe began to put the t-shirt on Bronte and then to help her with her painting. Greer tried to get Rafe *not* to help Bronte. She wanted Bronte to be free to express and explore without too much influence. Soon, they were all covered in paint, and Bronte was having a blast putting paint on everything and everyone. She made handprints, footprints, and body part prints everywhere and even snacked on some of the tasty paint.

Greer stole a few secret looks at Rafe. She was becoming more intrigued and enamored of her despite their fiery first meeting. She found herself thinking about her at unexpected times. She knew getting into a relationship with her would be hard, but it had never stopped her before. Rafe was a very strong woman with high expectations of herself as well as others. Maybe it was their similarity that drew her.

Watching Rafe interact with her daughter, Greer smiled at their antics. She loved children, though she hadn't felt the need to have any. She knew it would be difficult being in a relationship with someone with children. It was so easy to get attached and so hard to leave if things didn't work out. She could already tell she would love Bronte. It didn't hurt Bronte was so fun and precocious in an endearing way. Greer re-focused and began showing Bronte how to mix colors and help her make more hand and footprints in her art.

As they painted, Greer found herself moving closer to Rafe and using any excuse to touch her frequently. Rafe was oblivious because she was focusing her attention on Bronte. Greer fought off the jealousy niggling at her. *It was ridiculous,* she told herself, *for a woman with three PhDs to be jealous of a toddler.* She found focusing on the project helped, and she was soon enjoying her time teaching Bronte and chatting about small nothings with Rafe.

31

TURNING OFF HER car engine Eden Kingsley sat nervously in Rafe's driveway. Gripping the steering wheel to keep her hands from trembling, the memory of her confrontation with Jake was still troubling her. She closed her eyes to calm herself before dealing with Rafe because she knew she was an hour early again. This would be another confrontation she would have to try to get through.

She told Abby she would make her six o'clock dinner, and she wanted to be sure Abby would keep the situation with Jake to herself, so she didn't want to be late or cancel. She also knew if she made Abby change her routine or time schedule, she would talk to everyone about it, including Rafe. To keep her situation under control, and to keep Rafe from getting involved, it was worth dealing with Rafe's wrath about being early. She hated doing this, but she had convinced herself she didn't have a choice.

When Eden was finally able to break free of Letty, she left the Kiki and went to the hotel to get Bronte's costume and pack an overnight bag. It was too late to check out and save a little money. She would go back in the morning and check out. It was time for her to move again because she was not sure if Jake had found out where she was staying or not. Eden fought the anxiety she could feel building in her chest making it hard to breathe.

After another minute, she got out of her car to face Rafe. As she walked toward the house, she could hear laughter from the backyard. She quietly entered through the back gate and made her way to the deck where she found Rafe, Bronte, and someone she didn't know, a woman, sitting on the deck playing in paint.

"Hey," she said in a forced upbeat voice. "What are you guys doing?"

Rafe turned at Eden's voice, and Greer, following Rafe's gaze, looked in the same direction. Rafe smiled at Eden and couldn't wait to show her their art. She hoped she would be excited about Bronte's art lessons. "Hey, Eden. We're having an art lesson. Look what Bronte made! Is it six-thirty already? Sorry, we lost track of time."

Eden swallowed hard and braced herself. "Actually, it's just before five-thirty, I'm early." She saw the immediate change in Rafe, but Eden remained calm.

Rafe couldn't believe she was doing it again. She held in her anger as much as possible but couldn't hold back the frown from her face. "Why are you here so early? What's going on?" She waited for Eden's excuse and hoped Greer couldn't see just how angry she was right now.

"I'm sorry. I didn't know you were doing anything. I have a last minute dinner invitation at six for us, and didn't think you would mind if I got Bronte a little early."

"I do mind, Eden. You could have called."

"I should have. I'm sorry," Eden said again and wrung her hands nervously.

"Hello," said Greer looking at Eden curiously. She hadn't seen what this woman said to upset Rafe, but it was obvious she was angry.

"Sorry, Greer," said Rafe trying to calm herself as she ran a hand through her dark hair. "Eden, this is Greer. She is a professor at the Conservatory, and she is here giving Bronte her first art lesson."

"It's nice to meet you," Eden smiled and held out her hand.

Greer smiled back as she held up her paint covered hands as her excuse not to shake and gave a shrug. "I'm a mess, sorry. It's nice to meet you too. Bronte is sure to be a great artist. She's really showing a lot of interest for her age."

Eden pulled her hand back awkwardly noticing the woman's halting speech pattern. "Oh, sure," she hesitated. "Rafe and I hoped she would love art," she said and looked at Rafe hoping the small things they had in common would make this moment better.

Rafe, still upset and not wanting to make nice talk with Eden, stood and picked up Bronte. "I'll get her cleaned up," she said shortly and turned to take Bronte into the house.

Eden looked at Greer and gave her an awkward smile then followed Rafe inside.

"Rafe, I really am sorry. I wish I would have known. I think art lessons are a great idea." Rafe didn't say anything, so Eden followed her into the master bathroom.

Rafe turned on the shower and then took off Bronte's paint covered diaper and t-shirt. She could feel Eden standing in the doorway.

"I'm glad you think that the art lessons are a good thing," she said trying to remain calm, but she just couldn't keep her anger in check. She spoke calmly so wouldn't upset Bronte. "I just wish you would call if your plans are changing or come when you say you will, and not show up early or unexpectedly all the time. I really do want to spend all of the time I can with her. You're making it hard again."

She carried Bronte over to the toilet and pulled out a training seat she placed on the toilet and then sat Bronte down. "Can you potty?" she asked the toddler and waited to see what she would do.

"You're potty training her already?" asked Eden in wonder at Rafe actually thinking to do this.

"Yes," said Rafe annoyed. "She's in and out of the pool all the time, and it just made sense to make her go before and after. So whenever we come into the bathroom, we try. Plus, you can tell when she has to go most of the time. Right now, it's really just getting her use to the idea." She saw Bronte was finished, took care of her, and then carried her to the shower.

Eden shook her head in surprise. "I think this is great, Rafe. I'll start doing it for her too."

Rafe took off her smock revealing her teal swimming suit, and then put a towel down on the shower floor. She put Bronte on the towel, and then she got into the shower with Bronte to wash off all the paint from them both.

"You take her into the shower?" Eden asked surprised at this new fact and at seeing Rafe in her teal swimming suit revealing her smooth skin and contrasted nicely with her swarthy coloring.

Rafe gave Eden a look of annoyance. "Yes, she loves the shower. It's like playing in the rain. Isn't it, Bronte?" She soaped up Bronte with baby soap and then began to rinse her off.

"It's just... I always give her baths," Eden explained tentatively. "What if you slip or she slips out of your arms?"

"Eden, she can stand up on her own or sit down. She stands or sits on a towel, so she won't slip, and if I pick her up, I wrap a towel around her." She finished cleaning the soap off Bronte, and Eden handed her a towel. Rafe wrapped up Bronte, picked her up, and they got out of the shower. Rafe sat her on the counter and dried her off a little more. She put some lotion on her before rewrapping her in the towel. "There you go. All clean for Mommy." She held Bronte out to Eden. "Why don't you take her and get her dressed. Her bag is in the living room."

Eden took the baby and held her close while looking at Rafe, amazed at what she was doing for Bronte. She could also see she was not going to get a break from Rafe's anger.

"Okay," she whispered and walked out of the bathroom.

Rafe put her robe on over her swimming suit and followed Eden out. "I'll be outside with my company," she said and went out onto the patio.

Outside, Rafe found Greer cleaning up the paint and canvases. She started helping her move the canvases where they could dry and put away all the painting supplies. She knew every move told Greer she was unhappy, but she couldn't help herself when Eden made her this mad.

"Sorry we had to end the lesson early."

Greer touched her arm and smiled. "It's okay."

"No. No, it really isn't," said Rafe as she looked at Greer. "I don't do this to her. You know, she didn't use to be so erratic. I can feel something is wrong. I just wish she'd tell me what's going on with her. Sometimes, I wonder if she is doing it on purpose because she knows it upsets me." Rafe cut herself off as Eden walked out with Bronte.

"Okay, we're ready to go. Say bye-bye to Mama and teacher." Eden let Rafe kiss Bronte goodbye.

"*Addio, piccola bambina,*"[31] Rafe said to Bronte then looked at Eden. "I put her treat in the bag. I hope you take her to let Letty see her."

"I will," she said softly. She considered asking Rafe if she wanted to join her and Bronte tonight. She changed her mind when she looked at the auburn haired woman who was behind Rafe. The way she looked at Rafe made it clear she was not just there to teach art. Eden also thought about what Abby would say to Rafe if she got the chance. "I am sorry, Rafe," she said and hoped Rafe believed her.

Rafe shook her head with sorrow. "You're sorry a lot lately. I'm sorry too. Next time, please call and tell me when things change. I would really appreciate it."

Eden looked down avoiding Rafe's stare. "I'll try," she said and made her way to her car.

Rafe watched her walk away and then sat down in her deck lounger and watched Greer as she scraped leftover paint back into their appropriate tubs.

"She'll try," she said to herself with a sigh.

Greer could see Rafe's mood had gone from anger to sadness. She thought she might know just the way to cheer her up. She smiled to herself and walked over to her with the tray of paint. Sitting it on the table next to the chair, she then pulled

---

[31] Goodbye little baby,

Rafe's head up by her chin and looked into her eyes. She wiped off a spot of paint still on her face.

"Blue just isn't a good color on you."

Rafe gave a half smile. "What?"

"I think red is more your color," Greer said softly as she sat down on the lounger with Rafe. She scooped out a small amount of red paint with her fingers and wiped it gently onto Rafe's face next to her lips. "Yes, red is nice."

Rafe looked at Greer with amusement. "What are you doing?"

"Don't be blue." She climbed over Rafe and kissed her where the red strawberry-flavored paint was and then moved to kissing her on the mouth.

With an amused twinkle in her eye, Rafe laughed. "Is this my art lesson?" She was answered with silent kisses.

Greer pulled away and applied more of the edible paint to Rafe's face. She then slowly kissed it off her. She ran her paint-covered hands down the inside of Rafe's robe and slid it off her shoulders. She followed the trail of paint she had left with kisses, then looked up at Rafe and smiled invitingly.

Rafe looked at her as she felt Greer's hands run down her body. "What are you doing?" Greer just smiled and kissed her again. Rafe chuckled softly and held onto Greer's wrists so she would look at her. "So, am I to understand you used my daughter as an excuse to come to my house and jump my bones?"

"I would never use a child in such a way! I am so offended." Greer laughed as she pulled from Rafe's grasp and pushed back a lock of her dark hair. "Actually, I've been thinking about you a lot and trying to get your attention all day. But you were oblivious." She smeared a small dab of paint on the tip of Rafe's nose. "So, I just thought, since we're alone now, I'd make myself more... clear."

"Oh, really? Was I oblivious? Well, I get the picture now," she said as she closed her eyes and lifted her face to receive another kiss. Instead of a kiss, she felt more paint being applied and laughed. *Two could play this game,* she thought and reached for some paint.

Rafe looked into Greer's eyes as she dipped her fingers into the paint and ran them gently over Greer's lips and down her neck.

"Ah," grinned Greer, "so the Maestro appears." She laughed, and as a reward for getting the picture, Greer left red kisses on Rafe's chest and breasts.

"Maestre," Rafe corrected as she wrapped her arms around Greer and found her way under her shirt to unclasp her bra. With one smooth movement, the bra was loose, and Rafe had Greer's breast in her hand. She pulled the tank top up and over Greer's head and grinned as Greer ran her hands down her own chest and over her own breasts, leaving a trail of paint.

Without hesitation, Rafe followed the trail of paint with her tongue. As they painted, kissed, licked and touched each other, the heat grew between them until they both knew it was too late to stop.

Rafe broke away breathing heavily. "I think we should go inside."

She led Greer into the house to the master bath and turned on the shower. While the water warmed inside the shower,

Rafe slipped easily out of her bikini and made short work of Greer's shorts in her rush to feel her body and kiss her again. She wasn't sure exactly what this auburn-haired woman wanted from her other than sex, but right now, she didn't care. She just wanted to feel like someone wanted her, needed her, and would return the intimacy.

As the steam filled the room, and Rafe kissed her neck, Greer suddenly gasped as Rafe moved her hand between her legs. She pushed Rafe's head up caressing her face. "Shower," she rasped. She led Rafe into the shower, took control of the soap, and applied it to Rafe creating a silky lather over her body. She pressed her body against Rafe, and the lather was sensually shared between them. They kissed and moved their hands over each other's slick naked skin and let the warm water rinse away the lather as they exchanged passionate kisses.

Still naked and wet from the shower, Rafe led Greer into the living room with her kisses. Rafe quickly turned on the gas fireplace, and Greer pulled her down to the floor and pushed her back, kissing her and silently showing Rafe what she wanted with her hands, eyes, and mouth.

Rafe smiled and let Greer take control. As the water evaporated from their bodies, it was replaced by the moisture caused by the passionate heat created as their bodies entwined.

32

THE SUN SEEMED to be shining a little brighter these days, Rafe Salvaggio observed as she walked down the street holding Greer's hand. The last month seemed to fly by with all the things happening. She was making progress at work, Bronte's art lessons had, so far, been uninterrupted by Eden, and Greer was just fucking amazing.

This morning, they were stopping by The Kiki Bistro for breakfast before Greer had to go into work. Rafe had all Saturday to visit Abby and the gang and then go spend time with Bronte. As they walked inside, they saw the gang gathered around a table with a view of the street having breakfast.

"Good morning, everyone," Rafe said, smiling as she and Greer sat down. They quickly ordered breakfast and coffee from the attentive waitress.

"Well, aren't you two quite the pair," said Julia to Rafe trying to hide her lip movement with her hand. "Kissy, kissy," she teased like she used to in school when Rafe found a new girlfriend.

"It's nice to see you all again," Greer said with a smile just catching Julia's comment but not letting anyone know.

Abby moved closer to Greer excitedly. "Hey, I've been meaning to talk to you about doing a blog on art therapy. My promotion's people think it's a great idea." She liked Greer, and it was good to see Rafe happy. If the amount of time Rafe was spending at Greer's apartment was any indication, it seemed like things were going quite well for them.

"I'd love to do one," Greer said and reached into her back pocket. "Here is my card. Call my office and set up a time with Beth when we can meet, and I can show you what we do."

"Thanks. I'll set it up first thing Monday." Abby smiled happily and put Greer's card in her pocket.

"Sounds great." Greer nodded as the waitress brought her a to-go bag with her breakfast and a cup of coffee. "Well, I have to get to work," she said as she stood up. "I'm meeting Beth to go over my lecture for next week." She leaned over and kissed Rafe goodbye passionately. "Kissy, kissy," she said as she smiled mischievously and winked at Julia over Rafe's shoulder.

"Bye." Rafe laughed as she turned and saw Julia had turned bright red.

Outside the bistro, Eden was carrying Bronte on her hip. She looked inside just in time to see Rafe being kissed. She watched Julia's face redden with embarrassment before the beautiful art teacher walked away from the group's table. She started for the door of the bistro but then hesitated. She took a deep breath, readjusted Bronte, and then turned around and walked back to her car, avoiding the possibility of bumping into the art teacher or Rafe this morning.

After being caught out by Greer, Julia raised her hands in surrender and laughed. "So, Rafe, fucking the teacher now, are you?"

Shaking her head, Rafe chewed her food and swallowed. "No, Julia, the teacher is fucking me and doing a very good job at it too."

"So I guess this means no more wagers between us for a while," said Julia with raised eyebrows. "You've practically disappeared since I moved in," she said sarcastically because it seemed Rafe had been MIA for the last month unless she had Bronte.

"I guess." Rafe shrugged and took a sip of her coffee, ignoring the obvious old jealousy from their high school days rearing its head. The same thing happened almost every time she met someone new, and Julia was around, including when she met Eden.

Abby watched Rafe with suspicion. "So, do you love her?"

"What?" Rafe retorted as she looked at Abby with annoyance.

"Do you love her?" Abby repeated with curiosity.

"I don't know yet," said Rafe waving her question away. "But I do know she challenges me in a way no one has for a long time."

"Well, it's a start," said Abby and patted her on her leg. "I was worried about how much time you wasted waiting for Eden, but now maybe it was all worth it since you met Greer."

Rafe blinked and looked at Abby with a frown. "I don't think I was wasting time," she said softly and moved her leg away from Abby's hand.

"No, I didn't mean..." Abby tried to apologize for her thoughtless comment about Eden.

"So now you're dating older women?" asked Julia interrupting. "She's got to be in her late forties or early fifties maybe."

Rafe ignored Julia's criticism trying to stay in a good mood and spoke to Stacey instead. "Greer's an exciting woman. She makes me feel alive. I haven't felt this way for a while."

"Are you sure it isn't just the sex?" offered Stacey with a wink.

"Well, sex is definitely part of it but," she said thoughtfully then couldn't help but smile, "we also just connect. I can talk to her about art and work, and she understands where I'm coming from, even if she doesn't agree. We've had some incredible debates."

Julia scoffed. "How does talking work with a deaf woman?"

Rafe looked at Julia with a frown. "Being deaf doesn't mean she can't hear what I am saying. She reads lips, and she's teaching me to sign. And a lot of time, Beth is around to interpret. It really is amazing." Rafe took another bite of her food while Julia processed her words and the others ate. Rafe tried to keep her good mood, but she had lost her battle and Julia made herself the target. "Why do you do that?" she asked Julia suddenly. "You put down every girl I spend any time with. You even did it with Eden."

"I did not," Julia claimed and rolled her eyes.

"Yes, you did," said Rafe evenly. "You always find something wrong with them all. You didn't like any of the girls I dated in high school or the ones you met when we were in college, for any number of reasons. You didn't like Eden because first, you thought she was too young for me, then because she had anxiety problems, and now you don't seem to like Greer because she's deaf and older than we are. Are you still jealous after all these years?"

"I'm not jealous!" she insisted. "I'm your friend, so I'm just looking out for you."

"I don't need you to look out for me," she said and took a sip of her drink. "Can't you just be happy for me and keep your mouth shut?"

Stacey could not help her laugh. "So you've gone from cradle robbing to grave robbing? Nice, Rafe." She laughed again.

Abby scowled at Stacey. "Shut the fuck up," she hissed at Stacey, and Rafe just shook her head. "It's not much of an age difference," she looked at Rafe trying to make up for her own screw up earlier, "right Rafe? I mean Eden is like seven years younger than you—"

"Closer to six and a half," Rafe corrected Abby and looked at Julia daring her to say anything.

"Okay, six and a half," said Abby, "and Greer is what? Maybe ten years older than you?" She shrugged.

"Whatever," Julia grumbled because, in her mind, Rafe had snatched Eden up before she even graduated college and had just passed the legal age for drinking.

"Greer is fifteen years older than me," said Rafe and stared at Julia daring her to say anything about it.

"So?" Abby said quickly wanting to calm everyone down. "In the straight world, at our ages, it's perfectly acceptable."

"I just think you sometimes overlook things that wind up being a big deal in the end," said Julia not backing down from Rafe's stare. She would not be intimidated. "Eden, for example," she said wryly.

"Fuck you," said Rafe scornfully. "Her age had nothing to do with anything."

"Right." Julia laughed mockingly, and Rafe glared at her. She would have put another example of how she was right about Eden and her anxiety issues out there, but Jude piped in.

"It's good you've found someone, Rafe," Jude said hoping to make the mood of the table more positive.

"Yeah, we were all getting worried about you," agreed Stacey. She didn't understand why it took Rafe so long to get over Eden. She kind of agreed with Julia. Eden was a mess.

"Especially Abby," mused Jude. "Your three girl thing really freaked her out."

"I wasn't freaking out," insisted Abby trying not to be mortified. "I was worried. I thought you were going out of your mind."

"I think I *was* going out of my mind." Rafe sighed as she thought about all the pain she was dealing with over the past year. She pulled herself out of those thoughts. She smiled at Abby remembering her tirade after Julia took her on her walk of champions. *Time for a little fun*, she thought. She needed to get back into a good mood. "But honestly, it's much easier to make love to three women at a time than just one," she said and flashed a small smile at Jude, who she knew would catch on.

"What?" Abby screeched not believing what she was hearing.

Jude picked up the jest and continued the conversation in a serious tone. "Oh, I know what you mean."

Abby looked at Jude in disbelief. "What? How could that be?" She was certain it would be much harder to satisfy three women all at once.

"Well," explained Jude, "with one girl, you have to be the one who makes sure she's completely satisfied, you know?" She hesitated for effect.

Rafe gave Jude a conspirator's wink. "But when you get more than one girl in there, it takes the pressure off because they can take care of each other."

"Yeah," Jude sighed knowingly, "and it's less exhausting."

Looking at Abby's saucer-sized eyes, Rafe tried not to laugh. She turned her head toward Jude and gave her an impish grin before she took a casual sip of coffee. "You just have to make sure to give each one a small amount of very intense time, and then you can lay back, relax, and watch the show." She shrugged and took a bite of her food.

Abby was in shock her friends were so blasé about this matter. "You two are so evil, it should be criminal," she exclaimed.

Julia shook her head at Abby and her gullibility. She turned her attention to Rafe and changed the subject. "Well, I guess this means you're back on the straight and narrow path. Since you're so lucky to have someone like Greer now," she said not hiding her sarcasm and anger at what Rafe had said to her.

"She's lucky to have Rafe," interjected Abby.

"Thank you, guys," said Rafe and ignored Julia's sarcasm. "But I think we're both very lucky."

33

RAFE SALVAGGIO PULLED her father's Maserati Spyder into the scenic overlook and parked in the vacant parking lot. She sat for a moment and looked out over the trees to the view of the ocean and the sky. It was a beautiful December day, but also, a very sad one for her.

Her father had died on this day two years ago. It didn't seem very long ago. Sometimes, she felt like she had never been able to grieve for him like she needed to because of everything else going on in her life. She had to get out of the house and the office because of the bleakness she felt thinking about his death and everything happening around that time.

She didn't expect Greer to know today was important to her, but she was surprised no one else seemed to remember or care. Only Gabri had called her and shared consoling words. He also wanted to know when she was going to Italy to see him, meet the woman he had been dating for the last couple of years, and hear his new music.

She couldn't give Gabri an answer. She gave him a list of reasons from Bronte to her new job. What she couldn't tell him was how bad she felt about how things had turned out with her and Eden. She especially couldn't tell him how everything was still up in the air about Bronte's adoption after all this time. He was her best friend, and she was holding onto a lot of guilt around the possibility the child created with his gift might be taken away by Eden and Jake. It was heartbreaking and felt like a monumental betrayal of his trust.

She wasn't sure what Eden and Jake were doing. Though Eden had made assurances the adoption would happen, it still felt like the threat was there it might not happen. Eden was erratic in her promises about the time she could spend with Bronte. It seemed like Eden was purposely making it hard. She felt as if she had no choice but to take what she was given and to hope things would change once the adoption was final.

Rafe got out of the car, walked around it, and popped open the trunk. Inside was a portable easel and a paint box had belonged to her mother and next to it was a sealed cardboard box. She got them both out and took them over to the makeshift seating area. She could see someone had made a fire recently in the fire pit.

She sat everything down, got out matches and paper from the paint box, and re-lit the fire. After adding a couple of the logs from the wood stack to the fire and getting water in her paint jar from the spigot nearby, she sat up the easel and paintbrushes. She added a small piece of watercolor paper and set up her tubes of watercolor paint so she could use them easily.

She turned her attention to the cardboard box. Using the Exacto knife from the paint box, she sliced through the tape sealing it. She looked inside and sighed at the sight of the contents. She pulled out the ornately carved urn holding her father's ashes.

She had to have him cremated and planned to take him to Florence to be placed with her mother last year. She was going to take Eden and Bronte with her and hoped to introduce Bronte to Gabri, but it never happened. She had made one trip to Milan that year, and when she got back, Eden was gone. After that the funeral, so many things had happened with Eden and Bronte she felt like she had to stay in California. It seemed like whenever she left, something bad happened. First, her father died, and then Eden left without a word and the adoption unresolved. She didn't know if she could take anything more happening. She still could not bring herself to tell Gabri the real reason she couldn't come to Italy.

She sat the urn next to her and could feel the warmth of the fire as she looked out to the ocean. She forced herself not to cry and spoke to her father in Italian. "I'm sorry," she said softly. "I'll take you home as soon as I can." She turned her attention to the easel, and for the next few hours, she painted.

Rafe allowed her thoughts to meander carefully through her childhood and memories of her parents. Mary Lijia Carver-Salvaggio was a beautiful American art student who went to Italy to study and stayed after she married Ettore Rafaello Salvaggio, who, according to Mary, was her beautiful wild love.

Mary became an art teacher after graduation while Ettore was an *Agente Immobiliare,*[32] real estate agent, who quickly grew into international real estate brokerage. They had Rafe a year after they were married, and she was their only child, which was unusual in Italy.

Rafe thought maybe because Gabri was an only child too was the reason they became friends. They were different from the others and had a lot in common. They both had spent a lot of time alone and were given many freedoms. Finding each other solved the loneliness they would sometimes feel.

---

[32] Realtor

Rafe opened Gabri's world up even more because she got an allowance allowing her to include him on their adventures. She and Gabri, along with their friend Brettito, were almost inseparable for a long time. They were separated only by Gabri's music lessons, Brettito's *calcio*[33], and Rafe's art lessons.

As Rafe painted the scene in front of her, she fondly remembered her art lessons with her mother. Rafe had a natural talent but had difficulty spending too much time on any one thing. She was a fast learner and loved the praise her mother gave her when she finished projects.

She had been a wild child, according to her mother, all of her life. She was always moving and doing things and had a need to know everything. Her mother got her to settle by starting the lessons with a long walk to a plaza or museum. When she was older, Rafe was always walking out of school.

She told her mother she was bored and decided, after reading *Tom Sawyer,* she needed more adventure. So one day she just walked out of the school to find it. Some days she didn't make it to school at all.

It seemed like, at times, her mother knew when Rafe was going to decide to turn right instead of left toward the school. Those were the days her mother would decide to ride her bike to school along with Rafe, or even worse, make Rafe ride on the back of her bicycle.

It was on one of those days, when Rafe was twelve, her mother died.

Rafe had planned to skip school with her friends Gabri and Brettito and go spy on the *prole zingari*[34]—the gypsy or

---

[33] Football/Soccer

untouchable kids. They didn't know if they were really Romani or if they were just transient people. They had seen the large group of people hanging around the bridge for a few months, and they had been told by people they were *Zingari*,[35] so it was what they called them.

They had also been warned to stay away from the zingari kids and were told stories to scare them about how the zingari would steal bambini and sell them. But they thought they were too old for the zingari to care about and, instead of scaring them, it gave them—ideas.

Rafe suggested to Brettito it may be a good way of getting rid of his little sister, but in the end, they decided not to hand her over to them because Brettito couldn't stand the thought of his mother being heartbroken.

But it didn't mean they should not try to learn the *mistici segreti*[36] ways of the zingari they had heard about. It was their hope the zingari kids could teach them all of *la magia zingari*[37] and maybe even teach them how to read fortunes and cast spells.

No matter what Rafe said that morning, her mother wouldn't change her mind about riding to school together. So, after breakfast, they took off on their bicycles and turned left at the corner toward the school. When Gabri and Brettito saw her with her mother, they laughed and shrugged, then followed them to school knowing they were found out somehow.

---

[34] Gypsy children (offspring)

[35] Gypsy

[36] Mystical secrets

[37] the gypsy magic

At the school, they put their bikes in the rack, and Rafe's mother walked to the door of the school with her. Rafe pulled away at the show of affection her mother wanted to give her in front of everyone.

Her mother just smiled and told her, "*Buona giornata. Si può avere la vostra avventura dopo la scuola mio bambina selvaggio, stare lontano dalla zingari. Ti voglio bene.*"[38]

Rafe watched as she got on her bicycle and rode to the traffic light on the corner, wondering who told her about their plans and why her mother hadn't said earlier she knew about the zingari.

Gabri put his arm around Rafe and was starting to tease her playfully about their missed adventure when there was a crash and screaming. They all looked around and ran to the corner to see what had happened.

Rafe had stepped through the crowd, and the vision before her was of her mother lying motionless on the street and the wheel of her crumpled bicycle still spinning. She stood unmoving, not understanding why her mother was lying so still in the street. Then the vision was ripped away by a teacher who grabbed her and took her away from the accident.

Under her grief and guilt, she knew her mother was hit by an impatient driver who ran the light. But to Rafe, it seemed, if she had been better, if she had just gone to school and not skipped, making her mother feel the need to ride with her to school, her mother would still be alive. She was sure if her mother had told her she knew their plans to find the zingari,

---

[38] Have a nice day. You can have your adventure after school my wild child, stay away from the Gypsies. I love you.

they would have just gone to school instead and wouldn't have needed her to go that day.

In the middle of the night, she ran away as fast and as far as she could because she wanted to be as far away from her grief as possible. But the grief was not something she could outrun. Her father found her and brought her home in silence, for which Rafe was thankful.

Rafe felt she was defined by her mother and her death. She was a wild child. So, the skipping school and the adventure seeking continued and escalated. Her father looked the other way as long as her grades were not affected and he didn't find out or hear any complaints. So Rafe made sure her grades were acceptable to him, and she was not caught.

Then later, after her friend Brettito died, her father decided to move them and his real estate business to Milano, and then a year later to America, and Rafe's world changed again.

Living with just her father was a different challenge. He had very high expectations, was demanding, and for a long time, he was angry. School and schoolwork suddenly became an escape and at the same time, a prison. When she did well, she got the praise she needed from her father when he was willing to give it, but when she got bored, she could only think of leaving school for an adventure. She finally decided the adventure was much more important than his praise.

When school was not in session, she worked with her father a lot. He insisted she learn his business. It was at one of his projects where she found a reason to want to go to school.

Later in the year, on one of the days she and Julia had skipped school, they went on an adventure that led them to a museum. Museums were always good places to go because no one thought anything about kids being there, reasoning they were there for a school trip. Julia was bored and went to the gift shop. Rafe found a class where a man was talking about restoration and showing a restoration project done in the city. It was fascinating.

When she found out her father had purchased a building with historical status, Rafe told him all about the information on restoration she had learned. Her father immediately looked into the matter, and soon, they were both very interested in restoration—Rafe for the artistic and historical interest and her father for the money.

Rafe was able to meet with more people who did historical restorations and research as well as artists who did reproduction art and period style work. It all fascinated her, and she decided it would be her career direction. Her father was very pleased, and he helped her start the restoration business well before she finished her undergraduate work and started her graduate studies.

They made a great team, him with his construction management, real estate, and negotiation skills, and her with her restoration, architecture and art skills.

Rafe looked over at the silver urn for a moment and wished her father were really there for her to talk with. It seemed like they had just started having a better relationship when he got sick. They lived further apart, and maybe it was what helped their relationship.

The last time she visited him, they had a great talk about everything from the business to her mother. Then she went on her business trip to Italy. It seemed like he was doing well and was okay with his stay in the hospital. He insisted she go on her trip and to take care of the job she had restoring a villa outside Milan.

She found out after he died he had kept it secret how sick he really was. His cancer had spread throughout his body, and just ten days after she had talked with him, his body failed, and he was gone.

Rafe threw down her paintbrush and sighed. She looked at the painting of the scene before her of the vegetation, sea, and sky. The scene didn't capture her mood, and it made her feel worse. It was a beautiful scene to paint, but she could not enjoy it because of all the grief she was feeling.

She picked up her brush, dipped it into the black paint, and then added it liberally to the painted sky. Then, in frustration, she swiped her brush and inky blackness through the entire thing, leaving it ruined. She put down her brush, pulled the painting from the easel, and stood. She stepped over to the fire pit and added the painting to the fire, watching it burn.

She knew she should be happy now she had started a new job and Eden had promised the adoption would happen, but she felt like something was missing. Greer was making her happy. Spending time with Bronte was making her happy. Maybe she just needed more of them together.

The fact Greer loved Bronte was amazing. They had so much fun together, and Bronte was learning a lot from Greer. Rafe felt so calm and at peace when she was with Greer. She felt focused with her for some reason. She had considered asking her to go with her to Italy to take her father to the

Salvaggio mausoleum to be with her mother. For some reason, she always stopped herself. She just did not feel like she could leave right now. It was one of the same irrational excuses she gave to Gabri but couldn't help the feeling.

The ruined watercolor painting had been completely consumed by the fire. Rafe used a stick to separate the logs and went to the water spigot to fill up the fire bucket. She took it back to the fire and poured it into the fire pit until the fire was well doused. She sat the bucket down, brushed off her hands, and then began gathering everything.

When her mother's easel and her father's ashes were back in the trunk, Rafe got into the car and began her journey back to her life. She needed to fill in the missing place, and she hoped she could do it with Greer.

34

EDEN KINGSLEY WALKED out of her apartment and headed toward her car on her way to work early. Lydia was already inside finishing feeding Bronte breakfast and getting her ready for day school. After a month in her new apartment, she had finally gotten everything organized the way she wanted it. She only wished she could feel truly safe in her new place. She seemed to be doing better and finding notes pinned to her door and gifts or flowers left outside didn't affect her as much it did at first.

Eden rubbed her hands over her arms as she walked quickly to her car feeling the soft material of the light cover-up she was wearing. It was not cool out, but she still had marks on her arms from scratching at the pain and itching caused by the anxiety she was feeling.

She got into her car and pulled out of the driveway. From her rearview mirror, she could see another car had pulled out right behind her.

She knew it was Jake.

He was not keeping it a secret he was following her and watching her. The situation was wearing on her. She could see the haunted and hunted look on her pale face and in her eyes every time she looked into the rearview mirror. She forced herself to look straight ahead, and she never stopped anywhere before work anymore. She didn't want to be confronted by Jake on the street, or in a coffee shop, or anywhere.

Eden made it to the studio lot where Jake couldn't get in because she had placed him on a 'no admittance' list with security for her building. She made her way to her office building feeling a small amount of relief she could get physically away from Jake. If only she could get away from him in all other ways. Her co-workers just thought she was taking the break up hard. She tried to take their sympathy with grace, but she was happiest when they would just let her focus on work so she could forget her problems for a while.

In her office, she saw a large parcel next to her desk. In the stack of mail, there were more letters from Jake. She didn't open them. She put them in a file with others she had opened and wished she hadn't. She found, after a while, it was better not to read them until she was in a place where she could separate herself emotionally from them so her anxiety level could be controlled. She looked through a battered manila envelope at some information she had collected and then put it back.

She then gave her attention to the large parcel beside her desk. The envelope attached said it was from Rafe. She opened the parcel and found a professionally framed very colorful abstract painting. She opened the envelope and read the card inside.

The card read: Eden, This is one of Bronte's first paintings. I think this is the best one so far. We hope you like it. Merry Christmas, Rafe & Bronte.

Eden looked at the painting and was overwhelmed with emotion touched Rafe would remember her and send an early Christmas gift. "I love it. Thank you both," she whispered through her tears, grateful something good in her life had happened.

35

IT WAS A perfect December day to be outside and at the zoo in California. The weather was mild, and the animals were out enjoying the day as much as the zoo visitors were. Rafe Salvaggio pushed Bronte in her umbrella stroller as Greer walked beside them. They had even brought Beth along for the day, and she was happily signing to Greer about something. A week after her memorial trip with her father's ashes, Rafe was feeling better about life and about Greer. The more time she spent with her, the more she thought they could have a lasting, happy life together.

They edged their way up to the giraffe enclosure so Bronte could see them up close. "Look, Bronte," said Rafe as she pointed to the giraffe. "He has a long neck."

"What color is he, Bronte? Can you tell me?" asked Greer as she knelt next to her. "Orange, that's right," said Greer with a smile as Bronte made the sign for orange by repeatedly squeezing her little hand into a fist and then relaxing it. She smiled up at Rafe. "She sure knows her colors now."

"She does," Rafe agreed proudly, "and I'm sure it's all because of her beautiful art teacher. She really enjoys spending time with you, and so do I. Thank you for coming with us today."

Standing up, Greer gave Rafe a small kiss. "I feel the same. Come on. Let's get some lunch."

They found seats in the little café inside the zoo. Rafe took Bronte's jacket off her and put her lunch down in front of her, breaking apart a falafel for her. "Here you go, baby," she said and put a spoonful of hummus on her plate.

Greer looked at Rafe with some apprehension and, as she and Beth sat down, she signed to Beth she wanted her to interpret for her. Beth nodded and moved her plate and drink aside. Greer took a drink of her water and looked at Rafe.

"Rafe, there's something I need to talk to you about."

"Sure, what is it?" asked Rafe with a smile. Greer was beautiful today, and life was good.

Greer looked at Beth and then began talking with her hands. Beth spoke as Greer signed. "I've been offered a new position."

Rafe looked at Beth and then at Greer, not quite understanding why she was using Beth instead of talking to her directly. "You're going to head a different department at the Conservatory? I thought you loved what you're doing. Why is Beth translating? Why can't you just talk to me?"

"She wants to make sure she can tell you everything and you don't misunderstand, Rafe," said Beth as she signed their conversation. Greer began signing again, so Beth continued to speak. "I do love what I'm doing. I've been offered a position at Johns Hopkins in their new mental wellness division starting in January. They want to implement my ideas and want me to head their art therapy program. It's the job I've always hoped for."

"Johns Hopkins?" asked Rafe not really asking a question but just trying to catch up with what was happening.

"I'll get to work with patients alongside doctors and really help them, instead of just teaching other doctors how to use my techniques," Beth interpreted.

"When?" Rafe asked surprised. She felt a small crumble at the edges of her world. "When did you get the offer?"

"Well, after your friend Abby's blog with the video we made was put up, I got several calls, and one of them led to me speaking with some researchers at Johns Hopkins. They came out and talked with me last month, and they offered me the job. On Monday I had to let Clarice know what I decided, and I put in my two weeks' notice. I really want to do this." Greer watched Rafe's reaction to her news but couldn't tell what she was feeling or thinking.

"I see," she said and took a deep breath then let it out. She did see. She knew Greer's career was important to her, and she wanted her to be happy and successful. She couldn't yet process what it meant for them. "It sounds wonderful. I know you'll be a great asset to them."

"Rafe, you're okay, aren't you?" Greer voiced. "I'm sorry I didn't tell you earlier, but it all happened so fast, and we've both been so busy.

"Sure, I'm fine. I was just thinking about Bronte's art lessons," she said to give herself more time to process. She looked at Bronte, and the thought of being far away from her made her heart hurt. "Greer, I can't go with you. You have to understand—I can't leave her," she said and motioned to Bronte.

"I know, Rafe. I would never ask you to leave her. I can recommend one of my graduate students to take over her lessons. I think she should have them even if I'm not here. She loves them."

Rafe cleared her throat feeling the loss already. "So, where does this leave us?"

"We're good. We'll both be fine." Greer assured her through Beth. Greer could see Rafe was controlling her feelings and might need time to be okay with everything.

"I'm going to miss you," Rafe said quietly. "We're both going to miss you."

"I'll miss you too," voiced Greer, and she began to sign. Beth interpreted for her, "Rafe, we have a good thing, and we're great together, but I think my taking this job right now is the best thing for both of us."

Rafe shook her head in confusion because she was hoping Greer would be what was best for her. "What do you mean, for both of us?"

"Well, you've been through a lot, and I can see you're still not ready to get into a serious relationship. And it's okay. With this new job, it may be a while before I'm ready for one," Beth interpreted.

Not sure what to make of Greer's comment, Rafe was unsure how to react, so her defensiveness began to surface. "What makes you think I'm not ready? Is there something I can do to make you want to stay?"

"No, it's not about making me want to stay. I can't hear your voice, but I can see your eyes and the expressions on your face. I can see the little things you do screaming you're just not over everything that's happened during the last couple of years. For all I know, you may never be over them, though I hope it isn't true. It may be you have just closed yourself off because of the pain, or you may, in some part of your heart, still be in love with Eden."

"I don't think that's true." Rafe forced a laughed then looked seriously into Greer's eyes. "I'm with you, Greer. You make me happy. I want you."

Greer was flattered and smiled, but those words proved her point because none of them was about love. She looked at Beth and began to sign for her to interpret. "I want you too. You have so much passion inside you it's almost scary. And we have had fantastic sex in your living room, in your shower, in your pool, and at my house. But we have never made love in your bed. I don't think anyone has been in your bed since you asked Eden to leave it."

"I," Rafe hesitated, "I don't know what to say," she shook her head, "I didn't realize."

"It's okay. You've come a long way. You smile a lot more now." Greer grinned at Rafe.

Rafe smiled just for her. "Well, you do make me happy."

"I'm glad," Beth interpreted. "You know, it's just... I don't want to be the one who helps you through everything, and then you wake up one day and think you have to stay with me because of it. I want both of us to go into a real relationship whole and with both eyes open. Maybe someday we can try again."

"What do we do now?"

"I think we should keep doing what we're doing until I have to leave in a couple of weeks. Keep making each other happy. I love to see you happy." Greer touched Rafe's face and spoke aloud to her. "Remember, blue just isn't your color." She smiled at her fondly. "Can we do it?"

Smiling sadly, Rafe nodded her head. "Yes, we can do it."

"Great," Greer said and smiled back. "Now let's eat and go see some more animals!" Then she signed 'more' to Bronte. Bronte signed 'more' back to her, and they laughed as the baby giggled.

36

THE SHABBY STRIP mall looked abandoned, but it actually had one tenant. The space at the end of the building was the local headquarters of the religious group *Stewards to the Protection of the Innocence and Morals of Youths*. The sign above the space had the colorful letters SPIMY along with a friendly smiling character creating the illusion of innocence.

The founder and spiritual leader of this international group was Reverend Ezekiel Cazzak, a large and powerful man, who exuded charisma and demanded loyalty from his flock. From behind his desk, he looked at the two men sitting across from him, Jake and Daniel, and then he looked down at the file to refresh his memory of the mission they were assigned.

The Stewards had spent a lot of time and money grooming the Kingsley woman. It started when they found her online when she signed up on some artificial insemination sites they monitor.

They had targeted her almost three years ago because she was on the sites a lot posting questions, showing a need for advice and counseling by asking for help. When it was determined she fit the criteria for their mission, they created a file and a plan.

They were able to become several of her 'trusted' online friends and steer her based on the fears and anxieties she expressed on the boards. Soon, they were even able to infiltrate her life in small but powerful ways from internet spamming and real life chitchat in grocery stores or other places she might go regularly. They even influenced decisions from the mundane like what to make for dinner to more important life decisions like leaving her companion.

The Kingsley woman told them she felt at times like she was doing everything alone and felt like a failure when her second insemination had failed. She told them about her current life and a lot about her childhood. They were able to use her small town religious upbringing to subtly create more doubts, especially about the definition of a family. Through the illusion of their online friendship, they were able to find out about her issues with anxiety and use it against her in the attempt to sever her from her ungodly relationship.

Their initial goal was to convince her not to go through with the pregnancy. Due to their influence, it wasn't long before she was posting how she was afraid she was making a mistake in agreeing to get pregnant. With their subtle urging, Eden lied about her ovulation, and by relentlessly targeting and building on her anxieties, they kept her from communicating about how she really felt to her companion.

They listened to her worries and were able to add subtly other worries enabling them to influence her. With careful grooming, they were even eventually able to lead her into having cyber 'relations' with one of their members.

They were able to hack into her computer and had access to her camera so they could see a lot of what was going on in her life. They found out she was a lesbian and her companion was gone a lot. They saw she was vulnerable because of her anxiety issues. At times, they were even privy to private conversations about things in their lives including the therapy sessions she and her companion had attended. They were even able to influence her to choose a therapist who advised along the lines of their mission.

They thought they had been successful in preventing the pregnancy because the Kingsley woman had told them about the failure of her last insemination and there was no more sperm. She told them she was thinking about taking a break from trying to get pregnant because they had to go through the selection process again. They kept her on their watch list but didn't contact her again for a while.

In the meantime, it came to light the couple obtained a donor outside the system, and the then Kingsley woman did not go back to the chat rooms. It was during this time she used the donated sperm and became pregnant. When the Stewards checked in on her again, they saw she was pregnant and found she was no longer with her companion. It looked like their influence, though she was pregnant, was still working on her without their further action.

They kept tabs on her, and for several months, they thought she wouldn't take the innocent child back into a unholy life. Upon the next check-in, they found the subject had begun spending time with and eventually moved back in with her ex-companion. They knew then, as soon as the baby was born, they would have the mission of rescuing the innocent, either with the mother—or without.

They renewed their efforts to influence her and groom her for preparation to leave her relationship working on her anxieties and using the groundwork they had already laid. Though they were unsuccessful at getting her to have cyber-relations again, they flooded her with enough stimuli they knew from the choices she had made based on her online activity, and other real world choices, she was being influenced.

Soon, they knew the Kingsley woman confessed her feelings about men to her companion. This was when they sent in Mission Soldier Jake Thompson. His mission: get the Kingsley woman and her baby out of the clutches of the unrighteous life she was in by any means.

Jake was very good at what he did. He had saved dozens of children from the unrighteous, including his own son. His ex-wife tried to go into a relationship with a woman, and he helped the Stewards not only save his son but was able to get his ex into a proper relationship with a man. Jake was even able to recruit his family and others from his community in order to help him with his missions.

The Rev. Cazzak recognized Jake had a gift, and for this reason, Jake didn't remarry his ex-wife, and Rev. Cazzak put him with the Soldiers. Jake was very good at getting women to believe him, fall in love with him, and sometimes, even agree to marry him and do it quickly. He had been 'married' several times in the church, but they made sure no marriage certificates were ever filed, and there were no church marriage records to be found.

Within the Stewards, the Soldiers were special and were outside of certain rules because they were considered to be in the trenches. Just like military personnel have certain exceptions like lying to and killing the enemy without prosecution in times of war, the Stewards' Church Soldiers had special exceptions. The Soldiers could do things like marry Mission Subjects without being bound to them by the church, have sex outside of marriage in order to save the innocent, and lie in any manner that helped with the mission—they were allowed to do just about anything as long as it led to a successful mission.

Jake was especially good at lying and manipulating. He had a perfect track record because it was what was required. It only took one exposure or failure, and the Soldier would be considered 'dead' and a liability to the Church.

If they failed or were exposed in any way, they were cut off from any Church resources they would have as a Soldier. If they chose to, they could work in lesser occupations or make themselves available to be surrogate fathers of rescued children. But to have that the honor, they had to be married in the Church and be in good standing.

Jake and the Stewards were invested in this latest rescue project, and they seemed to be failing. Jake had spent more time on the mission than normal, and now things were not going well at all.

The reverend looked up at Jake unhappily. "Jake, what happened? The last time we talked, you had everything under control with your charge. You're one of our best Soldiers. What's gone wrong?" asked Rev. Cazzak with disappointment in his deep voice.

"I don't know what happened," said Jake in frustration. He dared not tell him she had disappeared for a week, and he had no idea where she had gone. "One day, she suddenly wanted to move out. I did everything right. I've sent her letters declaring my love, gifts for the baby, and I've left messages begging her to take me back."

Jake had never had this kind of problem and had never spent this amount of time with a Mission. He was at a loss about why it was happening. At first, he thought it was taking so much time because of Eden's anxiety and inability to make decisions quickly, but now he just wasn't sure.

It was supposed to be a simple mission. Get Eden Kingsley out of her relationship, get her to agree to marry and move away, move to the assigned town, his hometown this time, and get her and the child integrated into the community and the Church. Then await the news from the reverend on his decision about where he would place the mother and child and for instructions on the next assignment. It was a mission Jake had done successfully many times with others.

Everything seemed to be working out fine at first. Jake had started grooming Eden immediately after making contact with her. He got her to move in with him and break almost all contact with Rafe and her friends. Things went as expected with the friends. They considered her a traitor and pariah so cut her out or cut her down. It seemed like it hurt Eden the most when Abby had the harshest words for her. She seemed to always come home crying after seeing her.

He listened to all her problems and doubts about her friends as he comforted her, and he tried to get her to stay away from them. He knew she still saw them sometimes, which he didn't understand, but she limited herself because of how they had made her feel when she left Rafe.

The big surprise for Jake was the companion, Rafe. She didn't show up angry with demands or go after Eden with lawsuits as expected. It was what normally happened in these scenarios—fights, lawsuits, and threats. Eden was just as surprised as Jake was when none of it happened. Rafe finally called and asked for time with the baby, and Eden gave it to her. After Eden gave in, Jake made sure any time Rafe had with the child was very limited. It did cause arguments, but in Jakes mind, it was a good thing because it put distance between them and the companion.

All the while, Jake romanced Eden while slowly grooming her to be a good wife and for her future in the Church. Her background made many things easier because her parents were very devout, so many of their teachings were already familiar to her.

Jake blamed all of Eden's anxiety problems for the delays. Eden was hot and a great fuck, but she was a nightmare to deal with because she had so many issues. He couldn't get her to talk to his friends or go to church. She would practically shut down if there were more than two other people in the room. She took forever to agree to marry him and tried to break it off not long after she had agreed and had told his parents.

Eden would also never commit to letting him adopt the baby. She would either shut down or have an anxiety attack if pressed into an argument over the adoption or anything else by him or by Rafe. He bent over backward trying to convince her to reconnect with her mother hoping it would help, but for some reason, she was either too stubborn or too ungrateful.

One of the most frustrating things was it seemed like he was taking her to the emergency room every two or three months because she would break out in hives at night for apparently no reason at all. She kept telling him she didn't know why it was happening and how it hadn't happened to her since she was young. But from what his sources told him, she was just as crazy when she was with Rafe, though it was true she hadn't gone to the hospital. So Jake just thought it was a new bid for more attention when she was feeling insecure.

Apparently, Eden unloaded on Rafe all the time. It was in the report Rafe would just walk out and leave her crying sometimes because she was being so unreasonable. Jake sometimes thought he knew exactly how Rafe felt and they had something in common when it came to dealing with Eden. He had been tempted many times to see if he could convince Rafe to leave with him and take the baby. There was something about her he was drawn to but told himself it was probably just because he felt sorry for her having had to deal with Eden. Besides, it was always better for the Mission if they had the birth mother with the baby.

The sources also informed him Eden had a lot of worries, some reasonable and some ridiculous, about Rafe. She complained about everything Rafe did or said and was demanding and selfish when Rafe was dealing with her father's death. It was also reported at the time they were monitoring her Eden's mood swings were affecting her anxieties, and they may have been compounded by the hormones she was on. So they had exploited her moods too.

Jake thought maybe the pre-pregnancy team had made his job a little harder with all they had done back then to make her anxieties worse, but he could not be sure.

He thought he almost had Eden convinced not to allow Rafe to adopt the baby and to move away with him. He had attempted many times to get the baby's passport and was sure when he suggested the trip to Canada for Bronte's birthday, he would have it. Having a passport would make it easier to move the baby without Eden agreeing to let him adopt, if necessary. Instead of getting the passport, Eden just used the baby's birth certificate, to Jakes frustration. He thought he caught a break with everything that had happened in Canada and was sure Eden would want to get away from Rafe. But suddenly, she started letting her see the baby more and was adamant she didn't want to move away.

The next thing he knew, she had disappeared for a week. He thought something had happened to her. He searched for her everywhere and almost called Rafe. Then he realized Rafe had not called him. Surely, if Eden and Bronte had disappeared and Rafe was not getting her visitation anymore, she would be calling. So he drove by Rafe's house and saw she had the baby.

Then one day, he got an alert someone was in the apartment. He came home, found Eden was packing her things and wanted to end the relationship. Now she wouldn't see or speak with him. It pissed him off, and now he was sitting in front of the reverend looking like a rookie.

Daniel Fuller was excited he had been brought in to help and was eager to get started. He was a big man and knew when they called him they needed him for his muscle. But he wanted to prove there was much more to him than met the eye—he had brains too. He could see Jake was in a bad spot, and he wanted to help him out.

"Is there someone else? Did the other woman get to her? If she did, it's even more imperative we save the child."

Jake shook his head. "I've been following her. She isn't seeing anyone else. She spends very little time with those friends, and she only sees Rafe long enough to pick up or drop off Bronte. I've let her know I'm following her. I'm not sure if I'm scaring her away or making her think I really love her." He did not mention since Eden had found an apartment it was easier to find her and follow her.

"You're scaring her," Daniel decided. "But it's okay, because we may have to change our strategy. It's becoming clear we're in danger of losing the child to an immoral situation if the adoption is successful. Just don't scare her too much. She may decide to start talking to those friends. If that happens, she may be harder to reach."

"So, what's your suggestion for the next move, Reverend?" Jake was anxious to fix the situation and was annoyed Daniel was stating the obvious in front of the reverend.

Rev. Cazzak leaned back in his chair to think and form their plan. He saw the child was still allowed to be influenced by the immoral lifestyle of Kingsley's former companion.

He frowned at the word companion. *It was better than the word partner,* he supposed. Neither word, in his opinion, was right because they insinuated correctness or an approval of the relationship. He would need to talk to his media team about coming up with a more appropriate term. It should have a more negative connotation, especially for internal reports and for press releases. Maybe 'abettor' or 'cohort.' He would think about it more.

Cazzak gave his attention to the report again. It also looked as though the adoption petition would soon be on the docket.

He glanced up at Jake. "First," he decided, "we have to attempt to get the child away from her mother. We can give up on her, and you won't have to move her anywhere or marry her, but we cannot give up on the child. This is the fastest and easiest way to rescue the child, if successful. There's a family in the Midwest who can take her, and we have a secure way to get her there. Then we can get her out of the country if necessary." He looked at Jake sternly. "It's up to you, Jake. A failed attempt means they'll become more vigilant. If you fail in your attempt, we'll have no choice but to go through legal channels to stop the adoption or postpone it long enough we can intervene in other ways to rescue the child. We don't want the exposure. We like to keep a low profile, but it has worked in the past."

"I know," said Jake wanting to make things right. "I'll make my first attempt to get her tonight."

Rev. Cazzak stood up and walked around his desk. The two men stood with him. He shook both their hands.

"Good luck." He opened the office door and felt pride he sent those two godly men off to rescue an innocent child.

37

THE DAY AT the zoo had a lot of ups and downs, and both Rafe Salvaggio and her daughter, Bronte, were exhausted. Rafe was exhausted from keeping up the façade of being happy, and Bronte was exhausted from the fun of seeing all the animals.

During the drive home, Rafe realized she was calm and didn't really understand why.

They made it home, and Rafe put Bronte down for her nap. She grabbed a beer from the refrigerator and joined Julia, who was sitting outside on a lounger by the pool.

"Is she asleep?" asked Julia quietly.

"Yes, she fell asleep again as soon as I laid her down. She had a big day."

"It was a great day to visit the zoo. Did Greer enjoy it?" she asked trying to stay on Rafe's good side. She had kept her comments about Greer positive and her thoughts to herself. She still thought it was strange Rafe was dating such an older woman even if she did seem nice.

Rafe sighed at the thought of Greer and their conversation. "Yes," she said and took a swig of her beer.

Julia could see something more than fatigue was affecting Rafe. "Okay, what's wrong?"

"Greer and I are breaking it off."

Julia sat up in shock. "Breaking it off? But I thought you two were so happy. What happened?" She wondered if it had to do with the whole age difference.

"Nothing happened. She got a job offer at Johns Hopkins, and she's going to take it. It is something she's always wanted. It also turns out I'm still really fucked up."

Julia laughed. "Join the club. How are you fucked up?"

"Well, I'm passionate but unavailable emotionally."

"Wow!"

"I guess I'm oversimplifying it," said Rafe and took a sip of her beer. "We're breaking up, but the good thing is we're still going to see each other until she has to leave."

"Is it because you aren't mature enough for her?"

Rafe looked a Julia and shook her head. "Fuck off."

Julia chuckled then sipped her drink. "So, you're okay with everything? You don't seem very upset. A bit unhappy but not angry or anything," observed Julia wondering if Rafe would want to start hanging out again. The door was back open, and it felt good.

"I know," said Rafe and took a sip of her beer. "It's funny. With Eden, we met, and it was calm and sweet, then we broke up, and it was like world war three. It seems like we're still at war. With Greer, we started out at war with each other, and now we are breaking up, and it's almost sweet. We didn't fight or anything. We just talked." She looked at her beer bottle and shook her head. "I can't believe I feel this calm about it."

Julia watched Rafe take another drink and leaned back in her chair debating on whether or not to reveal her news. Finally, she decided to tell. It had been difficult living with Rafe and having Greer around. If Rafe started dating someone else, it would become hard again.

"Speaking of breaking it off, I've found a place of my own. I can be out by this weekend." Rafe was silent making Julia feel the need to fill the void. "Unless you think you need me to stay," she said hopefully.

"No, but thanks. I'm glad you found a place. Maybe you'll get some peace from all the drama around here. I'll be okay."

"I hope I do get a piece." Julia smiled at her own pun and hiding her disappointment it did not seem like Rafe would miss her. "It's been a while. I'm not sure why, but it's hard for me to attract someone with you around. When I tell them I'm at your place, it seems they just want to come to say they've been to Rafe Salvaggio's house. They act like they are walking on holy ground or at a P.T. Barnum production or something."

"Well, I haven't had any more towels or washcloths go missing," Rafe winked and gave a soft laugh, "that I know of, anyway."

Julia couldn't help but chuckle at the memory of the day the girls took Rafe's monogrammed washcloths. "I know it's selfish, but it may be the only reason I hate to see you and Greer break it off. I'll have you to compete with again."

"Don't worry. I think I need to figure out the issues pointed out to me today before I get into another relationship. They're all yours."

"Relationship? I'm just talking about sex." Julia laughed. "At least you'll save on bath linen."

The voices from next door began to get a bit louder as Rafe's neighbors Stacey, Jude, and Flynn came through the back gate and into the backyard. "Can we join the sex talk?" Stacey asked as she sat in one of the loungers.

"We just came over to see if we can swim," admitted Jude then dived into the heated pool.

"Sure, just keep the noise down. Bronte is sleeping," explained Rafe and then took a swig of her beer.

"No problem," said Flynn and jumped in the pool with Jude.

"So, what's going on?" Stacey asked seeing Rafe's gloomy mood.

"Well, Rafe has just had the most beautiful and sweet breakup in recorded history, and I have found a place of my own," Julia answered and held up her glass in salute.

"Rafe, you and Greer? I thought things were going good," said Stacey. "You two seemed so happy together."

"It's okay. We're just walking down two different paths right now," said Rafe appreciative of her concern.

"She got a great job offer and is leaving town," offered Julia and then took a sip of her drink.

The sound of Jude and Flynn splashing in the pool filled the silence. Suddenly, Rafe sat up and looked out at Jude. "Hey, Jude," she called out, "I have a proposition for you. You hold the master lease on your house, right?"

"Yep," Jude nodded as she hung over the edge of the pool.

"Greer won't be giving Bronte art lessons anymore, but she has a student who'll do it," said Rafe excitedly. "I was wondering if I could rent out your garage and make it into an art studio. Then the teacher can have more students and make some money as well as complete her graduate program."

"I guess it'd be okay." Jude shrugged. "But there's no water or anything out there. We don't use it because it's full of the landlord's junk."

"I'll talk to your landlord and see if I can get rid of the junk and install a bathroom and some sinks," said Rafe as she went into her planning mode. "I may be able to help the grad-student get a grant to help pay for it since she'll be using it as a graduate program project."

"It sounds great." Stacey nodded.

Julia shook her head and sighed. "And she's off, filling her time up with projects to keep her from getting out there again."

"I told you, Julia, I really do need to figure out some things before I get out there again."

"Okay, I won't bring it up again... tonight," said Julia with a smile. "I'm going to start dinner for us."

38

JUST BLOCKS AWAY at The Kiki Bistro, the shift change was underway, and they were getting ready for the dinner crowd. Eden Kingsley walked in the door and saw Letty was having an early dinner with Ephraim and Abby.

Abby waved her over to their table. "Hi, Eden. How are you? You look like shit."

Letty slapped Abby's arm. "Abby, leave her alone."

"It's okay," said Eden with a small smile. "I know. I've had a bad week at work," she said hoping her excuse was believable.

Letty stood up as Eden sat at the table. "What can I get you?"

"Oh, just a coffee, thanks. I'm only staying here until it's time to go get Bronte from Rafe."

"Hey, did you know Rafe and Greer are both doctors?" asked Abby curiously. "I just thought Rafe was a regular old architecture grad or something. I guess they have a lot more in common than we knew."

Eden looked at Abby and gave her small anxious smile. "Yeah, I know about Rafe. I didn't know she was dating a doctor, though."

"She and Greer took Bronte to the zoo today," Abby informed the table. She looked at Eden's stricken face and immediately regretted saying anything. "Oh, sorry."

"No, don't be," Eden reassured her. "I'm sure Bronte had fun."

"Yeah," she said and took a sip of her drink feeling awkward.

Ephraim could see the tension at the table and changed the subject. "Did you go to work on another Saturday? What's up with at the gold mine?"

Eden looked at him thankfully and smiled at his joke. "I guess I didn't have to go in. It's just better than being at home alone."

Abby took a sip of her tea and shifted in her seat. "So, you and Jake are really over? Since we haven't seen you, we thought maybe you made up."

"Yes, I mean no, we haven't made up, but he isn't getting the hint. He's been sending me letters and presents and following me to work. It's getting bad." She sighed softly.

"He's stalking you? I never figured him for a stalker," Ephraim said with concern. "Have you told the police?"

Letty had just made it back to the table with Eden's coffee and sat it in front of her. "Police? What's going on?"

"It's nothing," said Eden and pulled her coffee toward her.

"Jake is stalking Eden," Abby announced.

"I wouldn't go that far," said Eden as she shook her head. "I haven't seen him around since yesterday. Maybe he's finally given up," said Eden trying to believe it could be the truth.

"Should we be worried about this? It sounds bad from where I'm standing," said Letty as she sat beside Ephraim.

"No, Letty, it's nothing to worry about," Eden said with assurance. "Really," she added hoping what she had said was true. She smiled bravely at her friends and took a sip of her coffee.

39

IN THE DINING room, Rafe Salvaggio's dinner table was filled with plates and platters of Julia's amazing cooking. Since the neighbors had come over, she went all out and created a dinner party she was calling a 'last hurrah' because she would be moving to her new place soon. It was also meant to be a subtle little reminder to Rafe of what she would be missing when she left.

Julia held up her glass for a toast, and the others followed her lead. "To new beginnings," she offered, and the others repeated her toast.

"We're going to miss you as a neighbor," said Stacey while helping herself to more food.

"Yeah, Rafe doesn't cook like this," Jude concluded as she popped another morsel of food in her mouth.

"It's good." Flynn nodded with his mouth full.

Rafe laughed as she offered Bronte more carrots. "Well, maybe the grocery bill will be smaller now, and I might even have more privacy since you guys only come over to eat."

"Mmm, no," said Jude through her chewing, "we like to swim too." She laughed, and the others joined her.

"I'm sure Julia will invite you all over to her new place for dinner," said Rafe and put more food on Bronte's plate.

"Of course," said Julia happily. "It's a great place with all kinds of amenities."

The doorbell rang, and they all looked up from their meal. Jude looked at Rafe and could see her trying to control herself. "Maybe it's a sales person," she offered with a cringe wondering if Rafe was going to bite Eden's head off if it was her showing up early again.

"Right," said Rafe and threw her napkin on the table as she stood up. She straightened herself and walked over to the door as the others watched. She took a deep calming breath and opened the door.

"Hello, Rafe. How are you tonight?" Jake smiled at Rafe and could see she wasn't expecting him. *Why should she? This was going to be so easy*, he thought.

Rafe looked around for Eden. "I'm fine," she stated flatly. "Where's Eden?"

"Well, she had to take care of some things and asked me if I would pick up Bronte for her," he lied smoothly.

Rafe looked at this person she couldn't stand and then stepped out onto the porch and closed the door. She crossed her arms and looked at Jake calmly. "Eden didn't tell me anything about this."

"Well, she's been very distracted lately. I'm sure she just forgot. We're supposed to meet her for dinner in thirty minutes," Jake said as he looked at his watch and back at Rafe with an expectant grin.

Rafe looked intently at Jake and wanted to smack the grin off his face. She thought about what she saw in Eden in the last week. "She hasn't seemed very distracted to me for the past week. As a matter of fact, she seems like she has it back together. I can't believe she would forget to call me about something like this again."

Jake shrugged and smiled. "I don't know, Rafe. I'm just doing what she asked me to do."

Rafe had had enough. If Eden was really so distracted she couldn't even come pick up her own daughter, then Bronte would just stay. "You know what, Jake? The answer is no. This is too much, and I'm not putting up with it tonight. She can pick her up and do it at seven o'clock as she agreed. We're having dinner, and I'd like to finish."

"But we're taking her to dinner," Jake said calmly.

"Well, you guys can take her, but she will have already been fed."

Jake knew he had to change his tactics. He knew Rafe could be stubborn so he would just have to put some fear in her. "Eden isn't going to like it you're doing this."

"Eden will just have to deal with it. I'm tired of her doing things like this, and I'm not going to let it start again."

"Fine," Jake said and threw up his arms. "It's okay with me. You're just giving her more reasons to rethink the adoption. I'm part of their life now, and you have to accept it."

"What are you talking about? She isn't rethinking anything," said Rafe in a low, angry voice.

"Eden has changed, Rafe," Jake said as if it were a fact. "She's getting out of this immoral lifestyle. By doing this, you just give her more of a reason to want to marry me and move away to instill the traditional Christian values she grew up with in her daughter. And frankly, I thank you for it. Remember, it'll be your own fault when she decides to stop the adoption process."

Rafe could feel her anger flaring and fought to keep herself under control. He had said the right words to seal his fate. She would not put up with any more threats. There was no way in hell he was taking Bronte now. "I think you should leave."

"Are you going to give me Bronte now and keep your relationship with Eden civil, or are you going to risk losing her?" Jake offered. *She had to see it was better just to give him the child.*

Rafe was done. She was not going to be bullied or bribed into anything, especially by this man. "You're not getting Bronte. I suggest you tell Eden she had better come alone to pick up Bronte. You're not welcome here."

Jake could see he was getting nowhere and would have to back off if he were to get another chance to rescue the child. He would probably be better off dealing with Eden than this stubborn woman, anyway. "Fine." He sighed. "Your loss." He backed away then turned and headed for his car.

Rafe was so angry she was shaking as she watched Jake leave. She walked back inside where she found Julia and the others were listening through the door. "I can't believe Eden!"

Jude shook her head in disbelief at the situation as they went back to the table and sat down again. "Do you think he's brainwashed her? That didn't sound like things Eden would say. She wouldn't want Bronte to have a life without you in it, would she?"

Rafe sat back down at the table and gave Bronte her sippy cup. "I don't know. I don't know what she wants anymore. I do know when she gets here, she's going to have to come up with some good answers before I let her leave with Bronte," Rafe said very calmly.

Julia cringed at the calm tone of Rafe's voice. She may have been shaken up by Jake, but she could tell Rafe was saving up all her anger to blast Eden with it. "Just handle it calmly, Rafe. If she has been brainwashed or something, things could get ugly."

Rafe looked at Julia calmly and remembered Jakes threat. She knew she had to handle things right just in case Eden really was changing her mind about the adoption again.

"Julia, I need you to stay in the room with us. I need to make sure I handle this right. If anything he says is true—" she stopped in midsentence and fought to hold back her emotions.

"Don't worry. I'll stay. Let's just finish dinner." Julia looked around at Stacey, Jude, and Flynn. They were all in shocked silence. "You guys should hurry and finish then head back home." She watched as they all nodded and went back to the table and began to finish the food on their plates.

40

JAKE THOMPSON DROVE away from Rafe's house slowly and made his way down the street. He could not believe he didn't get the child. Why did Rafe have to be so stubborn? Anyone else would have been happy to hand the child over and hope they would still have a chance to be in the child's life.

He knew it because they all held onto the hope they could corrupt these children, but he would never let them. They would hand those children over to him, and he would rescue them from their evil clutches and send them on to people who deserve to raise innocent children.

He was frustrated, but he knew there would be other chances. He hit the dial button on his hands-free set. It clicked and connected.

"I didn't get her," he said angrily. "I tried everything on the bitch. I tried sweet-talking, guilt, and threats. No. I'm sure Eden hasn't talked to her about our break up, or she would have said something. Let's move on to the next step as soon as possible." He hung up the phone.

He would not fail.

41

RAFE SALVAGGIO PACED from the door to the living room, angry with Jake and Eden. She checked on Bronte who was playing with her toys on the living room floor. She checked her watch, and it was seven o'clock. Eden should be here any minute.

Julia had put all the extra food away and cleaned off the table. She then walked into the living room, bringing Rafe a glass of wine.

"Sit down, Rafe. Try to calm down," she advised as Bronte brought her a toy.

The doorbell rang, and Rafe abandoned the wine Julia had offered her. She rushed to the door ready to confront Eden. She opened the door roughly.

"Eden," she said angrily.

Eden took a step back, shocked at the force Rafe had opened the door and the shout of her name. She stammered in confusion, "Uh, hi."

"We need to talk. Come in," said Rafe and gestured for her to come into the house.

Eden walked in, and Rafe followed her into the dining room. She looked around concerned. "What's wrong? Is Bronte okay?"

Rafe pulled out a chair and pointed at it. "She's fine. Sit down."

Eden could see Rafe was angry, but she wasn't sure what she had done to cause it. She was here on time, just as they agreed, and she didn't like the way she was being treated. She sat down as told, hoping by showing she was cooperative, Rafe would calm down.

"Okay, what's going on?"

Julia followed Rafe as soon as she put Bronte in her playpen. She could see Rafe was ready to attack Eden verbally, so she made the decision to break in for some reason. Rafe had asked her to make sure she didn't do anything stupid, so she was determined to do as promised.

"Rafe, calm down now." She put herself between Eden and Rafe. "Eden, Rafe is upset about what happened earlier, and we're both just wondering what's going on with you," she explained.

"What happened? What are you talking about?" asked Eden shaking her head and feeling at a loss.

Rafe exchanged a look with Julia. Maybe she hadn't talked with Jake yet. It would be just like him to try to bait her into something so she would make a huge mistake. Maybe he didn't tell Eden what he did knowing she wouldn't understand why she was being confronted. He was probably hoping Eden would become angry enough to stop the adoption.

Rafe took another calming breath. She pulled out another chair and sat down next to her. "Why did you send Jake over to pick up Bronte tonight? Why didn't you call me if you were sending him, and why did he come so early? You promised you weren't going to do this anymore."

Eden looked from Rafe to Julia in confusion as a chill ran down her back. "Jake? Where's Bronte?" She stood up in in terror. "Did you give her to him?"

Rafe stood with Eden seeing her turn white with fear. "Of course not. She's in the living room."

Shaking, Eden went quickly to the living room with Rafe and Julia close behind her. When she saw Bronte, she collapsed onto the couch and tried to calm her pounding heart.

"Oh, my god. Oh, my god." She gasped as she shook visibly.

Rafe sat down next to Eden and took hold of her shoulders so she would look at her. "Eden, what's going on?" she asked firmly.

Eden wiped her face with her hands and calmed herself. Bronte was safe. Relief flowed over her as Rafe held onto her shoulders. She looked into Rafe's blazing gray-blue eyes and was very thankful she was so stubborn and possessive.

She had to make sure Rafe and Julia were not dragged into the situation with Jake and the Stewards, so she took a deep breath to focus.

"You just scared me," she said as she held her hands together to still their trembling. "Jake and I aren't together anymore. Promise me you won't ever give her to him."

"Don't worry, I have no intention of giving her to him," Rafe declared and gently let go of Eden. She never wanted to see the guy and his condescending smirks again. "If you aren't together, then why was he trying to pick up Bronte?"

Looking down at her hands, Eden shook her head. "I don't know. Maybe he just wanted to have a way to get me to talk to him. I've been avoiding him and not taking his calls," she admitted.

Julia looked at Eden and how relieved she was and felt like Rafe might be right about something else going on. She put her hand on Eden's shoulder to help comfort her. There were still some questions needing to be cleared up.

"Are you sure that's all? He said some things to Rafe," she hesitated. "Well, it sounded to me like both you and Jake were threatening her. He was talking about stopping the adoption and you leaving an 'immoral' lifestyle. What's that all about?"

Eden looked at Rafe, who nodded in agreement with Julia. She saw them both looking at her waiting for an answer she could not give them because of her fear. "Rafe, I'm so sorry," she said, desperate for her to believe her. "I'm not sure what he was talking about. He doesn't speak for me. You have to believe me."

Rafe stood up and paced in front of Eden and Julia thinking about how she wanted to respond. She was angry, and right now, she didn't know if she could trust Eden about anything.

"Eden, you have to understand," she stopped to try and gain control of herself again, "I'm so mad right now. I can't believe you didn't tell me you and Jake were over. What if I had given her to him? What if something happened?"

Eden knew she was wrong not to tell at least Rafe she had broken it off with Jake. She never imagined he would try to take Bronte while she was with Rafe. "I know." She nodded. "I'm so sorry," she repeated.

Julia didn't like Eden's short answers, and she could tell Rafe was nowhere close to being satisfied with her answers either. "Right then? So everything's out now, Eden? There's nothing else going on Rafe needs to know about, is there? You're not moving away or dissolving the adoption, are you?"

Shocked, Eden snapped her head up. "No!" She looked directly at Rafe. "I'm keeping my promise. The adoption is going forward, and I have no plans to move away. I don't know why he'd say those things to you!"

Rafe wanted to believe her, but she had been threatened like this one too many times. She was worried all of Eden's 'distractions' might be coming from making plans for something. Jake might have told her some small truth even if Eden didn't include him in her plans. "I think you should leave Bronte here tonight."

"What?" Eden said in disbelief as she stood up. "Rafe, don't," she pleaded.

Julia interrupted her with a wave of her hand. "Eden, I think its best too. Jake is saying and doing things you say you know nothing about. What would you do in Rafe's place?"

Eden looked at the two women in front of her and knew if she resisted and argued, they would just question her harder, and if she made even the smallest mistake, they would grab onto it. She had to keep Rafe out of her situation with Jake and the group she found he was part of people online called by the abbreviated name of the 'Stewards.' To win the war, she had to lose this battle with Rafe.

"Okay," Eden relented, "she can stay tonight." She looked at both of them and gave a small nervous smile. "I'll pick her up tomorrow morning," she said as she went over and picked Bronte up out of the playpen and gave her a kiss and a hug. "Goodnight, baby," she said softly. She put her back in the playpen and then stood. She looked at Julia and Rafe. "I guess I'll go," she said softly and headed for the door.

Rafe followed Eden and tried again to see if there was something more she had to say. "Eden, if there's something more wrong, you can tell me. Tell someone."

Eden avoided Rafe's gaze. "There's nothing, really." She walked out the door and closed it softly behind her.

Rafe watched the door close and turned to look at Julia. "Why is she doing this stuff? I really don't think I know her anymore."

42

INSIDE FAB BAB'S Cabaret Club it was overflowing with bodies. Abby Van Falkov was glad she got there early to save a table for the group. Most of the group anyway. Julia spent the week, since Greer left Sunday, trying to convince Rafe to get out of the house and apparently she had 'plans' for Rafe, so they were hanging out together. Abby was pretty sure those plans were nothing good.

The live music and Christmas themed drag show were about to start, and Abby was ready to meet and mingle. It was the day after Christmas but it did not stop the holiday themed parties where the singles could mingle. She looked around the room, and as the club name suggested, there was a lot of fabulous going on with all the 'Kings and Queens who make Bells Ring' were strutting their stuff and having a blast. She laughed at her own funny thoughts. She saw a familiar face in the crowd and let the others at the table know.

259

"Look, guys. It's Eden." She waved to get her attention. "Eden, over here." Eden saw them and waved as she made her way over. Abby had invited Eden, but she hadn't said for sure if she would be here.

"Just don't tell her she looks like shit again," said Jude remembering the conversation Abby told her about the last time she saw her.

"Hey! I won't," she said looking annoyed. "She actually looks good tonight."

Eden made it to the table and joined the group noticing Flynn and Erica were the only ones who had gone all out in drag tonight.

"Hi, everyone."

"It's good to finally see you out," said Abby glad Eden had accepted her invitation to hang out with her and the girls.

"Lydia was available, and willing, to watch Bronte tonight so I thought I'd get out of the house," she said as she smiled shyly and sat down with everyone.

"How have you been?" asked Flynn politely. He was looking particularly good in drag tonight wearing his flapper dress with a feathered headband and jewels strategically placed on his face sparkling under the club lights.

"I've been fine. Thanks for asking." Eden could see they were celebrating something. "So, what's going on tonight?"

"We're celebrating Rafe getting a grant to convert our garage into an art studio to teach art to children," said Stacey, who had been looking at Flynn proudly because she had helped him with his makeup. "She has a teacher lined up and everything. It's going to be really cool! Plus now we each can pay two hundred dollars less a month on rent for a while!"

Eden felt a sting of jealousy but pushed it away. "Greer will be the teacher, right? She is Bronte's art teacher." She looked at Abby. "Like you said, they have a lot in common. Now it looks like Rafe is already building her things."

Everyone exchanged looks wondering who was going to break the news. Abby took the lead for the group. The comment about Rafe building things was not lost on her. Rafe had built Eden a theater room not long after they moved in together.

"Eden," she paused, "Greer and Rafe aren't together anymore. After I did my blog and video special on Greer, she got offered this unbelievable job at Johns Hopkins. We had a going away party for her before she left for Baltimore."

"Here are our drinks," said Erica as she set a tray of drinks on the table before she sat down. She looked like a member of a boy band with her tight black pants, open-collared shirt, and her fedora hat. Her face had been made up to look like she had a little scruff, and if anyone's eyes lingered lower, they would see she was clearly packing.

Eden took in the news Abby had revealed as everyone grabbed their drink from the tray. Personally, she had not had a real conversation with Rafe for over two weeks. They had only exchanged pertinent information about Bronte, and that was about it.

"Oh," Eden said hesitantly, "no, I didn't know. I guess I need to start keeping better track of what's going on with everyone."

"Rafe is over there," announced Flynn and pointed to where Rafe and Julia were talking.

On the other side of the bar, Rafe and Julia were standing against a low wall by the dance floor. Rafe took a sip of her drink and then looked over at Julia.

"I can't believe you got me over here doing this again. But I admit I'm having fun." She grinned as she watched the girls glide by and look at her suggestively.

"Well, you can't stay home all the time. You'll go crazy. It's good for you to get out and be around people. Just look at those women drool over you," Julia said as she motioned to a group of women at the bar.

Julia looked Rafe up and down. She was not dressed in drag, but she was dressed like she was heading out to a construction site, and it was hot. Old jeans faded in just the right spots held up by a wide, worn leather belt. It was worn because Rafe always had a tape measure and other things attached to it when she was working. She had on one of her old sleeveless denim snap up shirts showing off her toned arms. The soft shirt was hanging open revealing the tight tank top underneath accentuating her curves. Julia had not forgotten how fit Rafe was under her clothes. Rafe's vanity had gotten to the point where she actually bought a set of weights a couple of months ago. Julia admitted to herself it was definitely not infandous to look upon Rafe in a bikini. To top it all off, Rafe had her construction site walk she couldn't help when she was dressed in those clothes and wore her work boots. Her walk drew eyes faster than the outfit or her toned body.

Rafe leaned in closer to Julia so she could be heard without shouting. "You know, the first time we came out together, I didn't think I could do it. I kept thinking about Eden. But then, something just clicked. It was like everything I was before I met Eden came flooding back." She gave a small laugh. "I felt like I was freed from a cage I had locked myself in." She paused musingly. "Hey, I thought you didn't want the competition. Why did you invite me out tonight?"

"Well, I've rethought everything," explained Julia thoughtfully as she played with the gold chain hanging from the pocket of her suit. She had not done a total drag king get up, but she butched it up in her own classy style.

"Really?" Rafe chuckled.

"Yes, I figure if I stick with you, I can wait for you to pick someone, and then anyone else left will be ready, willing and able for me by association."

Rafe shook her head in disbelief. "I don't understand you, Julia. You used to get any woman you wanted. You used to be a fucking dragon who could chew them up and spit them out. Why are you having such trouble now?"

Julia thought over the question not wanting to admit she had hoped Rafe would change her mind about her, and they could date each other.

"Yes, I know what you mean." She sighed realizing Rafe was not on the same page, as usual. "My best guess is since I've gone to a salary position in the company, I don't have the money confidence from all the big commissions anymore." She shrugged. "Now I'm on an even playing field, and I actually have to work at this."

Rafe rolled her eyes. "You poor thing." She looked at Julia thoughtfully knowing the real problem was probably she was still getting over her breakup with Andrea because Julia undoubtedly made a very good salary. She was the daughter of Ian Hawthorn, after all. She would never really hurt for money. "I'm going to let you in on a little secret," Rafe said with a slight arch of her brow. "Unless you tell them, none of these women know how much money you have or don't have. You're putting your money, or your lack of it, between you and any woman who might be looking your way."

Julia thought about her words and considered telling Rafe how she really felt, knowing she had just been giving Rafe an excuse. "Humph, I guess I am. Thanks," she said naming herself craven for not taking the risk again. But deep down, she already knew the answer. "Speaking of women looking your way, Eden is here." She pointed her chin toward Abby's table by the dance floor.

Rafe glanced over, saw Eden looking back at her, and brashly ignored her. She changed the subject back to their new bet. "Well, I've spotted who I want. What's your wager?"

"Which one?" she asked, and Rafe pointed out a girl across the bar. "Oh, my god. This is just not fair! The show hasn't even started yet! How do you spot these girls so fast?" Julia demanded with her jealousy showing.

"Actually, she spotted me." She gave Julia an evil grin. "She stares at me every chance she gets."

"So not fair! She already wants you! It's no challenge," she pointed out.

Rafe took another sip of her drink. "Do you want me to make her pick a friend to go with us?"

"No, no, no. I was berated enough by Abby the last time you did something like that. I don't want to deal with a nightmare again." She paused contemplating a wager she might be able to win. "I have it. You have to get her to have a drink, dance with you, and kiss you, and then you walk away from her." She paused again dramatically. "The challenge is you can't speak a single word to her. I've been told all about how you're back to using your seductive lines and Italian poetry by Abby and again by Carey. None of your affectations tonight. If she follows you out of the bar, I'll help clean the art studio this weekend. If not, you pay my tab at Kiki this month."

"How much do you owe?" Rafe inquired with a laugh.

"Oh, it's up to about two hundred and fifty dollars by now, and the month isn't up yet." She raised her eyebrows silently asking if the wager was accepted.

Rafe looked at the girl across the bar then back at Julia. "I'll take your wager." She smiled wickedly. "Get ready to get dirty."

Rafe picked up her drink from the half wall and then walked slowly and confidently with her easygoing construction site walk over to the fair-haired girl in the tight Levis and a ribbed tank top. She stood directly in front of her and smiled, then took a sip of her drink. She held her glass up to the girl, all while looking straight into her eyes with an inviting smile. With some trepidation, the girl took the glass from Rafe's hand. Rafe nodded to her, and the girl lifted the glass to her lips and took a sip. Rafe took the drink from her and gave it to a passing waitress. She held out her warm hand to the girl, and she took it. Rafe promenaded her to the dance floor, holding her around the waist with her right arm and holding her left hand in hers.

On the dance floor, Rafe pulled the fair-haired girl around so they were facing each other. She took the girl by both of her hands and pulled her close. Rafe placed the girl's hands on her hips and held them there. When the girl hooked her thumbs in Rafe's belt, she smiled and gently began to move to the slow rhythm of the music. As the girl held onto Rafe's belt, Rafe looked intently into the girl's eyes then lightly moved her own hands slowly up the girl's forearms to her upper arms and then to her shoulders. She leisurely moved her hands up so she could caress the girls face and gently moved her hair back so she could hold her face between her hands.

Very deliberately, Rafe pulled the girl close and smiled because the girl looked as though she was completely entranced. Delicately, she brushed her lips to the girls and pulled away. It was just a sign for the girl of what was coming, done by design so it would not be a mystery to the girl about what Rafe wanted from her.

Rafe leaned toward her for a second time, but only part of the way, and waited. The girl leaned forward making up the distance as if pulled by an undeniable force. Their lips touched, and they shared a long, deep, lingering kiss. Rafe knew she was in total control of the situation, and the girl had no question about what was happening.

Rafe smoothly pulled away and looked the girl in her eyes again, then backed away from her slowly while running her hands back down her arms until she was holding her hands again. When their arms were stretched out between them, Rafe broke her gaze and looked toward the door, then back into the eyes of the girl. She gave the girl a smile she knew could be interpreted as nothing else but an invitation.

She offered one more signal so the girl would be in no doubt of what Rafe wanted. She tilted her head toward the door, lifted her chin just slightly, and then slowly released the girl's hands. She stood there for just a moment and turned her body toward the door, breaking eye contact only after she had made a little more than half her turn, and walked away. Her steps were slow, deliberate and confident. They said 'follow me.'

The girl looked after her, hesitated, and then put her body in motion to follow Rafe. When she reached the door, Rafe turned and saw the girl had followed her. She looked over at Julia and gave her a nod and a triumphant smile. Rafe seized the girl's hand again and led her outside.

At the group table by the dance floor, Abby had been watching Rafe on the dance floor. She couldn't believe what she had just seen.

"Did I just see what I saw?" she screeched.

"I think everyone in the place saw it." Jude laughed as Julia approached the table.

Disconcerted about what had happened, Abby looked up at Julia. "Julia, what just happened with you and Rafe?"

Julia sat down and sighed. "I swore I would never wager with her again, and now I remember why. I think I come up with something impossible, and she does it. I think it was the walk she has—if that girl hadn't followed, someone would have.

Now I have a weekend's worth of work I have to do on the art studio. Are you guys coming to help too?" There were several nods, but they were more concerned with what had just happened.

"What was the bet this time?" asked Stacey with excitement.

"You saw it," Julia motioned to the dance floor and then took a sip of her drink. "She had to get her to take a drink, dance with her, kiss her, and follow her to the door all without speaking to her." She pouted then could not help grinning with pride. "I can't believe she did it!"

Stacey threw her head back and laughed. "We have just witnessed fucking greatness!"

Jude took a swig of her beer and chuckled. "I guess she decided to get back out since Greer is out of the picture. Rafe has always been a legend around here. I never thought I'd get to see her in action."

"Some of the stories about her are really unbelievable," added Erica hardly believing her own eyes. "But, after seeing her in action, I'm not so sure the stories are over exaggerated."

"Abby, you know how she was," Jude recalled mirthfully.

Abby was not enjoying the sideshow as much as the others. "Yes, I do," she said with a frown. "Julia, you really do have to stop betting with her. You're becoming a bad influence on her. I don't want her going back to her so called legendary ways."

"She's a big girl, as she just proved," Julia said coolly knowing Rafe could do things Abby would be much, much more upset about if she wanted. "She says she has broken out of her cage."

Eden looked up at Julia, stung by Rafe's suggestion she had been in a cage when they were together. She hadn't said anything about what she had witnessed. She stood up from the table. "I have to go," she announced suddenly and walked away.

"What's wrong with her?" Julia had scoffed before she took another sip of her drink.

Flynn watched Eden cross the bar. He thought it was mean Rafe acted like she did in front of Eden. He felt protective of her even though he didn't know her well. "Rafe didn't have to pick a girl up in front of her."

Julia had just gotten on Abby's last nerve. "Maybe seeing Rafe 'do her thing' was hard for her," Abby said indignantly. "She didn't know Rafe as her wildling self. She hasn't really been here to see Rafe do those things before."

"I'll go make sure she is okay," offered Flynn and he went after Eden.

"I can't believe Rafe!" said Abby, feeling sorry for Eden. "It's probably hard when you go from being Salvaggio's Paradise to seeing someone else who may end up taking your place."

"I think you're forgetting it was her choice," said Julia with little sympathy for Eden. She was happy Rafe was out and living again.

"Well, what choice would you have made if you were cheated on," asked Abby annoyed at Julia.

"She didn't leave because of her cheating," Stacey pointed out as she laughed. "She left to be with a man."

Abby gave Stacey a hostile look, angry she could not slap her, or deny the truth of her words.

43

A BLOCK FROM THE bar, Rafe Salvaggio was slowly walking her date to her car and laughing as they talked. Rafe didn't tell Julia she knew Tess who was a friend from New York in town for a visit. Tess had called earlier in the week, and they had met for drinks. When Rafe told Tess about her problems with Julia always pressuring her to go out, she offered to help out tonight.

"Tess, I'm so glad you came for a visit," said Rafe happily.

"Me too!" Tess laughed and held tightly to Rafe's arm. "It's always so exciting with you around."

"Did you see Julia's face? She was in shock!" She laughed and gave Tess a small kiss of appreciation. "You followed my lead really well!" she praised with a laugh.

"I told you I should be an actress." She smiled and struck a pose.

Rafe swept her up in a hug laughing loudly. "You saved me from her school girl wagers."

"I'm glad I could help. Tell me what the plan is now." She looked up and winked at Rafe as she wrapped one arm around Rafe's waist, grabbing her belt again and the other around her neck. "You do look really hot. Are you going to take me home?"

Rafe smiled at her, sighing as she debated if it was a good idea to take her home or not. They dated for a while years ago before she left New York but neither one took it seriously. She wondered if just having a good time was what she needed right now. Her phone went off, and Tess released her so Rafe could check it. She saw it was a text message from Greer.

"Congratulations on putting your passion into a worthy project for your daughter and others. I wish you and Annie luck."

After reading the text, Rafe looked at Tess who was waiting for her to lead her to the car. She hesitated and then made her decision. "I'm sorry," she said motioning to her phone. "I've just been reminded of something important." She ran her hand over her face and looked at Tess. "I just don't think I'm ready yet. Maybe another time, okay?"

"Of course," said Tess knowing Rafe was still getting over a breakup and needed time. She took Rafe's face in her hands and kissed her. "I'm glad we got to hang out while I was here. It was like old times in New York."

"It was," Rafe agreed. She smiled at Tess and hoped she could save the night for her. "I think you should go back inside. Enjoy the show and have fun with Julia. I think you'll like her. Just tell her I broke your heart or something. She loves to be the knight in shining armor. But don't tell her we know each other from New York. I'll never hear the end of it, and I want her to come help with cleaning the studio."

"I think I will." Tess chuckled softly and loved the fact Rafe was so thoughtful. She really wished she would take her home. She still remembered the last time they were together and was disappointed she wouldn't be with her again tonight.

Rafe gave Tess a small parting kiss of apology. "Have a great night," she said with a wink.

"See ya next year," Tess said returning Rafe's wink. "But, Happy New Year just in case I don't see you!" She waved as she turned to go back inside the bar.

Rafe gave her a wave then turned and made her way to her car happy to be away from Julia and alone again for a while.

44

OUTSIDE THE BAR, Eden Kingsley was pushing through the crowd desperate to get to her car and go home. She was still in disbelief about what she had seen and just wanted to get away as fast as she could. She heard someone call her name from behind her, and she turned around.

"Eden, wait," Flynn shouted. He saw her turn and wait, so he quickened his pace toward her. He was glad he decided on flats tonight. "Eden, are you okay?"

Eden hesitated, unsure if she wanted to talk with Flynn or anyone else right now. "I'm fine," she said shortly holding her arms across herself.

"Well, you left kind of fast. Was it because of Rafe? I've never seen anyone do something like that before."

"I'm not sure. I just had to get out of there," she said looking down at the ground.

"You know, everyone is kind of worried about you. You haven't been around. Abby said they thought you'd be around more since you left Jake," he told her hoping it would let her know they cared about her.

"I've just been really busy," she said turning to head for her car.

"Are you hiding out from someone?" he asked following her closely.

Surprised by the question, she stopped short, turned, and faced Flynn. "Why do you ask?"

"Well, you have a look I've seen before," he said stopping clumsily and almost running into her because he had been walking too fast in the tight dress. "It's kind of a haunted, fearful look. My mom had it when we were hiding from my stepfather. I know we don't exactly know each other well, but I can help you. I know what to do. You can tell me what's happening."

Eden looked at Flynn, thinking about how alone she was feeling in her situation. "Can you keep a secret?"

"I can, and I will." Flynn nodded, making the diamonds on his face sparkle.

"Come on. Let's go to my apartment, and we can talk."

Eden and Flynn walked into Eden's apartment, and Flynn pulled up a chair at the kitchen table. He began to remove the decorations from his face and the makeup Stacey had applied. Eden sent Lydia home and went to check on Bronte who was asleep in her crib. She went into her room and took a bankers box from her closet then carried it into the kitchen and sat it on the table. Opening the box, she took out a large manila envelope from inside with all the letters, emails, and other things Jake had sent her.

"This came a few months ago." She sat the large envelope in front of Flynn. "I've been trying to figure out what to do with it."

Flynn opened the envelope and pulled out all of the papers. He looked at everything and tried to understand what he was seeing. After listening to Eden explain what she knew, and then going online to look at things, he finally looked at Eden with concern.

"This is why you left him, right? You had to leave him."

"It was what tipped the scale." Eden sighed. "I was already having doubts and tried to break off the engagement once." She looked at Flynn and burst into tears. "I thought he was just really caring. You know, about Bronte and me. I was questioning myself. I was thinking my feelings of being pressured and pushed where I didn't want to go were all just in my head. I thought maybe my anxiety was what was causing me to have doubts. I was getting sick all the time, and I thought it was just because of all the tension between him and Rafe and my own fears that had built up. But when I got this," she hesitated, "I took it home, and... well, my eyes were opened. I didn't believe it at first." She picked up the photographs. "All these pictures," she said as she flipped through them, "I think they're all people who are part of the group and are fake families or," she hesitated and wiped her tears with the back of her hand, "they may be mothers and children who have been tricked and abducted. I was so freaking scared when I realized it. I still am," she said shakily. "I knew then I had to take Bronte and get out that day."

"What exactly is this group *Stewards to the Protection of the Innocence and Morals of Youths*?" Flynn asked as he looked at one of the pamphlets.

"I've looked them up online," Eden said as she wiped away more tears and pulled out printouts about the group and showed him the web address. "There's a forum where members described them as a group of fanatics who, by almost any means, try to take children out of situations they believe are immoral according to their beliefs. One of which is situations like Rafe's and mine. I fell into their trap, and I did it willingly just to be with a man, and for sex."

"You didn't know he was part of their group. How could you?"

"Flynn, I wasn't careful. I was too trusting."

"But it's who you are," said Flynn gently. He knew she was trusting because it was one of the things Abby and Jude said about her. "You can't stop being who you are."

"I've got to figure out what to do with this information. Jake has been following me and calling me, emailing me, trying to get Bronte and me back. I'm worried about what he and this group may do next. Look at some of the things they've done to people. They can be ruthless."

"So, this is why he tried to get Bronte from Rafe?"

"They told you about that?" She ran her hands through her hair anxiously. "Yes, I'm sure it is."

"We should tell Rafe what's going on. Warn her. Show her this stuff, and we should tell the police."

"What am I going to tell the police?" Eden asked with an almost hysterical laugh. "I have all of this information on this group and this guy. As far as I know, they haven't committed any crime yet, but they should do something about them? Oh, and by the way, I was screwing the guy."

Flynn was feeling at a loss, but he wanted to help. "We should at least tell Rafe then."

Eden could see Flynn just did not understand. "I can't, Flynn. I've tried. I've wanted to. She's not easy for me to talk to anymore. Did you see the look she gave me tonight? I know I hurt her by leaving the way I did and how I've been with Bronte. I know it. But I can't help my feelings. I wanted, I want—" she stopped because she didn't think she knew what she wanted. She felt like she was losing it and barely hanging on.

"What? What do you want?" asked Flynn softly.

"I don't know anymore," she answered anxiously. "You know, I've seen Rafe angry, upset, and sad, and in just about all other ranges of emotion. I've seen her make people shake in their shoes with just a look. But I have *never* seen her look at me or anyone else the way she looked at me tonight. It was like I didn't exist," she said hoarsely, "and then she—she did what she did. And I just," she choked on her words and couldn't continue.

"So, she took a girl home," Flynn reasoned. "It's not like it was the first time. You don't want her. Everyone says you want to be with a man, you made it clear you wanted to be in a traditional relationship. I know, Rafe is beautiful and what she did, it was... wow! But why do you think it affected you so much?"

"I don't know why," she said despondently. "I just want us to be able to get along. She used to make me feel safe and proud, and when those feelings went away after her affair, I didn't think I could feel any worse or more scared. I was wrong. She just makes me feel so cut off, and it's almost unbearable."

"Do you think you're jealous?"

"No, I don't think so," she moaned in despair. "You know, when I saw her so happy with Greer, I thought we had both begun to heal. Then I see her tonight so cool and confident surrounded by all those women who want her, and for a second, I thought I saw something sad in her eyes and my heart went out to her. Then she saw me and gave me a look. It was like a stab to my heart. She never made me feel like this before." She fought back her tears. "I don't want her to make me feel this way again."

Flynn stacked the papers and photos on the table wondering if Eden's anxiety was making the situation seem worse than it really was. He decided it was better to be safe than sorry and maybe talking to Rafe would be good for her anyway.

"If you don't tell her about these people, Bronte could get hurt."

"I just need more time," she begged hoping she didn't make a mistake in trusting him, "time to figure out what to do about this information, and about Jake. If I tell Rafe about this, I feel like she'll just have another reason to hate me. Look what's happening—not only do I tell her I want to be with men, but the first one I hook up with is a crazed cult member. I'm already making her angry enough."

"What do you mean? How?"

"Well, I've been trying to avoid Jake. So I've been changing my schedule around going into work at different times and dropping off and picking up Bronte at different times instead of the same time every night. Rafe thinks I am doing it on purpose, and I am, but not for the reasons she thinks. I've been doing better lately, but what if I have to start it again. Rafe will tear me apart," she said shakily. "I can't risk telling her about this until I have something solid, and I can do something about it."

"I'll help you," Flynn offered, knowing from what the girls had said Rafe was upset with her. It was also clear Eden was dead set against talking to Rafe, and she really did need help. "Let me start by looking at the emails he's been sending you and doing some digging. Maybe I'll find stuff that'll help you get a restraining order against Jake or something. Let me take your computer home for a couple of days. Computers are what I do. You worry about keeping Bronte and yourself safe."

"Thank you," Eden said as tears leaked out of her eyes. "You don't know how good it feels to have talked to someone about this." She took Flynn's' hand and looked into his eyes. "Flynn, you have to promise no matter what happens, you won't tell Rafe. It should come from me if she has to be told."

"Sure, I promise, no matter what. It's okay. I know what to do when bad things happen," he confessed. He was glad she was accepting help. He knew what it was like to feel like you were in an impossible situation without a friend. He was determined to help her in any way he could and to be her friend.

45

RAFE SALVAGGIO WAS up early Saturday morning, and the cleanup crew had been working hard to clear out the garage space soon to be an art studio. Annie Brown, the graduate student who would be holding the classes, along with Stacey, Jude, Abby, and Flynn, were helping clear out the garage while contractors took measurements to implement Rafe's plans. Rafe was in the middle of it all and standing over a table covered with the remodel plans she had drawn up.

The general contractor, Dean, was listening to Rafe explain what she wanted. "We want the bathroom here and the sinks and shower area over there. The plumbing permits have all been pulled so they can excavate today if possible. And I think we should build custom storage shelves along this wall," she said as she pointed from the plans to the areas where she wanted things.

"Well, I'm here," announced Julia as she strode into the chaos.

"Excuse me," Rafe said to Dean and walked over to Julia. "Glad you could make it." She looked at her watch, and it was almost noon. "Our deal was for all day."

"Well, I thought since you sent the girl back inside to me, you really only half won the wager. So, I'm here for half a day."

"I think you're mistaken," said Rafe as she crossed her arms trying not to smile because it looked like Tess made an impression. "I fulfilled all of the terms of the wager, and you owe me a full day."

Julia looked at Rafe bewildered. "But I took her home."

"Taking her home wasn't part of the bet."

"Oh," Julia said as she recalled the exact terms of the wager. "Well, I guess I should thank you then."

"You can thank me by grabbing a broom," Rafe said and could not hold in her laugh.

Dirt covered Abby joined them. "Okay, Rafe. I need a break. Hey, Julia." She smiled then turned to Rafe. "Can I go get some drinks and maybe some lunch for everyone?"

"Sure, Abby. I have everything in the house. Come on. I'll help." They walked out and made their way to Rafe's kitchen. "I really appreciate you guys helping out." They got out the ice and cups and began to fill them. "What do you think of Annie?"

"She's great for a straight girl," Abby quipped.

Rafe shook her head. "Abby!"

"Oh, right. I forgot you have a special place in your heart for straight girls." They both knew she was referring to Eden.

Rafe scoffed. "You know, Abby, *you* would probably have better luck with straight girls."

Abby ignored the dig. "So, did you see Eden last night?"

Rafe put the ice-filled glasses on a tray. "Yes."

"You didn't talk to her."

"Why would I talk to her? I don't think she has much to say to me."

Abby mixed the lemonade in the pitcher and pondered the situation. "Well, she hasn't been around, and you guys need to get along. Besides, she's not seeing Jake, and you're not seeing anyone. I thought you would want to talk to her. But no, instead, you turn into wild crazy Rafe again. I can't believe you were so insensitive. I thought you were different now."

"Well," Rafe shrugged, "I guess you thought wrong." She turned and got some fresh lemons from the refrigerator and put them on the counter.

Abby looked over into the dining room at the painting of Eden painted by Rafe. "What about the whole Salvaggio's Paradise thing?" she asked. "I mean, you still have the painting."

Rafe stopped slicing the lemons and looked at Abby with a frown. "The painting is called *Il paradiso terrestre, l'Eden* which means *Eden, Paradise on Earth.* You made up the whole Salvaggio's Paradise thing." She pointed at Abby with the knife. "So now you can just make something else up like 'shattered paradise' I guess because it's over," Rafe said irritably and finished slicing the lemon.

"But Rafe," Abby started then decided not to push her luck and stopped herself.

Jude walked into the kitchen and leaned on the island. "Hey, I'll take one of those." She picked up a glass with ice and held it up to Abby. "What are you guys talking about?"

"Last night," Abby grumbled.

Rafe put the lemon slices in the lemonade pitcher then took it from in front of Abby. "Besides, how do you know she hasn't kissed and made up with Jake? He is what she wants," she said to Abby. She turned to Jude and poured lemonade into her cup of ice. "Apparently, I'm a soul-possessing wildling and insensitive."

Jude laughed loudly. "Why?"

"Because I didn't talk to Eden last night."

"Why should you have talked to her?" Jude said with a small shrug.

"Exactly." Rafe nodded and gave Abby a smug look.

Abby angrily threw ice into another glass. "Rafe, after Eden saw you 'do your thing' she was upset and almost ran out of there. If you saw her, you could have saved her from seeing you 'do your thing.'"

Jude didn't understand why Abby was so upset. "So, when Eden is around, Rafe can't look for women?" She shook her head. "Abby, that's crazy."

"Besides, Eden doesn't care," insisted Rafe. "She likes men now, remember? And if it's not Jake, it'll be someone else."

"She's bi-sexual, Rafe, she can still have feelings for women! Including you," Abby exclaimed at Rafe's hard-headedness.

"Make up your mind, Abby," Rafe said wryly. "Is she a straight girl or bi-sexual?"

Jude laughed and almost choked on her lemonade. "Yeah, Abby! Which is she?"

Abby looked at Rafe sternly. "She's the woman you were with for four years, almost five, and the mother of your child," she said hotly. "She's not just another one of your conquests, and she has never seen your dark side. I think it really shocked her. It was probably worse than witnessing the parade you and Julia had in here."

"Hmph," Rafe grumbled. "Well, she won't have to worry about it again for a while."

Jude perked up thinking something new was going to happen. "Why? Did you meet someone? Is Greer coming back?"

"No, I was just reminded I need to figure some things out. I don't think I can if I am in a relationship or chasing girls. I really just want to focus on getting the art studio project going and start the classes right now." She put the final glasses on the tray and picked it up. "Come on. Let's get these drinks out there and then get lunch ready."

Abby watched Rafe and Jude walk out of the house, and she looked up at the painting in the dining room. The painting was in high Renaissance style and featured a very beautiful and erotic, scantily clad woman with golden blond hair, and a face blushed with pink, and she was holding an apple. It was clear to Abby and anyone else the woman was Eden. She was standing in an overgrown garden setting complete with an apple tree, and a mysterious vine covered marble structure with Greek columns in the background. Abby didn't understand why Rafe would keep the painting hanging in her house if she didn't still have feelings for Eden.

What really irked her was the fact she somehow convinced Eden to pose practically nude for a painting when she hardly knew her. She didn't know how Rafe was able to do things like she did and have girls just be okay with it. She knew it had something to do with those wildling ways she had. Lord knows she tried to warn Eden, but somehow, Rafe always came out looking golden. Now Julia was trying to get Rafe to start using her wildling ways on the unsuspecting women of California again, and if she did, then Abby knew everything would change—and not for the better. Rafe had been so much better since Eden. She just didn't understand how or why Rafe had screwed up so bad.

Abby frowned as she thought of Rafe's words about paradise being shattered. *You can't shatter paradise,* she thought. *It's not made of glass. They've just left it, and now they have to get back.*

Following Rafe out of the house, Abby decided to make it her business to try to help her out. She didn't want Rafe to go back to her wildling ways, and the only way she could think of to prevent it since Greer was on the other side of the continent, was to get Eden back in her life. Now, with both Rafe and Eden single again, maybe they could work things out.

In the hectic garage, everyone had stopped to take a break for the lemonade that had been brought out. Rafe watched them as they all talked and laughed together. She didn't know why, but she felt very apart from them all.

She knew they were her friends and they probably cared a lot for her, but she still couldn't help but feel the chasm separating her from everyone, including Eden and Bronte, over the past year. She felt like a stranger to them and wondered if she was growing away from them or if they were the ones growing away from her.

Lately, it seemed like she had to fight a lot harder to have good things in her life, and she was struggling to replace one lost thing with another constantly.

Since Greer was gone now, she wanted to make sure she didn't lose the time with Bronte she had helped create through the art lessons. Rafe hoped the art studio would allow her to spend some of the precious time she had with her with learning and fun.

Pushing the feeling she was alone away, even with people around, Rafe decided she needed to talk to Gabri again. She would call him tonight and let him tell her all about his music and the things happening with the love in his life. They would talk about Italia and her father and Paradise. She never felt alone when she talked with Gabri and could forget all the problems in her life for a while. He had been her best friend and confidant all her life. Maybe she would even let him talk her into moving back to Italy.

No, she thought, *I have to stay for Bronte.*

To be continued in Book Two - Blue Inferno...

Salvaggio's Light

Book Two
BLUE INFERNO

C.L. Cattano

NOTES

Herodotus— Wikipedia 2.20.2016 (*Erodoto -in Italian*) Father of History https://en.wikipedia.org/wiki/Herodotus

Translations: For translations of Italian, French and Spanish use: www.Babblefish.com

The chapters in this book were arranged with the intent of saving paper. This chapter style saved 36 pages. Original Total Book Pages 333 — Final Pages 297

Music mentioned in this book.

No financial incentive was given for the mention of the following artists in this work. The author is a fan and felt mentioning them worked in the story. For the use of their name, credit is given, and links to their work are below.

Enjoy!

Amanda Hughey

Website: http://www.ahmusic.co/
Facebook: https://www.facebook.com/amanda.hughey.376
Twitter: @AmandaHugh
YouTube: http://www.Youtube.com/amandahughey91

ABOUT THE AUTHOR

C.L. CATTANO LIVES in the Midwestern U.S. with her partner and their dog somewhere between the city and the forest. With a joy for traveling, she and her partner have visited many countries and have a love for meeting people and learning about the places they visit. When possible, she likes to include references in her work about the things she has learned, the places she has been and people she has met while on her travels and in her everyday life.

Cattano has a variety of creative interests including, but not limited to, creating fine art, writing, photography, and supporting women in the arts. She considers herself a 'Jack of All Trades' dabbling in what she terms the 'whimsies of her soul' pulling her toward happiness and fulfillment.

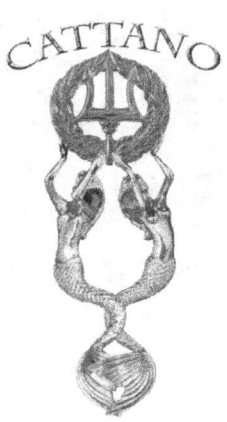

OTHER BOOKS
By C. L. Cattano

Cursed Hearts is a love story transcending time and gender. Separated from by a gift from a bored demon on All Hallows Eve two souls

connected by the power of love have been searching through time for each other and have been incarnated as both men and women.

Over time, the gift became a curse and a game for the demons.

Now the souls have finally met again, and they must fight for a life together.

Will love prevail? Will they finally be able to live together again for a lifetime? They have one night to figure out the riddle and get it right to break the curse.

NOTE: 18+ Lesbian Romance. Some light erotic moments.

Available on Amazon

REQUEST FOR REVIEW

Thank you for reading **Salvaggio's Light** — *An Epic Contemporary Romance Serial.*

I hope you enjoyed book one, **Shattered Paradise**. Your honest review will be greatly appreciated by me and other readers. It only takes a few minutes, so I encourage you to go now and leave a review!

Check out the Salvaggio's Light Facebook page to join in the discussions and fun! www.facebook.com/pg/SalvaggiosLight

Join the CL Cattano Mailing List www.clcattano.com

I love getting fan mail and you can contact me at
clc@clcattano.com